FACING EVIL . . .

The last room on the left was the parents' bedroom. There was a man in the bed. He was on his back, and I could see his full, long beard and bloodless face, eyes closed. He had to be the family's father, Thomas Kinderman. Grady was standing next to the bed, arms folded in his yellow hazmat suit. He walked over when he saw me. Danielle began to photograph the body.

Grady's eyes were troubled above his paper mask. "No signs of foul play. Nothing environmental . . . You ever seen anything like this, Harris?"

I shook my head. When I'd been a beat cop in New York, I'd occasionally been on calls to check on a neighbor, or investigate a foul smell, and found someone deceased. Many of those deaths were illness-related. But this? An entire family? And so fast too . . .

There was a loud knocking from downstairs. Someone was pounding on the front door. Grady and I looked at each other and both headed down. When Grady opened the door, the neighbor, Jacob Henner, was standing there with an officer in uniform. Jacob's face was wild. . . .

What now? I thought, feeling a new wave of dread.

Berkley Prime Crime titles by Jane Jensen

KINGDOM COME

IN THE LAND OF MILK AND HONEY

IN THE LAND OF MILK AND HONEY

JANE JENSEN

BERKLEY PRIME CRIME, NEW YORK

An imprint of Penguin Random House LLC
375 Hudson Street, New York, New York 10014

This book is an original publication of Penguin Random House LLC.

For more information, visit penguin.com.

Library of Congress Cataloging-in-Publication Data

Names: Jensen, Jane, author.
Title: In the land of milk and honey : an Elizabeth Harris novel / Jane Jensen.
Description: Berkley Prime Crime trade paperback edition. |
New York : Berkley Prime Crime, 2016. | Series: Elizabeth Harris ; 2
Identifiers: LCCN 2016009050 (print) | LCCN 2016015740 (ebook) |
ISBN 9780425282908 (softcover) | ISBN 9780698407213 ()
Subjects: LCSH: Women detectives—Fiction. | Murder—Investigation—Fiction. |
Amish—Pennsylvania—Lancaster County—Fiction. | BISAC: FICTION /
Mystery & Detective / Women Sleuths. | FICTION / Mystery & Detective /
Police Procedural. | GSAFD: Mystery fiction.
Classification: LCC PS3560.E583 I5 2016 (print) | LCC PS3560.E583 (ebook) |
DDC 813/.54—dc23
LC record available at https://lccn.loc.gov/2016009050

PUBLISHING HISTORY
Berkley Prime Crime trade paperback edition / August 2016

PRINTED IN THE UNITED STATES OF AMERICA

10 9 8 7 6 5 4 3 2 1

Cover art: *Amish buggy* © Willard/iStock/Thinkstock;
Landscape © Mischa Keijser/Plainpicture.
Cover design by Sarah Oberrender.
Interior text design by Kristin del Rosario.

For my husband,

who gave up a lot to move back to Lancaster County with me.

Love you Farmer Bob!

ACKNOWLEDGMENTS

Thanks to Kim Fielding for assisting me on criminal justice issues and my agent, Shawna McCarthy, and Berkley editor Katherine Pelz for encouraging the creation of this book. This story was inspired by the dedicated, passionate, and hardworking people in the Lancaster local foods movement.

PROLOGUE

Lancaster County, Pennsylvania, April 2015

"Mama! Mama!"

The strained cry pulled Leah from a fevered dream in which she'd been sewing and sewing. The stitches fell apart, disintegrating as she frantically worked. It was something important and she had to finish it . . . a bridal dress.

No. A shroud.

"Mama!"

Leah sat up in bed. Beside her, Samuel was asleep. She touched his forehead. It was still hot and dry with fever. But it wasn't Samuel who had called for her. It had been a child's voice. She left her husband to his fitful rest and went out into the hall in her white cotton nightgown and bare feet.

Coming! she thought. She left the reassurance unspoken because it was the middle of the night, and she didn't want to wake the rest of her children.

A shining band of lantern light peeked out from under the door of the upstairs bathroom the children all shared.

She knocked lightly. "*Hast du mich gerufen?*" she asked, her voice low. *Did you call me?*

"Mama!" Breathless and weak, the cry came from behind the door. Leah opened it.

On the floor by the toilet lay Mary. She was pale as snow. Her thirteen-year-old body had recently begun to develop a woman's shape, but she looked years younger now. Her long dark hair, loosened for bed, was sheeted around her, damp and oily at her brow. Her eyes were closed. One of her hands twitched weakly as if it wanted to reach for her mother. The smell of vomit and bile, sharp as the January wind on the open fields, hit Leah in the face. The lid of the toilet was open, small amounts of bile the only evidence of Mary's heaving. Her stomach was empty, poor thing. But the back of her nightdress was stained brown.

"Oh, Mary!" Leah fought her own nausea, exacerbated by the smell, and bent to help her daughter. She managed to get Mary sitting up and stripped off her soiled nightgown and undergarments. She cleaned Mary up with a wet rag and bundled all the stained cloth up together. Leah enumerated the tasks in her head. She had to put Mary in a clean nightgown and get her back into bed. And she had to see to it that Mary drank a glass of water too.

The doctor said water was important with all the vomiting and diarrhea, but it was hard to get the children to drink it. When they did, it often came right back up. After Mary was settled, Leah had to open the little window in the bathroom to air it out and take the dirty bundle down to the laundry room.

Mary was trembling like a leaf in the breeze, her eyes bleary. But at least she was able to sit up by herself. Leah draped her in a few towels to keep her warm and went to fetch a clean nightgown.

As she passed the boys' room she heard the muffled sound of crying—miserable, lonely gasps. She hesitated, wondering if she should first get Leah's nightgown, but the sound was too worrying. She pushed open the door to the boys' room.

"Aaron!" She hurried to the child's side. Six-year-old Aaron, who looked so much like his papa with their identical sandy-colored Amish haircuts, was sitting up on the lower bunk. He was crying, quietly but full-out, his mouth wide open.

She pulled him into a hug and checked his forehead. His fever seemed to have broken for the moment. His skin was clammy and covered with sweat.

"Was ist das?" she tsked quietly. Across the room in the other set of bunk beds, Mark, her twelve-year-old, was asleep on the upper bunk. He had his back turned to her. The bottom bunk the boys used for playing—at least until little Henry outgrew his crib.

"*Ich hatte einen Albtraum*," Aaron sobbed. A nightmare.

Leah felt a touch of relief. At least Aaron was not as sick as Mary, or as he himself had been earlier that evening. Maybe he was on the mend. Maybe they all would be soon, and her own nightmare would end. *"Es war nur ein Traum. Schlafen tu." It was only a dream. Go back to sleep.*

She tucked Aaron in, his eyes already drooping, and straightened up from the lower bunk. Her back ached deep and low, and she put a hand to it, rubbing. Chills ran though her, shaking her so hard the wooden boards beneath her feet creaked. *Dear God, let this terrible flu pass soon.* She should fetch her shawl. But first—Mary's nightgown.

She turned to go but decided to check on Will first. He was in the bunk above Aaron's. Her fourteen-year-old had been very ill all day, refusing food and going to bed at six o'clock after dragging himself through the daily chores. The cows had to be milked, no matter that the entire family was sick as dogs.

She stepped closer to the top bunk, went up on her tiptoes, and reached a hand out to touch William's forehead. He was a barely distinguishable shape in the dark. Her fingers touched wetness, partially dried and sticky. It was around his mouth, which was slack, open, and felt oddly firm. The smell of something foul came from where her fingers had been. Alarmed, she drew back her hand and paused for only a moment before reaching for the Coleman lamp on the bedside table. She turned it on. Keeping the other boys asleep was no longer the foremost concern on her mind.

"Will?" She blinked as her eyes adjusted to the light. She stepped on the lower bunk and pulled herself up to look at her son.

A moment later her scream echoed through the silent house like a gunshot.

PART I

The Curse

CHAPTER 1

I pulled into the driveway at the Yoders' farm and turned off my car. I forced myself to sit still for a moment instead of hopping out immediately. I needed to get my head out of my current caseload and hectic mindset before I could appreciate Amish hospitality.

It was early April. The weather had warmed early this year, and the signs of spring were everywhere. The dark brown wooden fence along the Yoders' pasture contrasted with the brilliant green of new grass and the white and purple of early-blooming crocus. The late afternoon light was just turning golden and soft. Several fawn-colored Jersey cows were completely engrossed in tugging up mouthfuls of the new growth. And the little decorative windmill in the center of the kitchen garden on the other side of the gravel drive spun in a light breeze.

The garden was still in its winter hibernation, dormant but cleared. I imagined it held its breath in expectation.

This is why I'd moved back to Lancaster County. Every once in a while I had to remind myself of that before I got bogged down with head-in-the-sand-itis. Feeling better, I grabbed Sadie's present and headed for the house.

Sadie Yoder had turned seven a week ago. This was the first chance I'd had to come by, having snuck out early from an afternoon of tedious paperwork. I'd debated what to get her. Ezra said dolls were acceptable for the Amish as long as they were modestly attired. No glam rock Barbie for Sadie, then. But I didn't want to reinforce the grow-up-and-have-lots-of-babies message, for no reason other than my core streak of feminism and innate rebellion. So I settled on a game of Chutes and Ladders.

I'd struck up a tentative friendship with the Yoders, specifically Hannah and a couple of her daughters, Sadie and Ruth. We were odd bedfellows—a female police detective and Amish womenfolk. But we'd shared a tragedy. Or, rather, the Yoders had tragically lost their daughter Katie, and I'd found her killer. I'd nearly died in the process.

There was guilt and gratitude on their side, and I couldn't even begin to untangle the mare's nest of motivations on mine. I felt protective of Katie's younger sisters and bonded to the family through the sympathy and pain of Katie's murder case—and I was curious. I wanted to learn about Hannah's way of life. Of course, I lived with Ezra, who was ex-Amish. But he couldn't tell me what it was like to be an Amish wife and mother, and he didn't like to talk about his life before anyway.

Also, if I were perfectly honest, I simply liked coming here. It made me happy. I went up the porch stairs and knocked on the door.

"Hallo, Elizabeth!" Hannah opened the door and welcomed me inside with a smile. She always looked so young for a mother of eleven—slightly built, her dark hair pulled back tight under a white cap and her face without a trace of makeup. Her plain, royal blue dress was covered with a large black apron that had traces of flour on it.

"Hi, Hannah." I smiled. I wanted to give Hannah a quick hug, but I refrained. Instead, I held up the gift. "I brought Sadie a birthday present."

"Ocht! You spoil her!" Despite her words, Hannah seemed pleased. "We're making strudel. Would you like to cook with?"

"Sure." Being in the Yoders' kitchen was soothing. And it would be fun to surprise Ezra by learning how to make something from his childhood.

The kitchen was crowded with girls and young women. The center pine table had been cleared and covered with wax paper, rolling pins, and large bowls of dough and chopped apples. Sadie's face lit up when she saw me. She ran over to give me a hug around the hips. The others all said hello. Sadie's older sisters, Ruth and Waneta, who still lived at home, were there, as was Miriam, who was grown now and had children of her own. There were two young women I didn't know. Before I could introduce myself, my dark pantsuit was covered by an apron and I was clutching a rolling pin. *En garde.* I bit my lip and refrained from saying it. They wouldn't find it funny.

The sheer volume of strudel they were preparing came as no surprise by now. I'd seen Hannah cook before. Not only did the Yoders have a large family, but they always made extra, either to freeze or to share with the community at some get-together or other. And the two young women I hadn't met before had probably come over to make batches for their own households. Cooking in a group made things a lot more fun.

We rolled out the dough, cut it into large square sheets, sprinkled on a sugar-cinnamon mixture, added raisins and nuts to some and not to others, and layered on small slices of apple before rolling them up and brushing the tops with melted butter and powdered sugar. The bushels of last fall's apples were from cold storage, according to Hannah. Those that hadn't been eaten over the winter had to be used up before they went bad. They were a tough-skinned green variety, and they were pared and chopped in an endless assembly line. And while trays of rolled strudels sat and rose in the warm kitchen, more and more and more were made.

It was a repetitive task that soothed me after a long week of work. This past week I'd investigated a man who'd killed his wife accidentally during a heated argument, a Jane Doe found near the highway, and a baby whose supposed crib death I suspected was really abuse. It all melted away under the steady motions and the pleasant singing in complicated-sounding German words.

I couldn't contribute much to the singing or the conversation. With the older Amish, most of my life was topic non grata. I was living in sin with Ezra Beiler, who was, in any case, an Amish man who'd taken the church vows and then left the Amish, and was therefore shunned. And my work as a homicide detective wasn't something Hannah cared to have her girls learn much about, even if she did respect it. But Sadie, as usual, had a million nonsensical questions for me like *Do you like grass?* and *Do you have red birds at your house?*

The last strudels were rolled. A few of the dough logs were stuffed into the warm oven, but most were wrapped in cling film for later baking. Hannah's guests left with cheerful good-byes and boxes bursting with strudel. Sadie opened her birthday present, thanked me for the "most wonderfullest gift" and ran off with Ruth and Waneta to play the game before supper.

I washed the dough off my hands at the sink. The window above the basin overlooked the fields outside. The sun was sinking, and I saw Hannah's husband, Isaac, and two of her boys heading home on a plow pulled by two horses. It was getting late—time to let Hannah get to their evening meal. Besides, the sight made me long sharply for Ezra, who would be ending his own day about now.

"Thank you for allowing me to stay," I told Hannah. "This was just what I needed to relax."

Hannah was placing two wrapped, unbaked strudels into a bag for me to take home. She paused, an odd look on her face, like she wanted to say something but wasn't sure if she should.

"What is it?" I asked.

Hannah looked troubled. "I meant to speak to you. . . . It is about a bad business."

"Of course." I stepped closer to Hannah and leaned against a counter, making it clear I was happy to listen.

Hannah sighed. "There ist some trouble lately, among the people in our church. Now a boy has died."

"Trouble? What kind of trouble?"

"My friend Leah Hershberger, her whole family is sick. They called in a doctor, and he said it was the flu. But . . . there has never been such a flu. So sick they were, and her son William, only fourteen and strong before now—he died from it."

"I'm sorry, Hannah." It was disturbing. There'd been word in the news that the flu was particularly virulent this year. Everyone at the station had been given a flu shot last November. But this was the first I'd heard about a local child's death. Of course, if he'd died from a virus, it wouldn't have come to the homicide team.

"Another family, the Knepps, got ill such like too. I hoped, maybe, you could look into this?" Hannah asked, her face uncertain.

I didn't understand. "How do you think I could help? It sounds like a case for a doctor, not the police."

Hannah tugged at her cap self-consciously, her eyes downcast. "Some believe it is not a normal sickness but *hexerei,* a curse."

I blinked rapidly as my mind tried to catch up. A *curse*?

Hannah looked up, her face hopeful. "There is a man, a

brauche man. He holds a grudge against our church. Maybe if you could just look things over, say what you think. I don't know what to believe myself, but if it is a curse . . . I don't ask for myself, Elizabeth, but for Leah and her children, and for my own children too."

I felt out of my depth, like the floor had gone wonky beneath my feet. A *curse*? What could I say?

"I . . . would be happy to take a look into the boy's death."

Hannah's face lit up with a grateful smile. "I knew you were a gut friend to us. Thank you."

Lancaster General Hospital was a big and open space, surprisingly modern and new. I was used to the old hospitals in Manhattan, with their cramped corridors and smell of centuries past. Like all things in Pennsylvania, this hospital's corridors were extra wide and ceilings extra high, as if its citizens could be counted on to be oversized, its families overblown, as if the population, in posterity, could only get bigger. There was something endearingly optimistic about that.

The optimism was nowhere evident in the patient room I entered.

Samuel Hershberger and his young son Aaron shared a large room, each in his own bed. Both were sleeping.

Samuel looked to be in his early forties. His long brown bangs and unkempt beard clearly identified him as Amish, even though he wore nothing but a hospital gown under the blankets. He must have lost a lot of weight, because the skin on his face appeared as if laid over a skull—drawn, loose, and colorless. An IV drip fed steadily into his veins. He appeared to be resting peacefully. I knew what it would take to get an Amish farmer like Samuel Hershberger into the hospital—near death. The loss of their son William must have been a wake-up call.

Aaron was quite young, maybe five or six. He was turned on his side and, although clearly ill, had a healthier skin tone than his father. He would probably make it, I thought. I certainly hoped so.

I decided not to wake them. There wasn't much Aaron could tell me, and Samuel looked too sick to disturb. Instead, I went off in search of their doctor. This wasn't how I'd planned to spend my Saturday off, but a promise was a promise.

"I can't say for certain what it is," Dr. Kirsch said, being perfectly blunt about his ignorance.

Thanks to my badge, I'd gotten the doctor to speak to me about the Hershbergers. I left out the fact that my investigation was in no way official.

"My best guess is it's a particularly virulent viral infection. But these things often remain undiagnosed. Both Hershbergers' blood work shows severe hyperchloremic acidosis, which can result from prolonged diarrhea and vomiting. We're giving them IV fluids. It's the best we can do for now. They should pull through fine."

"Do you know why the fourteen-year-old son, William, died?"

"Dehydration, possibly kidney or liver failure. I doubt there'll be an autopsy. There usually aren't with the Amish unless it can't be avoided. His mother said the whole family had been sick for three days, and William wasn't keeping liquids down. He worked on the farm that day too. His body just gave out."

Kirsch was an older man, early fifties, stocky, with a superior air. He clearly was a busy man and not overly curious about the medical mystery of the Hershbergers.

"If it's a viral infection you don't recognize, wouldn't it be the procedure to call in the CDC?" I asked.

Dr. Kirsch looked incredulous. "Well . . . no. Not without a lot more evidence that it's something unusual. It's flu season. There are dozens of common viruses going around. If we called the CDC every time we had a patient with flu symptoms, we'd need a CDC the size of the U.S. military."

"But a boy died."

Kirsch squinted impatiently. "There have been over forty deaths from flu so far this season alone in the U.S. It's tragic, but it happens. Dehydration can be very dangerous."

I pulled out my notepad—not because I really needed it, but to reinforce the message that I wasn't some dim relative he could bully. "Mrs. Hershberger says the entire family came down ill at the same time, overnight. There were also severe chills and tremors. Isn't that unusual for the flu? People in a family would normally get sick in waves, not all at once."

"It depends on when and how they were exposed to the virus." Kirsch leaned forward, elbows on his desk. He seemed to be taking me a bit more seriously, but I sensed defensiveness in his tone. "If they were all exposed to someone who had the virus—say, at the same church meeting—it's conceivable they would fall ill at the same time. And chills and shivering are to be expected with severe flu."

"What exactly did their blood work show?"

Dr. Kirsch opened the file on his desk. "I can't show you the results without permission from the patients, but in regards to this flu scare, the blood work is about what you'd expect. Electrolyte abnormalities, hemoglobin and red-blood-cell counts are elevated, and the acidosis . . . that's all typical for severe dehydration."

"Does it actually show the virus?"

"Viruses are detected via a swab culture, not blood work."

"And was a swab culture done?"

He gave a subtle huff. "No. Confirming the influenza virus via a swab test wouldn't change the treatment."

"I understand. Still. My i's dotted and t's crossed—you understand. Is it possible for you to administer a swab test now and confirm that it's influenza? Just for our records?"

Kirsch frowned. "You understand that we're conservative on our use of tests since these patients are not insured. It's not in their best interest to rack up avoidable expenses."

I gave Dr. Kirsch a brittle smile. "Run the test on Samuel Hershberger, please, doctor. Text me with the results today."

Ezra was working in the garden when I got home from the hospital. As I parked the car, my text alert went off.

> Rapid flu test negative in both Hershbergers.
> No influenza A or B virus present.

I read the message twice.

I typed:

> Meaning it's not the flu?

The reply took seconds.

> Inconclusive. Likely the virus has left the system
> and now it's complications. Treatment same.

Well. That wasn't very helpful. I'd been hoping for something concrete to report to Hannah. I sighed, got out of the car, and stretched my back. I also took the opportunity to check out my partner like a shameful hussy.

Since leaving the Amish a little over a year ago, Ezra had changed in many ways. He never had taken to T-shirts, but he loved jeans. In the warm April afternoon, he wore a denim button-down work shirt with the sleeves rolled up and a pair of jeans that clung to his narrow hips and long legs. I preferred his blond hair long, and he indulged me by keeping it shoulder-length. He had it tucked behind one ear, revealing his handsome face as he hoed between the rows.

The first time I'd seen Ezra, he'd been standing in his barn, his back to me, lost in a private moment of sorrow. Now, as then, he could make me forget to breathe. I gave in to the urge to go over and give him a hug.

"I'm covered in dirt," he warned, though his arms were welcoming.

"Mm-hum. You're so sexy when you're working in the garden."

Ezra's lips quirked. "'Tis so? Guess that explains why the Amish have so many children."

I laughed, feeling my mood lift like someone had pumped helium into it. "I suppose that could be a factor, though the lack of birth control might have something to do with it." I breathed him in for a moment and stole a kiss. Our golden retriever, Rabbit, panted happily and wove around our legs.

"Any news?" he asked.

"The doctor says Samuel and Aaron Hershberger will recover, so that's good. Unfortunately, the diagnosis is vague. Can I help you out here?"

"No. I was about to stop for the day. Need to do some chores in the barn already."

"Shall I make stir-fry?" On weeknights, Ezra usually cooked for both of us, since I worked late. So on the weekends, I liked to take care of him. I went to pull away, but Ezra tightened his arms in one last squeeze.

"Sounds good," he murmured into my ear. The nuzzle of his lips on my cheek held a lovely promise for later. I smiled.

"What's a *brauche* man?" I asked Ezra as we relaxed on the couch after dinner.

"Where'd ya hear that word?" Ezra sounded amused.

"Hannah Yoder. She said people thought the Hershbergers had been cursed by a hex-something. And she mentioned a *brauche* man."

Ezra settled down deeper into the couch and pulled me closer. "Ah. Well, a *brauche* man does a kind of magic. Sometimes it's called powwow."

"Magic?"

"They use prayers and plants and whatnot, but some say it's magic all the same. You go to them when you're sick or there's a problem with an animal or bad weather. They say special prayers and give you medicine that you take or . . . like bundles or tokens that you put under your bed or in the horse's stall. Things like that."

"Sounds like voodoo or maybe a witch doctor. I didn't know the Amish had a folk magic like that."

"Oh, ja. Have you not seen our hex signs? These are old beliefs, coming from Germany. But not many think anything of them anymore. My grandmother used to go to an old powwow woman."

"Yeah? Your grandma did?" I sat up so I could see Ezra's face.

"Yes." His face was serious, but his eyes twinkled.

"Okay. What did this powwow woman do for your grandmother?"

"Treated aches and pains. Though maybe there were other things she used powwow for too. My father didn't approve. He'd grumble about 'the work of Satan' and 'being in league with the devil.' Some don't like powwow, even when it's a gut church member that does it. But my grandmother just complained louder about her pain and didn't stop goin'."

"She sounds like a character."

"She was a woman who knew how to get her way. You didn't cross her. Reminds me of someone else I know." Ezra was smiling as he told this story, but suddenly his smile faltered and pain darkened his eyes.

I'm sorry. I'm sorry you lost all of your family in one blow.

I didn't say it out loud, but I laid against his chest and squeezed him tight. Just when I thought the anguish of being shunned had passed, it could crop up again. It probably always would. I still missed my own parents at times, and they were dead. They didn't live fifteen miles away and refuse to acknowledge I'd ever been born.

"So . . . a powwow man could hypothetically curse someone and make their crops fail or make them sick?"

Ezra shrugged. "Hex signs are to protect from curses. So yes, I guess the Amish believe in such things. Do you?" He sounded genuinely interested in what an English person—that is, someone who wasn't Amish—might make of it.

"Hmmm." I thought about it. "I think there are people who *believe* they can lay curses and send a lot of bad intent your way. But I don't think it could actually hurt you unless you knew about the curse and believed in it too. Then you might have a psychosomatic response."

"What does that mean?"

"If you expect to become sick—really, truly believe it—it can make you sick."

Ezra's body, so lanky and relaxed beneath mine a moment ago, grew tense. His hand had been stroking my arm. It stopped.

"Did I say something wrong?"

Ezra bit his lip, then shook his head. "Sometimes I wonder at how easy it is for you to dismiss anything outside of us humans, anything outside the mind. Not sure if I should admire you for it or just feel brokenhearted."

Leave it to Ezra not to pull punches. He didn't say things he didn't mean, and he rarely held back on the stuff that was hard to hear. Religion, faith in God . . . it was something Ezra struggled with. He couldn't be Amish any longer, but he wasn't an atheist at heart either. In his upbringing there was no such thing as a middle ground. Unfortunately, I had no faith of my own to give him as an alternative. I'd seen too much out there as a cop, experienced too much of my own heartbreak when my husband had been brutally murdered, to believe in an omnipotent being who cared and directed man's fate.

I cupped Ezra's face. "I don't dismiss everything outside of us. God . . . I don't know. But faith and love . . . absolutely. *Curses*, though?" I put a funny twist on the final words, hoping to get him to smile.

It worked. He huffed. "Ja, okay. Maybe curses don't work. Or I'd have killed off a few of my mules a hundred times over."

"Not to mention our furnace."

Ezra nodded solemnly. "It's a right bugger."

"And the shower."

"The hot water runs the other way when I get in there. Don't do a lick of good to yell at it." He was all laconic irony now.

Playing the game, I bit back a smile. "And I've heard you say some not very nice things to our stove once or twice."

"The flame on that right front burner has it out for me."

I relaxed back into him with a laugh. I breathed in the warm scent of his shirt, relished the shift of hard muscles under cotton, and felt heat stir inside me. "I missed you today." I raised my head to kiss his neck.

"Yeah?" His hand stroked my arm once more, but this time there was an electric intensity to it. He pressed up into me ever so slightly, causing my body to immediately heat, preparing for him.

Someday, our mutual attraction, the love we have for each other, and, yes, the quite lovely sex, might not be enough, I thought. It might not be a glue strong enough to hold us together. We came from such different worlds. I feared that day. But for now, I'd take all of Ezra I could get.

CHAPTER 2

I'd just arrived at the station on Friday morning and sat down at my desk with a cup of coffee, when Grady came bursting out of his private office. His expression was grim and his large face was an angry, mottled red. That was not a look you wanted to see on a man his size—six foot two and at least two hundred fifty pounds. It was also not a look you wanted to see on the face of your boss, which Grady was. He shot a glance around at the desks of the seven investigators who constituted the Lancaster Police Violent Crimes Department. Then he marched straight up to me. I'm ashamed to admit, but I hoped it was something more interesting than the cases I'd had lately.

"What happened?" I asked.

"A neighbor found an entire Amish family dead this morning,

south near Willow Street. It's our jurisdiction. We're meeting the coroner there. My car. Now."

My stomach sank. An entire Amish family could be a lot of people. "Homicide?"

"That's what we need to find out."

Grady used his siren and drove fast. On the way, he told me what he knew.

"The man who reported it is Amish. Says the family's been ill for a few days. His wife sent their son over there with a basket of food this morning, and he found the previous day's basket untouched. So the father went inside the house and found them. He phoned it in."

"How many are dead?"

"I don't know."

"My God."

Grady sighed in agreement. "He said it didn't look like there'd been any violence. Most of them were in bed. Maybe it's carbon monoxide poisoning, something like that. I alerted the hazmat people already, and they're on their way. But I wanted you along in case there's any sign of foul play."

"Of course." I was already considering another possibility. The memory of visiting Samuel and Aaron Hershberger in the hospital came to mind. "What if it's a pathogen? Like a virus? Should we be sending people in there?"

A semi pulled over for our siren, and Grady shot me a troubled glance as he drove past it. "Any reason to think so?"

I hesitated. "I see Hannah Yoder once in a while, Katie's mother? She said there's been a lot of sickness in their community. A teenage boy died from it recently. You said the neighbor reported that this family had been sick."

Grady tapped the steering wheel thoughtfully. "Yeah. But all of them dying of it at once? Doesn't seem likely."

I knew what he was saying. As a cop, you played the odds. Food poisoning, a gas leak, or even homicide were much more likely. Still.

"Call dispatch," Grady continued with a sigh. "Ask them to make sure the hazmat team has extra suits. You and I'll suit up and go in first, make sure it's safe for the team." He shook his head as the possibilities sank in. "Jesus Christ."

I did what he asked. As I spoke to dispatch, I felt that familiar surge of excitement and dread that always kicks in before I arrive at a new crime scene. And this one promised to be more upsetting and bewildering than most. What would I find this time? And would I be able to figure out what had happened?

At the Kinderman farm, we waited twenty minutes for hazmat to arrive. The Amish neighbor who'd called it in, Jacob Henner, was there. I interviewed him while we waited.

Jacob looked like he was barely hanging on, his mind bent under the weight of the horror like a sapling in the wind. "They'd been sick 'bout two days. My wife visited with Mary Kinderman a few days back. She said the whole family had the flu."

"Did Mary Kinderman give any details about their symptoms?" I asked.

"Ja. Said the children couldn't keep nothin' down. Bad chills 'n' shaking. Aches. Real weak like. I seen Thomas and his son Isaac out ta the barn, or I woulda offered to milk for 'em. We pretty much jus' stayed clear, not wantin' our young'uns to get it. But my wife sent off a basket with food once a day, jus' to help out. 'N' the last one weren't even touched."

"Did it appear they'd been sick when you went into the house today, Mr. Henner? Any sign of vomiting, piles of tissues, things like that?"

"I dunno. I jus' dunno. I was jus' tryin' to see if any of 'em was alive." His voice shook. "Poor lil' children."

With difficulty, I got Jacob to list the residents of the Kinderman household by name and give his best guess at their ages. I wrote it all down in my notebook. There were six children living at home, plus the parents and a grandfather.

He remembered seeing the bodies of Mary and Thomas Kinderman, the parents. But he couldn't remember where he'd seen them—maybe their bedroom, but he wasn't sure—or exactly who else he'd seen for sure or even how many. Only that they were "all dead." He said he'd forced himself to check in case they needed help. I could picture this rather awkward-looking Amish man stumbling around the house checking bodies for signs of life. His disturbing the scene wasn't really helpful for our investigation or for Jacob either.

By the time hazmat arrived, three Amish buggies were parked in Jacob's driveway across the road. They watched the Kinderman house intently, probably hoping for news. As Ezra said, never underestimate the Amish grapevine.

Hazmat pulled in with a large, converted RV. Grady went over to speak to them and waved at me to come along. The first man out of the truck appeared to be in charge. He was in his thirties and looked inherently open, wholesome, and nice the way so many Pennsylvanians did. It was not a facade I'd seen often in my years with the NYPD.

"Steve Springfield, hazmat team leader." Steve shook Grady's hand with a confident smile.

"I'm Detective Grady and this is Detective Harris."

Steve's eyes lingered a little too long, and his hand gripped mine too lightly, as if he was nervous. I didn't take it personally. Men had a tendency to react to any attractive female. I looked away to break eye contact.

"We don't know what we're facing," Grady said, "so I'd like to borrow some suits for Detective Harris and I. I also want to take in our police photographer, Danielle, and one of the medics. He wants to check for survivors." He pointed them out. The medics with the ambulance crew had been particularly upset about not being able to go inside right away, even though Jacob Henner swore that no one was left alive. But they didn't carry protective gear, and neither did the police.

"You're welcome to suits, but you should let us go in first. We can run a quick check for gas or chemical contaminants."

"I don't want a lot of people tromping around the crime scene," Grady said.

"It'd just be me and one other technician. It'll take five minutes. Then you'll know you're not going into danger."

Grady reluctantly agreed. It was another delay, which I found annoying. I hated these time-sucking protocols even though I understood the need for them. The detective in me was itching to get into the house, see things with my own eyes, witness the victims where they lay, try to get a sense of their final moments. There was always a fear that if I wasn't quick enough, some vital clue would slip away and I'd be unable to solve the puzzle, unable to avenge the dead. I knew it was largely irrational, but that didn't make me any less anxious to get inside.

But by the time Grady, Danielle, the medic, and I had put on the clownlike yellow-hooded hazmat overalls, orange boots, and aqua plastic gloves, Steve and his fellow technician were out of the house again. Steve took off his gas mask and strode toward us.

He was breathing hard. It wasn't the rapid breathing of exertion but that of distress. He face had a hint of green, and it wasn't a reflection off his hazmat suit. "No gas, radiation, or chemical leaks in there that our gear could detect. It's clear for you to go in. But—"

Grady impatiently pulled his arm away from the hazmat girl checking the tape seal on his glove. He was clearly as eager to get to work as I was. "But what?"

Steve swallowed. "It's pretty bad."

Grady nodded once and pulled up the paper respirator mask that was hanging around his neck. "Ready, Harris?" His voice was muffled.

I nodded and we headed for the house. I prayed it was all a ridiculous precaution.

Inside the modest home, the stench of death was thick, even through the face mask. I started breathing through my mouth and motioned Danielle to stay close and photograph each body as it was found. I pulled out my iPhone to record a video of my walk-through, talking as I went. The little details I found myself describing would be useful later.

The first body was in the living room, just inside the door. It was a girl, and she was lying on the couch. The medic checked her and shook his head, then he and Grady headed farther into the house while Danielle took pictures of the body. I leaned in for a better look.

"Adolescent female, approximately twelve to fourteen years old. Brown hair bound in a disheveled ponytail. She's wearing a long flannel nightgown. . . ."

The only sounds in the house were the ticking of a loud grandfather clock, the click of the photographer's Nikon, and my recitation. "She's lying on the sofa under an afghan as if she'd been sleeping. There's a bed pillow under her head, white pillowcase. No trace of blood or fluid on it. There's a large stainless steel mixing bowl by the side of the couch, possibly to be used if she had to vomit. There's also a book on the floor. *A Girl's Story Collection.* Maybe she was reading before she fell asleep."

The thick aqua plastic gloves made my hands feel awkward, but I carefully raised the afghan so I could look underneath. "Postmortem, hands are curled protectively around her stomach.

Possibly she was in pain. There's a sharp odor of excrement." I forced myself to pull the afghan up a little higher to confirm. "Looks like the deceased vacated her bowels before or after death. Material is liquid in nature."

I was glad for the face mask. Not just because it lessened smells, but because I didn't like the looks of this at all. The girl, likely named Sarah by Jacob's account, had been very ill. Which meant whatever killed her might be contagious. God, she was so young. The death of a child like this felt wrong, even obscene, as if life itself had a freak-show deformity.

I pushed aside my emotions and finished my observations. There were no signs of foul play, and it didn't appear that the body had been disturbed in any way. I motioned to Danielle, and we moved on to the kitchen. There was no one in it, but there were dirty dishes in the sink, glasses with dregs of milk, cups, and bowls of what might have been Jell-O and ice cream. I knew enough about Amish families to know it was unusual for them to leave dirty dishes in the sink like this. Whatever had happened had been bad enough to disrupt the normal cleanup routine for at least a day. On the counter I found a bottle of cod liver oil, a near-empty bottle of Pepto-Bismol, and a box of saltine crackers. I noted my observations on the iPhone video and Danielle photographed the items.

I headed back through the living room to the old farmhouse stairs. I met the medic on the way down. I couldn't see a lot of his face behind his paper mask, but his eyes were vacant. He shook his head. *None alive.* He practically ran from the house.

I looked over my shoulder at Danielle. I didn't know her well, but from everything I'd seen, the plump and acne-scarred young police officer was professional and unflappable. Danielle nodded. *I'm okay.* I continued up the stairs.

I spoke into the iPhone. "First bedroom on the left at the top of the stairs. Looks like a queen bed containing three bodies. Two girls around four and six and an older woman, possibly the mother, Mary Kinderman."

I paused as Danielle's camera snapped away. I felt the need to take in the scene without interference from technology for a moment. The two girls were side by side in bed, both ashen with hollowed cheeks and purple bruises under their eyes. Their eyes were closed, as if they'd passed in their sleep. The woman was in a nightgown and a thick flannel robe that closed with a fabric belt. She was above the covers and on her side, one hand protectively stretched over her children. Her fingers just brushed the top of one brown-haired head. Her eyes were closed too. On the bedside table were a box of Kleenex, another bottle of Pepto-Bismol, and a partially drunk glass of milk.

I took a deep breath and resumed the video. "From the position of the bodies, it looks like the mother came in to check on the girls and lay down for a moment. She died here. It's unlikely the girls were already dead when this happened, or the mother would have gone for help. She looks like she just closed her eyes for a brief nap."

Had the girls been alive? Or was it possible they'd already been dead and the mother, in her grief, had simply lain down and given up. But her face looked too relaxed, her body's position too casual. I thought my first instinct was correct. At least Mary Kinderman had been spared the horror of her children's deaths.

In the next bedroom there were two single beds and two deceased boys in them. There was vomit in a bucket by one of the beds, lumpy and vile. A third boy, a young teen, was sitting up on the floor and leaning his back against one of the beds. His arms were around his knees and his face was buried in them. There was defeat and despair in his posture. *This boy knew*, I thought. He knew at least some of his family was dead. He probably knew he was dying too. That especially hurt.

The last bedroom on the left was the parents' bedroom. There was a man in the bed. He was on his back and I could see his full, long beard and bloodless face, his eyes closed. He had to be the family's father, Thomas Kinderman. Grady was standing next to the bed, arms folded in his yellow hazmat suit. He walked over when he saw me. Danielle began to photograph the body.

Grady's eyes above his paper mask were troubled. "No signs of foul play. Nothing environmental . . . You ever seen anything like this, Harris?"

I shook my head. When I'd been a beat cop in New York, I'd been on calls to check on a neighbor or to investigate a foul smell and found someone deceased. Many of those deaths were illness-related. But this? An entire family? And so fast too.

A thought went through my mind—what if this had been Hannah Yoder's family? All of them dead—Sadie, Ruth, Hannah, Isaac, and the rest—strewn about the house like dolls in a dollhouse shaken by an angry child. The idea was unbearable. "According to Jacob Henner, and what I saw in the kitchen, the family's been sick for a few days at least."

"Could be food poisoning," Grady suggested. We both knew that would be preferable to some apocalyptic disease, and more likely too. "In any event, this isn't looking like a homicide."

"What about poisoning?" I asked. I wasn't ready to walk away from this, not yet.

Grady looked at me sharply. "You seen any indication of that?"

I shrugged. I wasn't about to tell my boss about *brauche* men and powwow, but I couldn't completely dismiss Hannah's fears in the face of this new tragedy. "Whatever it was, it was relatively fast and a hundred percent fatal. Poison would explain that."

"Christ." Grady went to rub his jaw and ended up crinkling up the paper mask instead. "Guess I should at least talk to the CDC. I don't really wanna bring in the crime-scene team, at least not until I hear what the experts say about protocol. But if you and Danielle want to continue to record what you can without disturbing anything—*or* taking off your gear—go ahead. I'm gonna go make that—"

There was a loud knocking from downstairs. Someone was pounding on the front door. Grady and I looked at each other and we both headed down. When Grady opened the door, the neighbor, Jacob Henner, was standing there with an officer in uniform. Jacob's face was wild.

Not wanting to expose the men to whatever was in the house,

I stepped out onto the porch. Grady followed and shut the door behind him.

"What is it?" he asked the cop, still speaking through his face mask.

"Tell 'em," the cop said, looking at Jacob.

His face was red and his eyes bright with unshed tears.

What now? I thought, feeling a new wave of dread. Was Jacob's family sick too?

"Th-thought I should tend to their animals," he stuttered, his voice thick. "Went into the barn. The cows . . . the cows're sick too."

"Show me," I said, starting off the porch. Grady followed.

The barn door was open, banging in the April wind that had sprung up. As we crossed the yard, I would have given a week's pay to be able to strip off the confining suit and gloves, to peel the mask off my face, and breathe as much fresh air as I could get. The toxic, smothering smell of death and bile and sickness inside the house had seeped into my skin, hair, and mouth. But I didn't dare remove anything. Would I have to be sprayed down with disinfectant? I didn't even know. I was so out of my depth.

Inside the barn, Jacob led us over to a bar gate that opened into a large stall. The end of the stall was open to the pasture. Jacob went inside and held the gate for us. I looked at the manure-and-straw-covered floor of the stall and realized that, if I went in there, there'd be no going back into the house, at least not without visiting the hazmat RV again to change boots. I paused for only a moment though—this felt important. I stepped into the stall, and Grady came in behind me. The uniformed cop stayed on the other side.

"This way," said Jacob, still shaky.

He led us through the stall to the pasture. Just beyond the barn was a dead cow. It was light tan in color and fairly small, probably a calf. I recognized it as a Jersey, the docile and cream-rich dairy breed the Amish preferred. The carcass was lying up against the white wall of the barn, as if it had been sheltering there. Flies buzzed around it, and its tongue was out and bloated, its legs stiff.

"That one's dead. 'N' that one's sick," Jacob said, pointing.

A few feet away, a full-grown light brown cow stood, staring at us with enormous eyes. It blinked and seemed to want to start toward us, but after one hesitant step it stopped. Its entire body shook, its flank trembling. It bleated out a cry. Foamy mucus hung from its nose in ropes.

Feeling sick, I put a hand to my mask.

"She needs to be milked," Jacob said, his voice tight. "Her udder's so full 'n' she's in pain. Probably been a whole day or more. But I dunno if I should touch her. Do ya think I should go ahead and milk her? She's sick, but she needs to be milked real bad."

Grady cleared his throat. "We should probably call in the ASPCA."

"She needs to be milked right away," Jacob repeated. This was a man used to taking care of things, not calling in someone else to take care of them for him.

As much as I hated to see the cow suffer, this felt all wrong, so wrong it prickled the hairs on the back of my neck in warning. "Don't touch her. We don't know how long she's been sick or what she has. She might even have given it to the family. Plus, the milk—"

My brain hiccupped mid-sentence. *The milk in the sink. Glasses of milk on the bedside tables.*

I looked at Grady, horrified. He shook his head as if he couldn't believe what I was thinking, what we were now both thinking.

"Fuck it," Grady mumbled. "I'm calling in the CDC."

CHAPTER 3

By Saturday morning, the Lancaster City Bureau of Police was overwhelmed with technicians and investigators from the Centers for Disease Control in Washington, also known as the CDC. They were the knights and wizards of food-borne illness, and with the high number of fatalities in the Kinderman case, they were rightfully concerned. So was the public. News of an entire family dying—an *Amish* family at that—had made local headlines. The story was picked up by the Huffington Post. It was lurid and frightening enough to draw attention.

I was neither officially on the case nor, thanks to my pleading with Grady, officially off it. I couldn't forget my promise to Hannah to look into the sickness in the Amish community. *The curse.* I never mentioned that conversation to Grady, but I did my best to convince him that the department shouldn't close the case until the CDC or the coroner determined the exact cause of death. Then again, there wasn't much for me to investigate until they did, and I had plenty of other work to do.

Within twenty-four hours, E. coli, the most likely suspect, had been eliminated. It wasn't found in the Kindermans or in their cows. Nor was a viral infection the cause. The CDC labs set in to dig deeper, looking for less likely pathogens. I knew they'd combed the Kindermans' farmhouse from top to bottom and were fanning out agents to speak to other Amish families in the area to see if anyone else had been ill recently. Remembering my own stonewalled investigation as an outsider a year before, I didn't envy them.

I decided it was time to talk again to a source of my own. I went to see Hannah.

"I can't believe it. The whole family!" Hannah's voice was mournful as she placed two cups of strong, black coffee on the table. Supper was over in the Yoder household, and the older children were upstairs giving their mother a break by bathing the younger ones.

"It's devastating," I agreed. Scenes from my walk-through of the Kinderman farmhouse rose up, my gorge rising with it. I swallowed down the burning acid in my throat. "It must be so hard on your church."

Hannah tsked. "We pull together in God. It's all we can do. This is in his hands. But ocht—ist hard." She shook her head, the white strands of her bonnet swaying, and took a sip of her coffee. Hannah's hair was as neat as usual, and her thick blue dress and apron were ironed. But her eyes were swollen and red and her face was grim. She looked like a different woman without her typically placid expression. Hannah always seemed busy yet somehow at peace. At least, before today.

"We all pray the Lord spares any more children."

"Me too," I agreed. "I want you to know, we're going to find out what caused these deaths."

"You're a gut friend," Hannah said, toying nervously with her cup. "Did you ever speak to Henry Stoltzfus, the *brauche* man?"

I felt a twinge of guilt, but I had to tell the truth. "No, Hannah. I went to see Samuel and Aaron at the hospital, and I talked to their doctor. He was convinced it was the flu, but the tests for it were negative. I wasn't sure what I'd say to this . . . *brauche* man. I can't accuse someone of a crime without knowing what's actually going on."

Hannah's lips pressed tight. "I don't see how anyone could be so evil. But some are now sure it is *hexerei.* We've never seen anything like this sickness in the cows. It's not natural."

There were plenty of "natural" things that were just plain evil, but now was not the time for a philosophical discussion. "Has anyone else noticed their cows acting funny?"

Hannah nodded. "Leah Hershberger said her husband mentioned the cow was tremblin' when he milked her. Thought she'd been scared bad by a fox out in the pasture. And that was jus' before they all got sick."

I made a mental note to tell that to the CDC liaison, Dr. Turner. "Anyone else notice sick cows?"

"One farmer's cow come down lame, real sudden like. Can't find a thing wrong with its foot. And Abe Miller on Willow Brook had a birthin' calf get stuck and kill the mother."

This was becoming less helpful, as far as I was concerned. If people were afraid, nearly anything could be blamed on a curse.

"Are any other families sick?"

"Not so far," Hannah said quietly. "Praise God. But I'm scared to death when one of mine so much as sneezes." Hannah poured some milk from a small pitcher into her coffee cup. And I suddenly realized I'd put milk in my coffee too—and had drunk it. I knew the Yoders had their own milk cow. Fresh, raw milk was as ubiquitous as water in these households. My stomach wanted to cast it up. I fought the urge.

"Hannah . . . it might be wise for you to stop drinking your cow's milk. Just for a bit."

"What?" Hannah looked shocked, like I'd suggested she fly to the moon.

"Look, the CDC is investigating the Kindermans' deaths, and hopefully they'll soon know exactly what caused them and if there's a link to Will Hershberger's death. But it's possible that whatever made them sick was passed on from the cows to the family in the milk."

"But our cows ain't sick!" Hannah looked distraught, as if the idea had not occurred to her and she found it shocking, repellent.

I leaned forward and covered her hand with mine. "We don't

yet know what's going on. It's possible a cow could be sick for a day or two without showing any symptoms. And meanwhile, this sickness could still be passed through the milk."

Hannah went pale, then paler still, as horrors passed behind her eyes. "But . . . they haven't said . . . The truck picked up yesterday like always."

I heard what was behind the denial in her words. Because there was Hannah's family, yes. But the Yoders didn't just have a family cow, they had a small herd and they sold the milk. And beyond this farm there was an entire community that sold milk by the tons and depended on the money from it.

I held Hannah's gaze, and we shared a silent dread. *Don't get ahead of yourself. The CDC knows what it's doing.* I forced a reassuring smile. "I'm probably being paranoid. But if there's even a small chance . . ."

Hannah got up abruptly and opened the door of her refrigerator. She took out a plastic gallon of milk and poured it down the kitchen sink. She spoke stiffly. "I can keep the kids from drinkin' it in my kitchen, but Isaac's not gonna wanna stop production. Not with no proof the milk's bad."

I was pretty sure she was right and that Isaac Yoder wouldn't be the only one.

Amber Kruger dropped off her dog, Lemon, at the neighbor's at six A.M. on Tuesday morning. She'd never been a morning person, and the first hour of her Tuesdays and Saturdays were a huge drag. But by the time her intern, Rob, arrived at her apartment and they'd driven to their first stop of the day, she was ready to smile and enjoy herself. She always felt a heady lift of spirits pulling into Willow Run Farm in Bird-in-Hand.

Amber loved her little business, and she didn't care what anyone said, particularly not her conservative jerk of an ex-husband. She'd started Lancaster Local Bounty a year ago with a vision of taking goods from Lancaster County Amish farms to the farmers' markets in Philadelphia and, eventually, New York. It was a ton of work, and it had taken her some time to find Amish farmers who would work with her. But she was hopeful that by next year she'd be turning a profit. She wasn't trying to get rich. She rented a one-bedroom apartment in an old row house in downtown Lancaster, and she drove an older pickup truck that was paid off. But she did have to pay rent and eat, and there were the booth fees at the farmers' markets and gas. She just wanted to do what she believed in and make enough not to go in the hole on a monthly basis. Her savings from years of working at a local health food market had about run out, and now that she was divorced there was no financial buffer.

But this—this right here—was why it was worth it: visiting, feeling a part of these beautiful small farms.

Amber and Rob got out of the truck. Levi came out of the house to greet them. He was wearing his standard garb—black pants, white long-sleeved shirt, black suspenders, wool jacket, and black hat. It looked like he'd just finished his "second breakfast," having probably been up for hours. He nodded at them.

"Amber. Rob. Mornin'."

Rob grunted. He wasn't much of a morning person either.

"Morning, Levi!" Amber said brightly. "Looks like it'll be a nice day."

"Ja. Think so." Levi looked at the sun, still low on the horizon. The sky was blue and without a cloud. The chill of night was still sharp. There was a touch of frost on the rolling fields. It was breathtaking. Daffodils bloomed in profusion around the Fishers' farmhouse porch, making it feel like spring despite the cold.

"Have everythin' ready ta go." Levi walked toward one of the cement outbuildings he used for cool storage.

Amber followed. She and Rob, Levi, and one of Levi's sons loaded boxes of early spring produce into the back of Amber's truck. There were three different kinds of lettuces, spinach, some small red and white radishes Amber thought would sell well, spring onions, bunches of lovely asparagus, and the first flush of strawberries. Amber took everything Levi offered. Fresh produce was sparse this time of year. He tallied it up, scribbling on a notepad.

"How much milk d'ya wanna take today?" he asked.

"How much can you spare?"

"Ten gallons. Gotta hold some back for my regular customers."

"I'll take them. I always sell out of the milk by noon, no matter how much I take."

He smiled at that, looking pleased. "It's gut milk." He added the gallons to the total.

Amber hoped she could pick up more milk at her next few stops. She liked to take at least twenty gallons to the Philly market, even on Tuesdays. She was currently working with five Amish farmers, all of them super nice people. From two other farms she got produce and milk, much like she did from Levi. The Red Barn sold her bundles of fresh herbs plus sugar and gluten-free baked goods made by Lyah Augsburger. And the Beacheys had fantastic cheese made from goat's milk.

Unfortunately, Amber had to pay the farmers up front. She'd tried talking them into letting her take the goods on spec, but they hadn't been interested. Still, they offered her a good discount. And usually she sold enough of it to cover her investment, if not much else.

She wished more people understood what a *privilege* it was to be able to get local produce raised chemical-free direct from Amish farms, and how important it was to support them by buying direct. Small family farms like this were all but gone in other parts of the U.S., replaced by thousand-acre empires farmed by huge machines. These people worked hard and had a challenging way of life. Why, just yesterday there'd been a story in the news about an entire Amish family that had taken sick and died, and the investigators still didn't know why. It was awful. Amber thought about mentioning the tragedy to Levi, but she wasn't sure how well he knew the Kinderman family, and she didn't want to upset him.

Sometimes the hippies at the Philly market turned up their noses because Amber's produce wasn't "certified organic." She explained that most of the Amish farmers didn't bother with that kind of government certification, but they raised their produce without all those toxic chemicals, and their animals grazed on real pasture and weren't locked up indoors their whole lives. But God forbid something not be stamped with a big old "USDA approved." Idiots. Everyone knew the USDA was in bed with Monsanto and big pharma and every other corporate evil you could name. Amber considered herself a commando against all that. She was involved in nothing less than a holy war.

"That 'bout does it," Levi said as he loaded the last of the raw milk into one of her coolers. "Total comes to two hundred fifteen dollars."

Amber peeled off the cash, trying not to feel anxious about it. This was business. It took money to make money. "Thank you, Levi! See you Saturday."

"Ja, See ya then. God bless."

Levi and his son walked toward the house, and Amber looked around for Rob. She snorted as she saw him squatting down, petting the Fisher's dog. Like most farm dogs, it was used to visitors and was a social creature. It was pretty too—a Bernese mountain dog. Rob scratched behind both of the dog's ears and the dog panted happily. That boy was such an animal lover. He was a lazy-ass intern but an animal lover all the same. And she paid pennies for his time because he wanted to learn about organic farming. She could hardly complain if he didn't bust tail.

She took the opportunity to open a gallon of the raw milk and fill up her empty travel mug. She hadn't had time for breakfast, but the rich milk would hold her for hours. She put the rest of the gallon in the cooler and opened up the driver's door.

"Let's go, animal whisperer!" she called out, laughing, to Rob.

Rob turned to her with a shy smile and headed for the truck.

"Ooh, fresh asparagus! Don't you wish we could have it all year long?"

It was a windy April day and almost closing time at the farmers' market. Amber was exhausted and ready to pack up the remains of their goods and head home. But the new customer was cute with her cropped blonde hair, boxy black glasses, and rosy-cheeked toddler in a carrier that wrapped around her torso. Amber couldn't help but smile.

"Fresh asparagus is the best," Amber agreed wholeheartedly. "It's really amazing when you can just snip it off the stalk in the garden, walk to your stove, and toss it into a hot steamer. But this is as fresh as you'll find it unless you grow it yourself."

"Ooh, gimme gimme!"

"How much would you like?"

"I'll take the three bunches here. Do you have more in the back?"

"No, sorry. This is the last of the asparagus today."

"Oh no! In that case, let me grab those quick. What about strawberries? I saw some at other booths, but they were from greenhouses. Your stuff is from Amish farms, right?" The woman looked up at the large banner Amber had designed. It depicted a painted farm scene with a red barn and the words "Fresh Direct to You from Amish Farms in Lancaster County," and "Chemical Free!" and "Raw Milk!" The woman tilted her head. "Are the strawberries coming in over there yet?"

"We had the first batch this week." Amber grinned. "So good! Unfortunately, I didn't have that many pints and I sold out. But I should have a ton more on Saturday."

"Damn." The woman lightly frowned. "I work an early shift at the hospital on Saturdays. Don't get home until three."

"If you're sure you'll be here before we close, I'd be happy to set aside a few pints for you."

"Would you?" The woman looked like she'd been promised a winning lottery ticket. Then again, the first spring strawberries straight off the farm were close. "I can *definitely* be by, like, three thirty?"

"We close at four, so yeah, if you can make it by then that would be great."

"That's amazing! Thank you so much!"

Amber smiled at the woman. They were definitely on the same wavelength. And her baby was such a cutie. Lucky baby to have a mama like this one.

"And I suppose you're completely out of raw milk?" the woman pouted.

"Oh, yeah! Sorry. That goes fast."

The woman sighed. "I figured. Oh well!" She jostled the

brown-haired munchkin strapped to her chest. "We'll have to get our moo moo at the store tomorrow!" she cooed to the little girl. "Lilah's crazy about the stuff," she told Amber.

"Well that's something she and I have in common." Amber leaned forward to touch the baby on the nose. She was rewarded with a smile.

"They have it at the natural food store in town, but it's a pain getting over there. We're so lucky, aren't we? I have a friend who's a mom in Maryland. Sometimes she'll drive up for a visit just to pick up raw milk. I can't imagine not being able to get it whenever I want it."

This was a topic Amber felt passionately about, and her tiredness from the long day faded as her blood rose. "I know!" she agreed. "Technically, I'm not supposed to sell it to anyone who'll take it over the state lines. But screw that. Anyone who wants to buy it from me, I'm not asking questions. If they happen to mention they're from Jersey or Maryland, I'm just like, 'La la la! Didn't hear that!'"

The woman laughed. "Good for you! So how much do I owe you for the asparagus?" The woman pulled a wallet out of a pouch in the carrier.

Amber hesitated. "You know, I have a gallon of milk in the truck I poured one glass out of this morning. If you want it, you can have it. Just so you have something to hold you over till tomorrow. No one drank out of the carton or anything."

The woman looked unsure. "Seriously? I don't want to take it if you were keeping it for yourself."

"Oh, I still have most of a gallon at home. I'm good."

"Well . . . okay. That'd be wonderful! Would you like some milk, Lilah?"

"Moo moo!" the little girl said happily, kicking her legs.

Amber laughed.

CHAPTER 4

The CDC held a VIP emergency debriefing at the police station on Tuesday morning, four days after the Kindermans had been found. The heads of a few state agencies came down from Harrisburg, and only the top brass of the police were invited. Fortunately, Grady stopped at my desk and nodded at me to come along. He knew I had a real jones for this case, even though the CDC were in charge of it.

Dr. Glen Turner from the CDC led the meeting. He was in his mid-thirties with sandy hair, a goatee, and a "hip scientist" vibe. His button-down oxford shirt and khakis stood out among all the suits. He came across as very intelligent and firmly in charge. He was pretty cute too. Not that I cared one way or the other. It was just an observation.

"Our lab has identified the toxin." Dr. Turner had his laptop plugged into a projector, and he put up a photograph of a plant. It had long stems and a wide head made up of tiny white flowers. "The Kindermans died of tremetol poisoning. It was in their cow's milk. Tremetol is found in a few wild plants—most commonly *Eupatorium rugosum* or white snakeroot." He waved at the picture on the screen. It looked like the sort of flowering weed you'd see along rural roads. "Also called deerwort, tall boneset, and richweed. The animals eat the plant, get sick, and develop tremors and weakness. The tremetol is passed along in their milk and meat. In sufficient concentrations, it's fatal to humans."

I had a million questions, and I wasn't the only one. A dozen hands went up, but Dr. Turner waved them down. "Let me get through this information, please. I'll take questions later."

He clicked to a photograph of the Kindermans' farm. "We've already been in touch with Pennsylvania's DCNR—the Department of Conservation and Natural Resources." He nodded to a man in the room, and the man put up a hand in acknowledgment. "They tell us white snakeroot isn't native to Pennsylvania, and they aren't aware of any growing here in the wild. We've checked the feed supplies the Kindermans were using for their dairy cows. They grew and harvested their own hay and bought grain feed from a local supplier. There's no sign of the tremetol in the feed. So that's a good thing, because a lot of farms use that same supplier."

Holy shit. The possibilities spooled out in my mind.

"Our most important concern at the moment is to locate the source of the tremetol on the Kindermans' farm. It is possible we're looking at an invasive-plant problem, so we're working with the DCNR. We'll be checking every inch of the Kindermans' fields. But it's also possible the cows got the toxin some other way—something brought onto the farm like livestock medicine, ear oil, insect repellent, whatever. We'll find it. And yes, we have prepared a press statement we'll be releasing in about an hour. Questions?"

This time only about five people raised their hands, but I found myself speaking before Turner could call on anyone. "Excuse me, but what about the milk?"

Dr. Turner blinked at me. "I'm sorry. What's the question, exactly?"

"What about all the other local farmers and their families who are still drinking their cows' milk? Not to mention selling it? Shouldn't we be warning people?"

A man in the front row stood up. He was definitely a state agency man, probably in his sixties. He wore a navy suit that somehow fit around his extremely wide middle, and he had the thick white hair and pleasant face of a character actor—or a politician. He shook his head ponderously, his hands making a "no, no" gesture. "I'd like to speak to that, if I may. Miss—?"

"Detective Harris," I said firmly.

"Right. Thank you for your service, Detective Harris."

Patronizing much? I folded my arms across my chest and waited.

"I'm Mitch Franklin, Pennsylvania Department of Agriculture. The situation here is that we only have one farm, the Kindermans', where this problem has occurred—"

"But there have been at least two other Amish families who've had unknown illnesses, and a boy named William Hershberger died of it. Isn't it possible that was tremetol poisoning too?" I pointed out.

The man made that same refuting gesture. "I was only aware of one other family, the Hershbergers, but so far there's no *evidence* they were exposed to this tremetol toxin. The boy's death certificate lists influenza, and he's already been interred."

I struggled to keep my voice reasonably pitched. "There *was* no influenza virus. I had the doctor culture Samuel and Aaron Hershberger to check."

"I read their file. The attending physician noted that the virus had likely already run its course before they did that test. Now, having *said* that . . ." He changed on a dime to a placating tone. "I know Dr. Turner and the CDC won't stop until they've traced down every single *remotely* possible case. But as of this moment, the situation is that we've got forty-five hundred farms in Lancaster County and over ninety-five thousand dairy cows. We can't stop the flow of the ocean because of a single bad drop. So far the only confirmed victims drank the milk from their *own* infected cows, and they didn't sell that milk to outsiders. The CDC is going to resolve this thing as fast as they can. Once they've found the source of the tremetol, we'll have a good idea if any other farms might have been exposed to it. In the meantime, we're not going to overreact."

A few men in the audience murmured in agreement. I shut my mouth tight and didn't respond. Mitch Franklin sat back down.

Dr. Turner glanced at me curiously. "Any more questions?" he asked the room.

Amber Kruger pulled her truck onto the wide shoulder of Route 30 and slowed down, then stopped. The cars and trucks whizzing by her driver's-side window caused her to jerk and wince. They were too loud, too close, too fast. She wiped the back of her hand over her forehead and encountered clammy moisture. Her ears were ringing loudly.

"Amber? Are you okay?"

Rob's voice sounded distant through the cacophony of white noise in her head. She was so tired it felt like an effort to open her mouth and answer. "Not feeling great."

Rob's concerned, boyishly plump face came into focus as he leaned in to study her. "Christ, you don't look good." He felt her forehead. A chill racked her body at the touch of his warm fingers.

"I'm okay. Just woozy. Shouldn't be driving."

"No shit. I can drive."

Amber had never let Rob drive her truck, but she nodded and opened the driver's-side door to switch places.

The fresh air revived her a bit as she walked around the truck. But then the diesel fumes of a passing semi hit her and turned her stomach. She put a hand on the back of the truck to steady herself. As the nausea faded, she yawned hugely.

Rob's hand was on her shoulder. "Okay?"

"Yeah. Wow. Really tired."

"Come on." He steered her around to the passenger side and opened the door.

She snorted. "How gallant."

"You must not feel *too* bad if you can still pick on me," he teased. He closed the door and went around to the driver's side.

He started the truck but hesitated before pulling out. "Um . . . what should I do? Do you need to go to the ER? I can take you to the one in Lancaster. We could be there in half an hour."

"No!" Now that Amber was back in the car, she mainly just felt tired. Tired and weak. Rob was driving, so she could close her eyes and not have to worry about the way her vision was blurring. She yawned again. "Just go back to my place."

"If you say so," Rob said doubtfully. "But if you feel worse on the drive, I'll be happy to take you in."

"'Kay," Amber said. It was the last conscious thought she had before falling asleep.

After the debriefing, I was left feeling restless. I had six other open cases on my plate right now—but most of them were pretty much open-and-shut, needing routine paperwork, reports verified, and facts triple-checked. It was hard for me to focus on any of them. I couldn't stop thinking about the Kindermans, Will Hershberger, and Hannah's family.

Giving in, I pulled out a book of detailed maps of the county and compared the locations of the Kindermans' farm, the Hershbergers', and that of another family Hannah mentioned, the Knepps. The Hershbergers and the Knepps were both in Paradise and not too far apart. But the Kinderman farm was south of Lancaster near Willow Street, not close at all to the other two geographically. It didn't make sense.

"Hello, Detective."

I looked up to find Dr. Turner standing at my desk. "Oh. Dr. Turner. Hello." I felt self-conscious and stood up from my ungainly position leaning over the maps on my desk. I tugged down my suit jacket.

"Call me Glen." He smiled.

"All right. Glen."

"Listen, I just wanted to follow up on what you said in the meeting."

"Okay."

"You mentioned the Hershberger family, and we've already reviewed their records. I was wondering if you have any specific reason to believe their case is related to the Kinderman family? And you said there were others."

I told him what I'd learned from Hannah. "The Knepp family was also sick with what they thought was the flu. But it was supposedly much like the illness the Hershbergers had. An older woman died. It seems like an obvious connection to me."

"I understand." Glen looked serious. "It's part of our protocol to check out any and all similar cases and verify or eliminate them. So absolutely, we'll check into it. As far as the Hershbergers go, it's not as straightforward as I'd like. Most of the family didn't have blood work done, and there was no autopsy on the boy due to the family's wishes. The tests we do have on the father and his other son from the hospital, well, they certainly didn't test for tremetol, and the blood samples they *did* take weren't saved."

I folded my arms and half sat on my desk. "Would tremetol show up in blood work if you took it again now?"

"I don't know. Honestly, we don't have any experience with tremetol poisoning. It's rare, to say the least. But I do know it's usually fatal, so if most of the people in these other families had it and survived, they'd have to have ingested a pretty small dose. I do want to check their blood again, just to be thorough. Assuming we can get the Hershbergers to cooperate."

I stood and pushed the open map book closer to Glen. "Take a look at this. Let's say the Hershbergers and Knepps *did* have low-level tremetol poisoning. What doesn't make sense to me is that their farms are so spread out. The Knepps and Hershbergers aren't that far apart, but neither are close to the Kindermans." I showed him where I'd marked the farms on the map. "That's gotta be at least ten miles as the crow flies. If this is caused by an invasive plant, why didn't it show up at the farms in between? And even if the Kindermans are the only ones who actually had tremetol poisoning, why them? Their farm is in the middle of dozens of other farms on all sides. How could a dangerous plant show up there and nowhere else?"

Glen leaned over the map with interest. "Well, first, it is possible for a bird to drop a seed miles from where it ate a plant. So it's possible a nonindigenous plant *could* show up on one landlocked farm. But also, we haven't ruled out the possibility the tremetol was in some product or hay bales or feed the farms were using and not a plant on the farm itself. We need to locate the source. We're going to be combing the Kindermans' pasture for the plant today and checking everything in the barn and farmhouse too."

"I suppose some of these other farms might have had sicknesses and not reported them," I admitted, skimming my hand over the map page. "In fact, that wouldn't at all be unusual with the Amish. They're not the type to run to the doctor at the first sign of a sniffle."

"So I gather. I didn't have much luck questioning the Kindermans' neighbors. 'Stoic' doesn't begin to cover it." Glen studied my face in a way that made me uncomfortable. "I, um, hear your boyfriend is Amish."

I was surprised at the mention of my personal life. Had he asked about me? "Yes. Well . . . Ezra is ex-Amish anyway."

"Oh. I'm sorry to have that confirmed."

I looked up at Dr. Turner to find that our heads were close together over the map. I straightened up abruptly. What did he mean? Why would he be sorry Ezra was ex-Amish?

Glen blushed a little, his cheeks going rosy. It was a strangely boyish look on a mature man. "Sorry. I'm sorry. I just meant . . . I'm sorry to have it confirmed that you have a boyfriend. That's a stupid thing to say, and I apologize."

"Fairly stupid, yes," I said coolly. Actually—and I'd never admit this—I felt a little flattered. I glanced at his left hand and found the ring finger bare. Dr. Turner was an accomplished man and apparently not married, so at least he wasn't a jerk on top of being overly friendly.

"You just seem . . . dedicated to the work. And bright. I admire that. And, well, obviously you're attractive. You can probably tell I don't get out much." Glen laughed self-consciously. But I didn't think he was as shy as he was pretending to be. "Um . . . anyway, back to the point—too late. Since you *do* know the local Amish, do you think your boss would object to you checking in on some of these farms? Say, specifically, the ones between the Kindermans' and the Hershbergers'?" He tapped the map. "Ask if they've had any illness in the family or with their animals, and maybe if they've seen the plant we're looking for? I can get you photos. I really need to be supervising at the Kinderman farm today, but if you're willing to do some legwork . . ."

"I'd love to," I said without hesitation. "If you put in a word with Grady, I'm sure he won't mind. To be honest, I'm really worried about this. And . . . I sort of promised a friend."

Glen nodded grimly. "I don't blame you for being worried. But hopefully we can figure this out quickly, and it won't cause any more trouble."

Those sounded suspiciously like famous last words.

CHAPTER 5

By the time I got home from work on Wednesday night, I was deeply out of sorts. I walked into our kitchen just after eight to find Ezra reading a local paper, the *Lancaster Farmer.* He closed it and smiled.

"Glad you're home. Got some grilled chicken and potatoes on."

The table was already set. Ezra went to the stove where there was a cast iron skillet and several pots covered and awaiting my arrival.

"You're the best. Just let me change." I felt exhausted.

I went into our bedroom and took off the charcoal gray suit and white silky blouse that was part of my detective wardrobe. I put on oversized flannel pj bottoms and a long-sleeved thermal shirt. Although it was April, the nights were chilly and I preferred to wear warm, comfy clothes until the summer heat made them unbearable.

Back in the kitchen, Ezra had dinner on the table. He cooked simple things like grilled chicken and baked or mashed potatoes and steamed veggies. But the food was from local farms, if not raised by Ezra himself, and it was always delicious. Right now, though, I needed a hug more than I needed to eat. Sighing contentedly, I put my arms around his waist. I loved the sense of strength and security I felt when his arms closed around me. He rubbed my back.

"All right?" he asked after a moment.

I shook my head.

"Bad day, then?"

"People expect me to be some sort of Amish whisperer, and I'm so not."

He chuckled. "Well, you do pretty gut with me."

I smiled against his chest. "*You*, yes. And I've gotten to know a few people in the community. But most of the Amish still treat me like I'm a scarlet woman."

"You are a scarlet woman. That's part of your charm."

I laughed at his teasing and pulled away. "Well this scarlet woman is hungry. Anyway, I could have wings and be glowing and I'm not sure I'd fare much better when it comes to interviewing the Amish." I plopped down in my chair and picked up my fork, then hesitated.

Ezra sat down and looked at me. "Go on and eat."

"Did you . . . want to say grace?" There was always an awkward moment when we started a meal. I knew Ezra was used to saying grace, and I wasn't. I sensed he missed it. It was in the way he always hesitated at the start of each meal. "It's fine with me if you want to."

"Not sure what I'd say." Ezra shrugged and frowned down at his food. As if to prove a point, he cut off a piece of chicken and took a bite. "Who were you interviewing today?"

I sighed and let it go. "I stopped at about thirty farms between the Kindermans' and the Hershbergers'."

"What'd you learn?"

"Not much. No one else has been sick, and that's great. That's a relief. But when I, or Glen, ask to see their animals, or suggest they lay off the raw milk for a bit—"

"Glen?"

Ezra's tone was merely curious, but I felt a guilty heat flush my neck. Damn it. I had nothing to feel guilty about. Yes, Dr. Turner was interested in me, but I hadn't encouraged him. "Dr. Glen Turner. He's, um, with the CDC. He met up with me this afternoon to help interview. Do you know they've scoured every bit of the Kindermans' farm and haven't found any trace of white snakeroot? Or any other source of the toxin, tremetol?"

Ezra watched me with calm interest. "That's good news. Not so?"

"Well . . . yes. But that means we still don't know where the toxin came from. And until we know that, it could show up somewhere else. It's frustrating that nobody is taking this seriously. I mean, when we go to these farms and say we're there to look at their animals and make sure they're not sick, you'd think we were threatening to shoot their cows or something."

"A man's protective of his animals. He doesn't like people thinkin' he's not taking good care of them," Ezra pointed out. "And they don't know you."

"But people have died! And when I suggest they refrain from drinking their cows' milk, just until we've figured out what's going on, they get angry!"

"Elizabeth."

Ezra's voice was calm but pointed. I realized I probably sounded a wee bit too intense. I took a deep breath and tried to relax. I'd felt like such an idiot this afternoon. It was one thing when the Amish farmers treated me like a strange and threatening creature, because I was not only English—an outsider—but a female and a police officer as well. But it was particularly embarrassing to be treated like a pariah on my home turf in front of a government agent like Dr. Turner.

And that wasn't even what really bugged me. I was frustrated about the case. My gut was telling me something was wrong. Hell, I'd walked through a farmhouse full of corpses, an entire Amish family dead after having no doubt suffered horribly. And most of the Amish acted like it had nothing to do with them. It was tragic but somehow "God's will." They would rather pray about it than take easy steps for their own protection. At least, that's how it seemed to me.

"Sorry," I muttered.

Ezra picked up his glass of milk and held it up. "You don't

know how it is. To the Amish, a man, his family . . . they don't just buy this at market. They raise their animals like they raise their gardens. Eating the fruits of that labor is a blessing and a responsibility. You don't let it go to waste. You don't turn your nose up at it. You thank God for it. Anything less would be the worst kind of blasphemy."

"But it's just milk!"

The gulf between me and Ezra rarely felt this wide, but he was looking at me with his brow wrinkled in confusion. He gave a frustrated grunt. "No such thing as 'just milk.' When you have a family cow, you drink milk at every meal, and between meals too. It's free and it's gut for the body. If you're feeling peaky, you drink milk. If you can't sleep, you drink milk. If the milk jug is empty, you go milk the cow. If the cow is dry, you go milk the neighbor's cow. And if the neighbor's cow is dry, well . . . in that case it's time for a general meetin'."

He was trying to be funny in that laconic way of his, but I wasn't in the mood to be amused. "I'm not asking them to give up milk forever. It's just until we've figured out where the toxin is coming from. You'd think parents would worry about their children. Hannah poured out *her* milk."

Ezra shook his head. "Hannah knows you. And she knows the Hershbergers gut too. You won't convince most Amish that there's somethin' poison in the animal he raised on his own land, and milks with his own hands."

I crossed my arms over my chest. "They'd damn well better hope I'm wrong then."

Ezra set his glass down, giving it a guilty glance. Suddenly, I felt uneasy. "That's the milk I brought home last night, right? From the store?" I got up and went to the refrigerator. Inside was the half gallon of pasteurized milk from a national brand in its carton with a grinning cartoon cow. Unopened. Next to it was a plastic unmarked gallon I recognized all too well, the top quarter already gone. "Ezra! For God's sake!"

Ezra's voice was steady but had a trace of apology in it. "Happened to go by Henry's Fruit Market today and . . . I was thirsty."

Feeling sick and angry, I strode to the table, picked up Ezra's glass, and carried it to the sink. There my temper and frustration overcame me, and instead of pouring it down the drain as I'd planned, I threw the glass of milk into the sink where it shattered and sent drops of milk flying everywhere.

"Elizabeth!" Ezra was out of his chair, his face red.

"How could you do that? You say Hannah knows me. How could *you* get that milk and drink it when you know—" My voice cracked. I was at a loss. "You didn't see them, the Kindermans! You didn't go into that house!"

"Hush!" Ezra strode over in two big steps, put his arms around me, and pulled me close. "I'm sorry. You mentioned it . . . but—I truly didn't know it meant that much to you. I won't drink it again. Don't be upset."

"Ugh!" I remained stiff in his arms. The thought of him waking in the night, vomiting . . . seeing him die in agony. One part of me knew I was being ridiculous. I was overreacting, like some kind of PTSD reaction to seeing those bodies, those *children*. The likelihood of there being anything wrong with *this* milk was minuscule. But still—

There was a knock on the front door.

"Who would be callin' at this hour?" Ezra made no move to get the door, just kept soothingly rubbing my back.

"I'd better see." I pulled away, not entirely done being mad at him. Christ. If my own boyfriend didn't listen to me about this . . . I wiped my eyes and walked to the door.

I opened it to find Glen Turner standing there looking unhappy. "Sorry to bother you at home. I tried your cell, but it went right to voice mail."

"The battery's probably dead. Sorry about that." I stepped back. "Come on in. What's going on?"

Glen stepped into the living room. He looked around curiously—and his eyes found Ezra, who'd followed me from the kitchen. The two men studied each other silently with a distinct air of sizing each other up.

"Um . . . Glen, this is my boyfriend, Ezra. Ezra, this is Dr. Glen Turner."

"Call me Glen." He held out his hand.

"Ezra." Ezra shook Glen's hand, but his face was closed off.

"What's happened?" I repeated.

Glen straightened back up, his expression turning grim. "I'm on my way to Philly right now. People have been showing up at emergency rooms there with symptoms that sound like tremetol poisoning. Five people have died, two of them children."

"Oh no!"

"The thing is—when doctors questioned them about what they'd eaten, all of them had consumed raw milk. And they all got it at a farmers' market there in Philly, from a booth called Lancaster Local Bounty. The milk came from *here*, Harris."

"Oh my God!" I put a hand to my head as if that would make the information easier to absorb. Maybe I should have felt a touch of vindication for my gut's sake, but I felt nothing but horror, horror for what had already happened and fear about what was still out there.

I turned and glared at Ezra. "What did I tell you! And you were drinking it at supper!"

"Sorry," he said sheepishly. "I'm sure I'll be fine."

Glen watched the two of us warily. "Anyway, I talked to Grady and he said maybe you could contact the woman who runs that Lancaster Local Bounty booth. Find out where she got the supply she sold at the market on Tuesday, and find out if she sold it or gave it to anyone else. I'm sorry to ask, but my staff and I need to check out this Philly outbreak. If you can get a list of from her tonight, my team can run it down in the morning."

"Of course. I'll go right away."

"Thanks. You should call Grady. I think he wanted you to go with a partner. The woman's name and address were sent to your e-mail. I'd, um, better go." Glen looked at Ezra. "It was nice to meet you." His tone was stiff and overly formal.

A nod was Ezra's only reply.

An hour later, I stood outside a row house where Amber Kruger lived. It was squeezed on both sides by identical homes, like lovers trapped forever in an embrace. The street was in one of the trendy old neighborhoods of downtown Lancaster, the sort frequented by young urban professionals. It was gentrified enough that I was surprised to see recent graffiti. The narrow residential street had the word "cotton" spray-painted on the asphalt in two-foot-high neon yellow letters.

Manuel Hernandez came jogging up with a welcoming smile. The ex-soldier was a relatively new detective and younger than me. He was my favorite peer in the department. Hernandez was tough but had a gentle spirit and was always eager to provide assistance, no matter how boring the grunt work.

"Hey, Harris."

I returned the smile. "Hi. Guess we're both working late tonight." I checked my watch. It was just going on ten o'clock, so hopefully our target would still be awake. "Grady give you a rundown?"

"Just that you need to interview someone, and there might possibly be more legwork tonight, depending on what you learn."

"That's close enough. Ready?"

"Always! Let's do this, boss," Hernandez quipped.

I rolled my eyes. I wasn't Hernandez's boss, but his light attitude made me relax, and I was grateful. I was glad I'd gotten Hernandez tonight. The Lancaster Police Violent Crimes Department was so small that I often worked alone or with whomever was available.

I knocked on the row house door. It was opened by a thin young man in sweatpants, a T-shirt, and thick socks. "Hi. Can I help you?"

I held up my badge. "Detectives Harris and Hernandez, Lancaster Police. We have some questions for Amber Kruger. Is she available?"

The guy looked surprised. "She, um, rents the apartment upstairs. I'll go knock."

We stepped into the hallway while the guy took a set of stairs two at a time. The old row house had been converted into two apartments—one up and one down. The door to the downstairs apartment was slightly cracked open, and we could hear the faint sounds of a TV. The staircase turned so we couldn't see the top of it, but I heard knocking.

"Amber? There're some people here to see you." Pause. "Amber?" He knocked again.

The guy came back down looking regretful. "She's not answering." He went to the front door and opened it, peeked out. "Her truck is here. Maybe she walked a few blocks to a restaurant or something, but I'd be surprised. She sounded pretty sick last night."

I felt the hair on the back of my neck prickle. "Sick? How do you know that, Mr. . . ."

"Nick. Nick Smith. Well, my wife and I heard her in the night. Her bathroom is right over ours. It sounded like she was in a bad way, so my wife went upstairs and checked on her. But Amber just wanted to go back to sleep."

"Have you seen Amber today?"

"No, but my wife and I both work. What's this about?" Nick looked uneasy.

"You have a key to that apartment, bro?" Hernandez asked him with a voice like velvet over a sledgehammer.

"Um . . . yeah. Sure. We swapped in case . . . you know. Fire or whatever."

"Get it," I said.

I instructed Nick to stay in his own apartment while Hernandez and I headed up. Knocking got no response, so I unlocked the door and cracked it open. "Amber? This is the Lancaster Police."

Nothing, not a sound. The air in the apartment felt stifling, suffocatingly hot, as if the occupant had turned up the heat hours ago and never turned it down. The heat made the cloying smell of the sickroom worse. I started breathing through my mouth, and Hernandez wrinkled his nose. It wasn't pleasant, but it didn't smell like death, thank God. I knew exactly what *that* smelled like.

"Amber?" I stepped farther into the apartment and nodded at Hernandez to go check out the kitchen. I headed for the hall and the bedroom.

I found Amber Kruger in bed. She was on her side in baby blue pajamas, covers cast off, knees curled up protectively into her chest. Her skin shone yellow-white, like the moon, and there was a sheen of sweat cast over her features. She looked young and petite with frizzy red-brown hair and freckles. And she lay so heavily on the bed she looked partially sunk through it.

"Amber?" I knelt by the bed and put my fingers to Amber's throat, dreading to find the flesh stiff and cold. But it was soft and there was a pulse, faint and slow like the final notes of a slow orchestral march. Thank God! As if to confirm the diagnosis of life, a tremor racked through Amber's body. I had the strangest thought—that Amber was in the crack between life and death and her body was trying to shake her loose one way or the other. She didn't waken.

"Shit." I pulled out my cell phone and called dispatch. "I need an ambulance right away. And call Lancaster General and have them ready for a critical patient with tremetol poisoning." I gave Amber's address. Thankfully, the hospital wasn't far. As I put the phone in a pocket, Hernandez touched my shoulder.

"She gone?" he asked quietly.

"No, but she's going." I stood up, ignoring the hand he offered. As a female police officer, I'd learned to never accept any gesture that underlined my femininity, no matter how innocent the intention.

And now what? I felt useless. If this had been a heart attack or hypothermia, a broken leg or car accident, my training would tell me what to do. But I had no idea what might help tremetol poisoning. I wished I'd asked Glen Turner that question.

"Can you get a warm, wet cloth from the bathroom," I asked Hernandez. I sat on the bed. "Amber? Amber can you hear me?" I picked up her left hand—it was damp and chilled—and rubbed it briskly.

Hernandez brought the cloth. "Should you be that close?" he asked worriedly. "I mean, is she—"

"It's not contagious. Not like that." *At least, I hope not.*

Amber's eyelids flickered briefly.

"Amber? Can you stay with me? The ambulance is on its way. Hang in there." *Please don't die. You don't deserve this, and I have to know where you got that milk, and where you sold it.*

From the distance came the blessed sound of sirens.

By the time Hernandez and I reached the hospital, Amber was already in the ER.

"You gonna wait?" Hernandez asked when it was clear there wouldn't be news anytime soon.

"Yeah, I'll stay. But you should go home. There's nothing you can do, and we can't both fall asleep at our desks tomorrow."

"If you say so, boss. Promise you'll call me if you need me?"

"Pinky swear." I smiled.

Hernandez gave a jaunty salute and left me to my solitary vigil in the waiting room.

I texted Ezra to let him know I wouldn't be home. Then I phoned Glen Turner and told him about Amber's condition. "I did a quick search of her bag and her truck, but I didn't find anything like a list of suppliers. I'm going to wait here to see if she wakes up."

Glen sounded tired. "If you could, that would be helpful. I'll be in Philly all night. Text me if her condition changes."

"Will do."

There was nothing else I could do, so I closed my eyes, hoping for a few hours of uncomfortable sleep in the waiting room chair. I must have drifted off, because a voice woke me up.

"Detective?"

"Yes?" Blinking awake, I stood up, still half-asleep.

I swayed, and the doctor, a thirtysomething Indian, steadied me with a hand. "Sorry if I startled you."

"No. It's fine." I shook my head, trying to dislodge the fuzz that coated my brain. "Amber Kruger?"

"She's in ICU but stable for the moment. I'm Dr. Ambati. Can we talk?"

"Yes, of course."

I checked the time. It was just after four A.M. The doctor led me out of the waiting room and into a corridor. Poking his head in a small examining room to verify it was empty, he gestured me inside. He half sat, his hip on the exam table, and clasped his hands in his lap. There was a frown of concern on his otherwise smooth face. "I heard they have this tremetol poisoning in Philadelphia right now as well. And the CDC is working on this?"

"Yes. We believe Amber is connected with the Philadelphia outbreak. It's vital that I speak with her."

The doctor nodded. "She isn't conscious yet. But I'm hoping in the next few hours . . . Her blood work shows severe metabolic acidosis, certainly enough to kill her. But I spoke to the CDC, and they confirmed a treatment of intravenous bicarbonate. That should reduce the acid in her blood that's caused by the tremetol and, hopefully, enable her to recover. I suspect it will take a few days or even weeks for it to pass through her system though. And from what I've read, she may have permanent weakness in some of her muscles."

"So there is a cure for this?" It was hard to believe. I'd begun to think of tremetol like strychnine—a one-way pass to certain death.

"Yes, it's pretty straightforward. We need to counteract the acid in the patient's blood using an IV solution until the body has flushed the toxin enough to rebalance itself. Unfortunately, the toxin works fast. The CDC says it can kill within twenty-four hours. If patients don't know to seek treatment—"

Or won't. Like the Amish.

"Have you seen any other cases at this hospital?" I asked. "Amber had to have gotten the milk that made her sick from a local farmer."

The doctor shook his head. "I've been on since eleven, and I checked with the nurses. We haven't had any cases in the past twenty-four hours at least. Or if we did, we didn't know what we were looking at. That's what scares me, Detective Harris. Because it would be easy to diagnose this as flu if a GP didn't do the blood work. Sending a patient home with the advice to rest is the worst thing they could do."

"I understand." By now, sleep had fled and I was already organizing in my mind. I had to speak to Glen Turner and Grady. They needed to make some kind of public statement and soon. And it was bad news that no other patients had appeared at Lancaster General. Someone else local had to have gotten sick from the milk Amber was selling, if only the farmer's own family. If they weren't coming into the hospital, they could die.

"Well, I'll send out an e-mail to all our doctors and staff so we can be looking out for it," Dr. Ambati said.

"Thank you. As soon as I get a chance to speak with the CDC liaison, I'll let him know what you said. Would it be possible to see Amber now?"

"You may. Though I'm not sure when she'll wake up, or how cognizant she'll be when she does."

I looked at my watch. "I've got nothing better to do until at least six A.M."

"Very well. This way."

I dozed off again in the chair next to Amber's bed. A crick in my neck woke me. The light of sunrise was just appearing outside the window. I looked at the figure in the hospital bed. In the dim light of the room, Amber's eyes were open. They were a deep brown, and they glistened with tears.

"Hey." I leaned closer. "Do you need me to call a nurse?"

"Where am I?" Amber whispered.

"Lancaster General. You've been very sick. We found you in your apartment and called an ambulance to bring you here."

Amber snuffled a breath, as if she would normally get upset about that but she was just too damn tired. She started to close her eyes.

"*Amber.* I'm Detective Harris with the Lancaster Police. It's very important that I speak to you."

Amber's eyes opened again, but they were hazy and unfocused. "Me?"

"Yes. You got sick from raw milk. And so did a number of people in Philadelphia who bought milk from you at Tuesday's farmers' market." *And some of them died.* I didn't think that would be helpful information at the moment.

Amber's eyes widened. "No. That's not possible." There was disbelief in those eyes, and pain. In Grady's rundown he'd mentioned that Amber was twenty-nine, only three years younger than I was myself. But right now she looked childlike and completely adrift.

It might not be protocol, but I took Amber's hand anyway. It felt clammy and limp, completely lacking in strength. "I'm afraid it is. It's very important that you tell me where you got the raw milk you sold on Tuesday. Others may get sick if we don't find the source."

Amber swallowed. Her eyes searched the bedside table. There was a glass and a small pitcher of water there, so I poured some and helped Amber lift her head and shoulders off the bed and take a sip. Even that much effort exhausted her, and I laid her back down when her strength gave out. There was a miasma of heat and stale sweat and something bitter coming off her. God, she was sick. No one should be this ill, not from eating or drinking something they thought was good for them.

Amber muttered something.

"What?"

"Is it . . . E. coli?"

"No. It's not E. coli. It was caused by a plant the cows ate, and the toxin was passed on in the milk. Please, Amber. I really need those names."

"So tired." Amber blinked her eyes open, hard. "Got milk at three farms Tuesday. Levi Fisher, Willow Run Farm, Bird-in-Hand. Amos Bender on Driskell in Paradise. Jacob Keim, Soudersburg Road."

Oh, thank God. I drew a notepad from my pocket and quickly wrote the information down. I needed to get this to Glen immediately.

"Am I . . . dying?" Amber asked. Tears rolled down her cheeks. She shifted her hand on the bed, seeking mine. I took it and held it again.

"No, Amber. The doctor said what they're giving you in the IV will take care of the toxin. You're going to be okay."

Amber took a shaky breath. "Feels like I'm dying." She closed her eyes.

"No, honey. You're not dying."

No, Amber would be one of the lucky ones.

PART II

Straw Man

CHAPTER 6

I was still towel-drying my hair as I turned on the TV in the living room to catch the nine A.M. press conference.

Ezra came in from the kitchen. "Thought you were gonna get some sleep after your shower."

"I will, babe, but I want to see this."

After leaving the hospital, I'd stopped by the police station. Glen had just gotten back from Philly, and he looked even more sleep deprived than I felt. He took the list of names I'd gotten from Amber so his team could contact them. Then Grady insisted I go home and get some sleep. I was tired, but it was hard to ramp down knowing what was about to hit the fan. News on the deaths in Philly was supposed to break this morning, and the brass was scrambling to put together a press conference. Glen had been on a call with the state's agricultural department when I'd left.

I turned to the local news channel and sank down onto the couch. They'd cleaned Glen up and put him in front of the microphone. I wasn't surprised at the choice. Put the CDC man in front. Everyone respects a doctor. But Mitch Franklin, head of the Pennsylvania Department of Agriculture, was standing to Glen's right looking grave and authoritarian.

"I'm Dr. Glen Turner with the CDC. We've been investigating a small outbreak here in Lancaster County for the past week, and we now have word that some cases have shown up in Philadelphia as well. At this briefing we want to fill you in on what we know about this illness, what we're doing about it, and what people at home can do to keep themselves safe."

The noise of camera shutters and flashes was so loud it sounded like firecrackers. Turner came across well, I had to give him that.

"That's the man who was here last night." Ezra sat down next to me on the couch. "He's an important person?"

I wasn't sure how to answer that, but I supposed it was true. "He's in charge of the investigation into what's causing the sickness."

"So far there have been twenty-nine confirmed cases and nineteen fatalities."

Murmurs were audible in the press audience.

"This is not—I repeat, not—a contagious illness. It's a food-borne sickness, and the only way to get it is by consuming a contaminated food source. We've confirmed that this outbreak is caused by a toxin called tremetol. The confirmed cases have all been linked to raw milk from cows that have ingested a nonindigenous plant that contains the toxin. This makes the cows ill, and the tremetol gets passed on in the milk. The CDC is cur-

rently investigating how and where the sickened cows got access to the plant, but in the meantime, there are some things you can do to keep yourself and your loved ones from getting ill."

Ezra had his arm around my shoulder on the back of the couch, but he pulled away and leaned forward, looking worried. I felt nothing but relief. Finally, they were telling the public what they needed to know to stay safe. Then again, how many Amish families would see this press conference? None.

"First, as of eight o'clock this morning, the Pennsylvania Department of Agriculture has suspended all raw-milk sales in Pennsylvania until this matter is resolved. Second, we'll be distributing information to the farmers in the county about what symptoms to look for in their animals and what plant they need to check for in their pastures. Third, we recommend that no one consume raw dairy products until we can be sure all affected milk is accounted for. And finally, this illness is treatable if those who are sick report to their local hospital immediately. If you have any of the following symptoms: muscle weakness, trembling, stiff or slow movements, nausea, vomiting, or unexplained exhaustion, please report to your doctor or the closest emergency room and get checked out. We'll be working with the hospitals and physicians in the area to make sure they know what to look for and how to treat it. That's all we have to report at this time."

There were more flashes from cameras, and a dozen reporters called out questions, but the news station cut back to their talking heads. Ezra turned down the volume. He stood up and paced. "This is bad. This is very bad."

"Surely it's better for them to act quickly and make sure no one else gets sick."

"You don't understand!" Ezra said vehemently. "Who sells raw milk? The Amish. And they've had to fight the government to do it for years. They want to regulate us. They don't like that anything is outside their control! They'd put us out of business if they could."

I thought Ezra was being overdramatic. I had a hard time sympathizing with his distrust of government, since I'd always worked for the city in one way or another. "It's only until the CDC is sure they know exactly where that toxin came from. We need to make sure it's not going to affect any other farmers' cows. That's common sense."

Ezra shook his head. "And what if they never find it? Or just say it's so? And next it is not only raw milk, but any food sold off the farm. And what about baking? The Amish bake with milk. What if customers no longer want to come look at my mules because Amish farms are . . . dirty?"

"Ezra! None of that is going to happen," I said with a surprised laugh. "You're the one who likes to say 'Don't borrow trouble.'"

Ezra looked unconvinced, a frown on his brow. On the dining room table, my phone pinged. I got up and answered it. It was Hernandez. "Hey, Harris! Did you see the press conference?"

"I did."

"Well, it's nuts here. They're gearing up teams to go out and talk to the Amish, ya know, because they don't have TV and all that. Grady said anyone in our office could volunteer to help out today if they didn't have anything else urgent. I'm gonna go. Thought I'd see if you wanna go with me."

I raised my eyes to find Ezra watching me. "You didn't get any sleep. You should lie down for the morning," he said.

"I slept some at the hospital," I countered.

Nevertheless, I wondered if this was the best use of my time today. They would have a lot of men out there passing out information to the Amish. And I could just imagine the warm reception that was going to get. I could probably push off my other tasks at work one more day, but should I?

The thought of focusing on my other cases made me wince. I wasn't ready to let this go. I doubted I could get engaged in another task—or sleep. The press conference should have eased my mind, but it hadn't, not deep down where it counted.

There was an anxiety sunk deep inside me, and it wasn't appeased. Shit. This was my war. I just wished I understood who the enemy was and what the battle was about.

"I'll come," I told Hernandez. "Meet you at the office in twenty."

Back at the police station, Grady rolled his eyes as I passed him in the hall as if to say, *Can't stay away, can you?* Hernandez was not at his desk in the Violent Crimes room. His chair was pushed in neatly—military habit.

I was about to text him when Glen Turner walked up. "Morning. Again." He smiled at me sheepishly.

"No rest for the wicked," I countered. "Nice job on the press conference. You looked so prime time."

His mouth fought to rein in a prideful smile. "Well, someone has to be the guy with the bull's-eye on his forehead. So, um, Hernandez mentioned you were coming in to volunteer. You sure you're up for that after last night?"

I tilted up my chin. "I had a shower. I'm fine."

"That works out for me, then. I was hoping you'd be willing to give me a hand today."

"Oh?"

"I need to do interviews at the three farms where Amber got her milk. I've already sent agents out to stop them from drinking or selling it, and to see if anyone is sick and needs urgent care. But I need to go myself and do a face-to-face. Since they're Amish, I thought you might be helpful." He ruffled his hair in frustration. "The DCNR is going to check those farms for white snakeroot, and I hope to God they find it. We still haven't found the source of the tremetol at the Kinderman farm or the Hershbergers', and we've gone over those pastures multiple times. The DCNR guys say white snakeroot is a woodland plant that only grows in shady and damp areas. Both the Hershbergers' and the Kindermans' cows are kept in fenced pastures, and even where the pasture gets shady from nearby trees, there's no sign of the plant. We also haven't found it in anything we sampled from the barn—the water, the feed. . . . We've dismantled and tested over two hundred bales of hay. Hell, we even tested the sparrow and mouse droppings in the barns. But we still haven't found the source of the tremetol."

"That's not good." I could feel Glen's frustration, and my own mirrored it. If they couldn't find the source of the toxin, they couldn't be sure other farms hadn't been exposed. Which meant there'd be no quick lift on the raw milk ban. Farmers would be angry and the public would be scared.

"I didn't have a lot of luck questioning Mr. Hershberger," Glen continued. "Maybe you can get more out of these farmers than I can. Or maybe you'll think of something I didn't, notice something I didn't—knowing the Amish as you do."

I was flattered by Glen's faith in me, especially after we'd gotten more than one cold shoulder when we did calls the other day. But I wasn't about to remind him of my lack of effectiveness. I wanted to be as close to this case as I could get.

"I'll go with you. I should let Hernandez know. I was going to volunteer with him today."

"He, um, already left. I told him I'd be needing you today."

I raised my eyebrows. "That's . . . efficient of you."

He had the grace to look guilty. "I didn't think you'd mind. If you prefer—"

"Nope, I'm good," I said briskly. "Let's go."

We pulled into the driveway of Levi Fisher's farm in Glen's unmarked sedan. The place was already crowded with several SUVs bearing DCNR decals, a CDC van, a police cruiser, and an unmarked white truck with a back cab. Three Amish children, looking perfectly healthy, watched us from the farmhouse's back doorsteps. Their faces were blank, as if they were watching a flock of birds or some other ordinary occurrence and not the invasion of their family farm by medical and police personnel.

As we walked by the pasture, I noted a number of men in green shirts scouring the area. I assumed they were DCNR agents looking for white snakeroot. Good.

Inside the barn it was quiet, a heavy silence that felt weighted, like at a wake. An Amish man, likely Levi Fisher, was seated on a bale of hay. He held his black hat in his hands, and his head was bowed. He wasn't old, maybe early thirties, and his still boyish face was tight with grief. He looked so miserable I felt sure some member of his family must be very ill or dead. My sympathy went out to him. I was easily able to picture Ezra or perhaps Hannah's husband, Isaac, in his place.

"Dr. Turner?" A young CDC officer approached us. She was dressed in the agency's white coveralls and gloves.

"Hi, Elaine. This is Detective Harris from the Lancaster police. How's the search going?"

Elaine nodded in acknowledgment at me. "Hello. They're checking outside now. We took samples of the feed and hay, but we haven't done anything in the stalls yet. We wanted to give the vet some space." She tilted her head toward the stalls. "Come see for yourself."

The barn had a long, open pen for the cows. There was an old wooden half wall on the interior side that came to my chest. A wide door, now closed, led out to the pasture. Inside the stall were six brown cows, all Jerseys, all with milk-engorged udders.

And they were sick. One lay on her side, panting, her eyes rolled back in her head. A man in blue coveralls, who had to be the vet, was kneeling beside her, injecting her with something. The other cows were in various stages of distress. One stood with her head in a corner as if she were trying to hide. The rest milled about, stumbling near the wall. They were trembling, their flanks shaking like they were being stung by an invisible horde of bees. Mucus dripped from one cow's nose. They looked like the Kindermans' cow to me.

I exchanged a dire look with Glen. There was little doubt the Fisher farm had tremetol poisoning.

"Once the vet is done, I want samples of everything in that stall," Glen ordered. "Straw, feces, urine, their water and any traces of food in the trough or on the floor, birds' nests in the rafters, everything. And get saliva and blood samples from the cows."

"Right," agreed Elaine crisply.

"What about the family?" Glen asked her.

She shook her head. "None of them appear to be sick. We checked the milk supply they had in their kitchen—two gallons' worth. The expiration dates written on them were yesterday and today, so that milk is over a week old. According to Mrs. Fisher, they drink the older milk themselves so it won't go bad. The new milk goes into their shop for customers. It's possible they dodged the bullet on this. But we'd still like to run blood work on the whole family, if you agree?"

Glen nodded. "Yeah. Of course." He looked at me. "Will they have a problem with giving us blood?"

I glanced back at Levi Fisher, who now had his head in both hands. "Shouldn't be a problem. The Amish do get modern health care when they need it."

"Good. Now what about their customers?"

Elaine gestured toward the door. "Come with me. You need to see their shop."

She led us out of the barn and across a wide gravel area to a little cement-block building that was coated with white paint. It had a tin roof and looked something like a bunker. An old wooden door faced a parking area big enough for no more than three cars. A sign on the door said "Farm Store. Open 8 A.M.–6 P.M., Mon–Sat." Another handwritten sign said "Raw Milk!"

Elaine pushed open the wooden door. A rusty old spring set at the top of it creaked.

The room inside was very spare. The whitewashed cement floor was clean. A wobbly wooden stand just inside the door held a few loaves of homemade bread. A folding table along one wall was covered in produce baskets with bunches of green onions, red leaf lettuces, radishes, and peas still in the pod. At the back of the room was an old white refrigerator, and on the left of the wall were the glass doors of a cold case. There were rows of plastic gallon milk jugs, stacks of egg cartons, and blocks of homemade cheese on the cold case shelves.

Glen stepped up to the case and looked at the shelved milk.

"We'll have to test all of these. There are expiration dates on them. We should be able to pin down exactly when the tremetol starts showing up in the milk."

"Yup. I was just waiting for you to see this layout before we take everything. We should test the cheese too. It's made here, though it's considerably older, so it's probably clean. The fridge has hamburger and raw butter, also made here."

"Test it all," Glen said. "Any way to find out who bought milk here in the past week?"

"We're in luck there." Elaine picked up a spiral notebook that was lying on a counter and handed it to Glen.

I knew what to expect before he opened it. I'd been to places like this before. The counter had a slot for stuffing in money and checks. The notebook was cheap and had been heavily written in. I took a step closer and looked at the page with Glen.

"Most farm stores work on an honor system," I explained. "You sign this notebook and write down what you took and the total you paid. The money goes into that slot." I looked over the top page and studied the dates written next to the list of names. "Looks like they get about twenty customers a day. They don't leave addresses or phone numbers, but there're probably some checks in the slot. Those will have addresses. We should be able to track down all the names if they're local."

Glen looked over the notebook, turned pages. His face was tense. "Christ. Thirty-three . . . thirty-*five* bought milk since Tuesday morning."

"And people who buy a gallon of milk are likely feeding a family," I added, feeling my gut twist at the memory of the dead children at the Kindermans'. Christ, we had to get a handle on this and fast.

Glen grimaced. "Elaine, get someone on this list. The police can help us find addresses." He looked at me. "Come on. We need to talk to Levi Fisher."

CHAPTER 7

We were invited into the Fishers' kitchen. Mrs. Fisher hustled the children out of the room, and we joined Levi at the table. He sat dispiritedly in one of the chairs, his posture curled in on itself defensively. He didn't meet our eyes. I pulled out my iPhone to record.

"This is Detective Elizabeth Harris with the Lancaster Police. I'm here with Dr. Glen Turner from the CDC. We're speaking to Levi Fisher of Willow Run Farm in Bird-in-Hand."

I nodded at Glen to begin.

"Mr. Fisher, can you tell us when you first noticed your cows were getting sick?"

Levi shifted his weight and gave a determined sigh. "When we did the milkin' Tuesday night, two of the cows were shakin' all over. They seemed kinda restless Tuesday mornin', and a few was off their feed, but I didn't think much of it till they was way worse Tuesday night."

"The milk you sold to Amber Kruger, do you know the date that was milked?"

"It was from that same mornin'."

"Tuesday morning," Glen confirmed.

"Ja. Tuesday mornin'." For the first time, Levi looked up at Glen. His eyes were red-rimmed and haunted. "I figured since she was takin' it all the way to Philadelphia, might as well give her the milk with the longest shelf life."

"I see. And the rest of the milk from Tuesday, the morning and evening milking both, went into your farm store?"

Levi nodded, his mouth in an unhappy line.

"Does the milk get sold or distributed to anyone else? Besides your farm store and to Amber Kruger?" I asked.

"Sometimes, but not for the past few weeks." He bit his lower lip and looked out the window. "By yesterday mornin', the cows . . . well, I milked 'em. You can't just leave 'em. But I set the milk aside. I wasn't sure. . . . The way they was actin' . . . I haven't sold any of the milk from Wednesday or this mornin'."

Well, that was something, I thought. "Have you heard anything about there being trouble with milk in the Amish community?"

Levi shook his head. "Not till youse showed up this mornin'. We don't normally go out anywheres during the week."

"Have you heard about the Kinderman family?" I asked, keeping my voice gentle. It was hard to believe, but we'd discovered the Kindermans only six days ago. It had been big news in the area though, and certainly was among the Amish.

Levi met my eyes for the first time. His mouth dropped open. "The Kinderman family that all died? That was . . . that was like this? Their cows was sick too?"

"I'm afraid so."

Levi digested that, looking stunned. His eyes flickered to the doorway through which his wife and children had disappeared, as if imagining what could have happened. His face went a peculiar shade of red. One hand clutched the table, and he muttered something in German that sounded like a prayer.

"It's all right, Mr. Fisher. Try to relax," Glen urged. He leaned forward to put his hand on Levi's shoulder.

While Levi got himself under control, facing the horror of what might have been, my mind rooted insistently at the situation. I felt hungry for something, some information I felt was missing, but I wasn't sure what it was.

"Have there been any strangers on the farm, Mr. Fisher?" I asked when Levi's color faded to a less alarming hue. "Have you noticed anyone hanging around that shouldn't be here?"

Glen looked at me oddly, but he didn't interrupt.

Levi focused his gaze on me reluctantly. "Customers come and go from the shop all the time. Haven't noticed anyone where they oughtn't be. And our dog, Tangle, he sleeps in the barn at night. He'd bark his fool head off if someone came around after dark."

"Have any of your farm-store customers reported getting ill, Mr. Fisher?" Glen asked.

Levi shook his head. "No. But . . ." He looked down at the table. "There's a lady comes by every other day for milk. Stops on her way home from work. She's got four or five kids at home. She was here Monday but didn't come last night, Wednesday. I noticed 'cause she always comes."

"Do you know her name?" I asked.

"Ja. Susan Traynor. Lives somewhere close by." His voice was rough, and I could well imagine what he was thinking.

"We should be able to locate her." It was true but not much of a comfort.

He rubbed his eyes and looked first at me, then at Glen. "I didn't know about the milk being dangerous till this mornin'. I guess they'll take my license. Will I go to jail? I surely didn't mean to hurt anyone. God knows I'd never want that. But I suspect that don't matter. It's just . . . my family."

"That's why we're here, Mr. Fisher," I said. "We need to determine how this happened, where your cows got the plant that made them sick and poisoned the milk." I didn't add *Likely the most you'll be charged with is manslaughter*, because it didn't seem like Levi Fisher needed to be thinking about that at the moment, and it was too soon to know what we'd find. One thing I absolutely believed though, was that Levi Fisher had done none of this on purpose. He was a sturdy man, and right now he looked like a stiff breeze could knock him over, and maybe he wouldn't care to get up again.

"Youse will check on all my customers? With the list in my

notebook? Make sure they're all right?" Levi looked at Glen, as if asking man to man.

"We'll track down anyone who might have had access to your milk," Glen assured him. "Get them help if they need it. That's our job."

"Thank the Lord. Please, God, let no one else die." Levi put his elbows on the table, folded his hands, and began to pray.

By the time we were done interviewing Levi Fisher, the CDC medics were at the door wanting to take blood samples. I left them to it and headed back outside. It wasn't that I was squeamish at the sight of blood, but crying children were another matter. I was already heartsick enough today. Out near the barn I found the vet packing up his truck.

"Is this sickness fatal? For the cows, I mean?" I asked him.

He gave me a quick once-over. "Hi. Are you with the CDC?"

I inwardly chided myself for my impatience. As a cop with the NYPD, we rarely did things like introduce ourselves. But what was normal there was considered rudeness here. "No, sorry. Lancaster Police. I'm Detective Harris."

"Ah." The vet's expression didn't relax. If anything, he grew tenser. "What was your question again?"

"I was asking if these cows will die—and if tremetol is always fatal for cows or if it depends on how much they consume?"

"Hum." He stripped off the gloves he was wearing and tossed

them in a receptacle in the truck. "I'm not sure. I suspect the two worst-off ones here won't make it. But I gave them all a strong dose of sodium bicarbonate and vitamins, so the rest may recover."

The vet was in his early thirties, overweight, and a bit geeky. It was clear he'd never been an attractive man, but he was confident and aloof.

"You're Doctor . . ." I prompted.

"Dr. Richmond." He didn't offer his hand. Then again, that could be because he'd just been tending some very sick animals, latex gloves or no.

"Are you familiar with this problem, Dr. Richmond? Tremetol poisoning caused by cattle eating white snakeroot?"

He shrugged. "I wouldn't say 'familiar with' it exactly. I've never seen it myself, but we read about it in vet school. In cows it's called 'the trembles' or 'the slows,' because the stiff muscles affect the animal's gait. And it's not just white snakeroot. Certain species of goldenrod contain tremetol too. It's more of a problem in the southwest I think."

"So you've never seen it around here?" I pressed.

"Nope," Richmond said briskly. "Not until today."

"I guess other animals, like horses or goats, would get sick if they ate the plant too, right?"

"Sure. And before you ask, no, I've never seen any animal sick like that around here."

It suddenly occurred to me that we should be talking to local vets—not just this one, but all of them. They might know of cases the police and the CDC had missed. Plus . . . An idea niggled. Not many people would know about white snakeroot and what it could do. But vets would. I looked at Dr. Richmond more closely.

He must have seen something on my face, because he shifted uneasily and rubbed his jaw with his thumb. "I . . . saw the press conference this morning. About the raw-milk ban."

"Yes?"

He narrowed his eyes and looked off toward the pasture. "That's really going to hurt the farmers. Take it from me, the dairy animals in Lancaster County, particularly the ones on Amish farms, are some of the healthiest you'll find anywhere. Almost all of them have access to fresh air and grass all year round. And they're not fed cheap feed with fillers or hormones." His voice shook with intensity. "My wife and I drink raw milk. You do know it's tested by the state? Farms with raw-milk licenses are tested regularly for bacterial contamination."

I didn't know that, actually. I was surprised it hadn't been mentioned in the CDC debriefing. "Thanks for the information, Dr. Richmond. I can assure you, the CDC is working hard to determine where this toxin is coming from. No one wants to hurt the farmers, but we have to keep the public safe."

Dr. Richmond grunted and shut the back of his truck. "Then I hope you find it soon," he said stiffly. He headed for the driver's-side door.

"Dr. Richmond?" I pulled a card out of my pocket. Something about Richmond's attitude didn't sit well with me, but I gave him a polite smile. "Would you please ask around with other large-animal vets you know, see if they've seen any cases, or suspected cases, of tremetol poisoning? If so, we need to know immediately."

I'd ask Hernandez to call around to all the local vets too, but it couldn't hurt to get Dr. Richmond trolling for us. He took the card and gave me a glance that was noticeably less hostile. "Of course. I'd like to help in any way I can. I'm sure all the vets in the area feel the same."

"Thank you." I turned on my heel and went into the barn.

I watched three CDC agents go over the Fishers' cow stall taking photographs and samples. They wore paper face masks now, along with white coveralls, gloves, and booties, and they carried sheaths of plastic evidence bags on their hips, clipped onto a loop on their coveralls. The door to the pasture was now open, and most of the animals had disappeared. Only two cows, too sick to make their escape, remained in the stall. The one who'd been down before was still lying on her side, eyes half-closed, insensible to what was going on around her. It made me feel sick to see her. The pain of animals and children is always the hardest to bear.

The encounter with Dr. Richmond worried me. If a vet who'd just treated these very sick cows was against the raw-milk ban, we were in deep trouble on the PR front. And that wasn't the only problem. Levi Fisher hadn't heard about the raw-milk warning, and we'd been working to spread that word in the Amish community for several days now. Ezra's famous "Amish grapevine" wasn't working nearly fast enough. Which meant there could well be other families out there who were sick or dying.

Elaine, the CDC agent I'd met earlier, started examining the feeding trough inside the stall. The trough was fixed to the other side of the half wall where I was standing. On my side, there were bales of hay and a chute from the upper story. It would be easy for the farmer to load the trough with feed without having to go into the stall. Elaine shined a high-powered flashlight over the old metal surface of the trough and leaned in to peer at it carefully.

I watched her, but my mind was elsewhere. *This is the first case the vet has ever seen. Why here? Why now? How are they getting this damn plant?*

The DCNR agents were still out in the pasture. Would they have any more luck finding a toxic plant growing here than they'd had at the Hershbergers' or Kindermans'? I hoped so, but I'd be surprised if they did.

"Detective?" Elaine's voice was serious.

I was immediately alert. "Did you find something?"

She motioned with her gloved hand for me to come closer. I took the few steps down the half wall and peered over the edge.

"There are bits of a green plant here," Elaine said. Using the flashlight and a pair of tweezers, she drew my attention to several small green leaves that were stuck to the bottom of the trough. "It doesn't look like hay."

No, it didn't. It looked like the remains of a green, leafy plant. I was familiar with what Ezra fed his mules, and this didn't look like anything he gave them. A shot of excitement went through me. Sometimes in my work I had moments that were rather like what I'd imagined an archaeologist would feel uncovering that first bit of a valuable artifact. Of course, sometimes it just turned out to be a buried penny.

"Should I go ahead and bag it?" Elaine asked.

I shook my head. "Let's get some photos before anyone touches it."

"We can do that." Elaine called for the CDC agent with the camera around his neck and he came over.

I fidgeted with the cell phone in my pocket as I watched. I was half tempted to call Grady and suggest a crime-scene team, but a few bits of leaves were hardly a smoking gun, and the CDC and DCNR people were already here. This multi-bureau work was so complicated.

More than a dozen photos were taken of the trough, and then Elaine looked at me. "Good?"

I nodded. "Yeah. Thanks. Go ahead and bag it."

She did, carefully picking up the bits of green with tweezers and placing them in a plastic bag. "I can courier this to the CDC lab for testing. If there's any tremetol in this plant, we'll know by tomorrow morning."

"That's fantastic. Thanks, Elaine."

I meant every word. If this was a breakthrough, we'd know soon. Maybe working with the CDC wasn't a hardship after all.

Glen got a phone call just as he and I were getting into his car. He took it outside while I checked e-mail on my phone.

When he got into the driver's seat, he looked pleased. "The cows on the other two farms where Amber got milk look healthy, and there's no sign of sickness in the families. We'll still confiscate all their milk and test it, and the cows too. But so far it looks like we're in luck there. Do you have a preference which one we hit first for questioning?"

"Actually, if it doesn't look like those farms were affected, I'd like to follow up on the Hershbergers. You said you didn't have much luck questioning Samuel Hershberger?"

"Not really. It's probably a good idea to go back there with you."

"The green plant your team just found in the trough—you didn't find anything like that over at the Hershbergers'?"

Glen gave me a worried frown. "No. But we did our investigation several weeks after the family first got ill. If there was something like that there, it might have been long gone."

"Right. Well . . . yeah. It's worth going back there. If you need to be elsewhere, you can drop me at the station and I can takc my own car."

"Nope, I'm in," Glen said firmly. "As you say, it doesn't look like the other two farms where Amber got her milk were affected. My team can follow up with them." He gave me a smile that was a degree too warm. I gave a weak one in return and looked out the window.

I was distracted by thoughts of those few green leaves. There hadn't been enough left of the plant for the DCNR people to be able to identify it. And Levi hadn't recognized it as anything he fed the cows. His best guess was it was a weed the cows had picked up in the pasture that had gotten dislodged from a cow's mouth as it ate at the trough. His explanation made perfect sense, but I couldn't help feeling it was significant. Until the test results proved otherwise, I was suspicious of those green leaves.

As if reading my mind, Glen spoke up as he drove. "We should have the lab results soon."

"Good."

Leah Hershberger was working in the garden with two of her young daughters when we pulled into their driveway. She eyed me warily as I got out of the car. I took the bull by the horns and walked right up to her. I held out my hand. "Are you Leah? I'm Detective Elizabeth Harris. We have a friend in common—Hannah Yoder."

Leah's face relaxed from worry to welcome. "Ja, Hannah told me about you, Elizabeth. You were the one to find out what happened to Hannah's Katie, and her English friend too."

I was pleased. "That's right."

Leah glanced at her own two girls, around seven to ten in age. "Such a terrible business. I know what was done to *you* too, and we were all so sorry about that."

For a moment, I had a visceral memory of that night over a year ago. I'd come so close to death I'd felt its chill in my bones along with the numbing cold of the water I'd nearly drowned in. I almost took a step back from Leah, but I caught myself in time. I pasted on a smile. "Thank you for saying so. I was hoping I could speak with you about your family's illness. I'm sorry I haven't been out earlier."

"Your friend the doctor was here. Spoke to my husband." Leah nodded at Glen, who was standing by the car trying to look like he wasn't watching us.

"I know. That's Dr. Turner. He's with the Centers for Disease Control. They investigate unusual illnesses in order to prevent widespread outbreaks. We're still trying to understand what's going on here in Lancaster County."

"That Dr. Turner told my husband it was the cows eatin' somethin' and poisonin' the milk." Leah looked doubtful. "But we ain't had any trouble since we all . . ." Her voice caught, and I knew she was thinking of her son who had died, William. "Since my husband and Aaron got out the hospital. No trouble since then. The cows are actin' normal, and no one's been sick again, thank the Lord."

"You've been drinking the milk?"

"Sure."

She admitted that in such a straightforward fashion, I had to hold in a visible cringe. "Oh. Well . . . I really wouldn't recommend that, Leah. We don't understand exactly where the plant's coming from, and next time, you might not be as lucky. It's possible your cows wouldn't show any obvious symptoms until after the milk was already poisoned. Do you understand?"

Leah looked at me for a moment, as if taking my measure one more time. Then she sighed in resignation and handed her hoe to one of her daughters. She wiped her hands on her apron. "I didn't think on it like so. Thank you for tellin' me. I will talk to Samuel about it. Now what can I do for youse?"

Glen walked me through the Hershbergers' barn showing me everything the CDC had checked and sampled. He was clearly hoping I might think of something they'd missed, but they'd been extremely thorough.

The Hershbergers were crop farmers, and they didn't have many animals. There was a lone Jersey cow they milked for the family and four horses used for farmwork and pulling the family buggy. They also had a few goats and a dozen or more chickens. Samuel Hershberger brought their cow, Ginny, in from the pasture on a rope lead and tied her to a beam in the barn. She was incredibly tame, chewing contentedly on some hay Samuel put into the feeding trough for her. She watched us with a placid expression.

We entered the stall, and Glen ran his hands over the cow's flanks, clucking his tongue softly.

"Know much about cows do you?" I asked with a trace of humor.

"Not a thing." Glen waggled his eyebrows at me, causing a funny spot of warmth in my belly.

I shook it off and turned to Samuel Hershberger. He and Leah were in their late thirties or early forties, I guessed. They were close in age to Hannah and Isaac Yoder. Samuel looked younger and certainly healthier than he had in the hospital. His skin no longer looked stretched over his skull, though he was still pale and thin. His beard was nearly to his breastbone, and its chocolate tones showed no hint of gray. His brown eyes were warm.

"Hannah Yoder mentioned to me that, just before your family got sick, you noticed the cow trembling when you milked her. You thought she might have been spooked by a fox in the pasture?" I asked.

Samuel stroked his beard. "Ja. 'Tis so. I remember."

Glen, still petting the cow, raised his eyebrows with interest. "How many days did you notice the trembling?"

"That day at the evenin' milkin'." He swallowed. "When I mentioned it at supper, Will—he was my oldest son that passed—he said he thought he noticed it a bit that mornin' too."

Glen spoke up. "And the next day? Did you or Will take notice of the cow?"

"Can't say. Will milked both turns, and by then the little uns was sick and we didn't talk about the cow. It was Will's job to milk, and he didn't say nothin' about it, and then he . . ." Samuel swallowed again, his lips tight. "He was taken to our Lord. Leah can tell ya who done the milkin' while I was in the hospital."

I looked Ginny over. Her big brown eyes were clear, her fawn-colored flank smooth and still. "She looks healthy now."

"She might have gotten a small dose of the plant," Glen said. "That could also explain why most of the family recovered."

"Did you happen to notice anything unusual around the cow's feeding trough, Samuel?" I asked.

"What d'ya mean?"

"Something leafy and green, perhaps? Maybe you thought it might be a plant the cow brought in from the pasture."

"Don't recall such like, no. Can't say as I've ever noticed somethin' like that."

I was disappointed. If Will was the one who'd milked the cow more often before the family got ill, he would have been the person to ask. But Will was dead.

A face had been peeking around the side of a post in the opening to the pasture for the past few minutes. Children were always present at Amish farms, usually in energetic flocks. This one was a boy, maybe twelve, slim and lanky. Like all Amish boys, he wore black pants and suspenders over a long-sleeved shirt. He had a store-bought wool jacket over the top. His hair was very blond, and he had a narrow, curious face. He made me smile. He reminded me of what Ezra must have looked like when he was a boy.

"Maybe one of your younger sons milked Ginny while you were in the hospital?" I said, looking right at the boy.

"Maybe so," Samuel agreed. "If they weren't too sick."

"How about you?" I asked the boy directly. "Do you ever milk Ginny?"

The boy, knowing he'd been seen, stepped out from behind the post. He fiddled with the zipper on his jacket and looked at the cow with a thoughtful press of his lips, as if considering it.

Samuel spoke up. "Mark. Answer the question now."

Mark nodded a yes at me.

"Did you do any milking while your dad and brother were in the hospital?"

Mark nodded again. "I done it all."

"How was Ginny then?" Glen asked. "Did you notice her shaking at all? Any foam or mucus around her nose and mouth? Did she stumble or have a stiff walk?"

"Try to remember gut now," Samuel added firmly but not unkindly.

Mark bit his lip and contemplated the question, his eyes rolling skyward. He tapped his chin, which made me fight back a smile at his drama. He probably wasn't used to holding the spotlight. "She was movin' kinda slow. Had to prod her gut to get her into the milkin' stall. She shook her head a lot. But I thought she was just missin' Will." He pressed his lips tight, his eyes growing bright.

Damn. Will's death must have been hard on Mark.

"If she was shakin' her head, she might have been sick. They can also do that if they get stubborn or mad," Samuel explained.

"You didn't notice any—" Glen began.

"Oh!" Mark said, as if he'd just remembered something.

"Don't interrupt your elders," Samuel scolded.

"Sorry," Mark muttered. Then, as if worried he hadn't been contrite enough to appease his father, he repeated it louder, looking at Glen. "I'm sorry I interrupted."

"It's okay, Mark. What did you remember?" I asked.

Mark shrugged.

"Anything that occurred to you might be important, no matter how small, Mark. We'd like to hear it."

Mark shrugged again. "All right. Well . . . I just remember. The way Ginny was actin', I thought maybe someone had been messin' with her agin and had made her mad. And she was takin' it out on me."

I exchanged a confused look with Glen. "Messing with her?"

"It was just a dumb idea."

"Who messes with Ginny? What do you mean?" I encouraged him, keeping my voice mild.

"Speak up," Samuel said. He folded his arms and looked at Mark as if he didn't have a clue what the boy was talking about either.

"Well, people at the road." He looked at his father, as if Samuel should know. "Ginny likes to eat the grass by the fence, and sometimes people stop their car and take her pitcher or pet her and stuff."

Samuel's shoulders relaxed. "Ja. 'Tis so. No harm done." He shook his head, his expression saying that he didn't understand the appeal of a stranger's cow, but then, English were crazy anyway.

"Hmm." Glen looked thoughtful. "Mark, when Ginny was being stubborn and shaking her head, do you remember if she was shaking in her legs too? You might have noticed . . ." Glen went on, but I stopped listening.

Messing with her.

Messing with Ginny. At the road. Again.

This time it was I who rudely interrupted. "Mark? Was someone else messing with Ginny earlier that week? At the fence line?" My voice came out more worried than I'd intended.

Glen fell silent, obviously getting the gist of my question at once. Mark nodded, biting his lip.

"Who? Can you describe the car? The person? What were they doing exactly?"

Mark glanced at his father as if asking permission. Samuel nodded.

"I saw a man when I was muckin' out the barn." Mark pointed to the wall, where thin slits of daylight shone through. "There's cracks and you can see outside. I noticed a car was stopped, and Ginny was at the fence. A man was pettin' her and givin' her somethin' to eat. I watched a minute, but he didn't seem like he was gonna hurt her or anythin', so I kept workin'."

A warm gush of certainty filled my stomach. My body had a mind of its own, and it was usually right. "What did he look like, Mark?" I asked.

Mark puffed out his cheeks and gave a big sigh, thinking about it. "Didn't see him gut. He had a hood up. Like English boys do? It was black."

A hooded sweatshirt maybe. I'd have to get some photos and show them to Mark for verification.

"And the car?" Glen asked.

Mark shrugged.

"Was it a car and not a truck? Do you remember the color?" I pressed.

Mark looked down at the barn floor as if uncomfortable with the questions. "I didn't look real gut at the car. Don't think it was a truck though."

"And what was the man feeding Ginny?"

Mark glanced at his father. "We seen 'em givin' the cows and horses carrots and stuff, the people who stop. Or once a lady gave Ginny an apple. I didn't see it gut this time though. Dunno what it was. I remember thinkin' it was probably carrots, but . . ." He shrugged again.

A cartoon image of Bugs Bunny eating a carrot came to my mind. "Did you see the orange of a carrot? Or maybe it was the kind that had a leafy green top?"

Mark's face cleared and he smiled. "Yeah! I saw something green and bushy like. Like a carrot top."

I looked at Glen. He was shaking his head, not at Mark or at me, but at whatever was going through his mind, as if he couldn't believe it. But he was CDC. I was a homicide detective, and I recognized the sick feeling in my veins.

This? This was murder.

CHAPTER 8

Ezra rolled his pickup truck as silently as possible into the driveway of his parents' farm and cut the engine. He sat behind the wheel feeling fear and was irritated with himself for feeling it. The very act of driving a truck onto his parents' farm felt like a slap in the face to them. He'd considered parking down the road and walking in. But it seemed ridiculous when they all knew he was driving now. He didn't want it to look like he was trying to lie, or to admit what he was doing was wrong before he even knocked on the door.

This was hard. He sat there a moment, feeling dread. But he was a man, and men got on with it.

There were no signs of his brothers and sisters. The younger ones were at school this time of day, but the older ones, the ones still living at home, should have been around. Jacob. Mary. And

Martha, of course. He suddenly wanted to see them all so badly his ribs ached with it. They used to just be around, the way the sun rose in the morning. You took them for granted until they weren't there anymore. His father would likely be in the barn. Ezra made himself relax his fists and went to find him.

Amos Beiler looked just as Ezra thought he himself would look in his older years. At fifty-five, Amos was handsome and sturdy. His hair had always been as blond as Ezra's and was now lightened further by strands of gray. His beard was long and ragged on the ends, and his straw hat, the one he wore around the farm while he was working, was stained from sweat and dirt. He didn't look at Ezra when he came into the barn, but his face went tight and unnatural.

"Jacob, go to the house," Amos ordered in German, without looking at Ezra.

Jacob set down the tools he'd been using to help their father mend a wagon wheel and slipped out without a word. He dared a glance at Ezra as he passed though, hurt and longing in his eyes. Ezra offered him a tight smile but didn't speak. The door banged as Jacob went out, and Ezra felt that bang like a stab in the heart. Jacob was, what, thirteen now? He'd always been the goofy one. Ezra longed to see that side of him again.

"Father," Ezra said.

Amos continued his work. There was a bad dent in two of the wheel spokes. Amos was using the flat end of a hammer to pry off the rubber rim so he could work on the spokes. It was a tough job for one person. Hating to see his father struggle, Ezra picked up a heavy screwdriver. He could hold the rim up while his father worked around to loosen it.

"Don't." Amos's tone was flat and absolute. It was one you didn't ignore. He stood frozen with the hammer holding up part of the rim until Ezra put the screwdriver down. Then his father began working again. Not once did he look at Ezra.

Ezra stepped back, feeling his cheeks burn and his stomach sour. "I came to warn you 'bout this sickness in the milk. Maybe you know my girlfriend, Elizabeth, works for the police. It's killed a lot of people yet. Cows eatin' some plant that poisons the milk. They don't know where all this plant is growin', so it's best to keep the family off the milk for a time."

His father said nothing, nor did he pause in his work. He cursed under his breath as the rubber rim slipped back in place. "Ah, *klere*!"

Ezra had to clench his fists to keep from reaching out to help again. "I'm sure you heard 'bout the Kinderman family. Best not to take chances, especially not with the little ones."

Ezra's mother had had her last baby only eight years ago—little Ameron. Ezra supposed she was too old now to have any more. But his older brother and sister had their own toddlers running around when they visited.

"Might pass the word on to Henry and Jane too," Ezra added, now that he'd thought of them and their babes.

Ezra had no idea if his father would listen to him or not. But Ezra had come and said it in person. That was all he could do. Maybe his father would take it more seriously coming directly from a son than from some stranger, even if that son was dead in his eyes.

"If you need me, Da, I've still got the same cell phone number I did before for work. And I wrote down my address." Ezra took a piece of notepaper from his pocket and laid it on the worktable.

The rim slipped back into place again and Amos cursed. He put the hammer down, turned to the worktable, crumpled up the piece of paper Ezra had put down, and tossed it into an old barrel that was used for a garbage can.

Amos turned and left the barn. The door banged hard on his way out.

Ezra made it about a mile down the road before he had to pull over, his eyes blurry and his breathing harsh and pained. He sat on the shoulder of a country road clutching the steering wheel hard. On all sides were Amish fields. It was a warm, blue-sky day, and the April crops were lush and green in their newness, only inches from the earth but holding the promise of eternity. In the distance, an Amish man rode through the rows of his field on a horse. His small son sat behind him. The boy's bare feet bounced on the horse's flank as his little arms encircled his father's waist.

Ezra felt a pain that seemed to swarm out of the core of him, as if its wellspring were a sulfurous black hole in the center of his soul. He'd lost so much—his first wife, the baby she'd carried, his birth family, and all of this—this way of life, this community. Everything he knew was gone. How could he miss it so fiercely and at the same time know it was irrevocably lost to him, not because of some outside agency, but because of a flaw of faith in his own heart? He reminded himself that he had a new life now, with Elizabeth.

He took out his cell phone and rubbed his thumb over the edge. He didn't like to bother her during the day when she was working. He didn't want to distract her, didn't want her to feel like he was clinging. But right now, he needed to hear her voice. Maybe he could just mention that he'd warned his family about the milk.

She sounded confused when she picked up. "Ezra? Is everything okay?"

He took a shaky breath. "Sure. Just wanted to talk a minute. You busy?"

"Well, yes, actually." He heard her speak, muffled, to someone else. "Turn here."

"You in the car?" he asked.

"Yes."

"With Hernandez?" The words were out before he'd thought them through. He'd only wondered. He liked Manuel Hernandez. But it had come out all wrong, hard sounding, the words of a jealous man.

"No." Elizabeth hesitated. "I'm with the agent from the CDC you met the other day. Glen. I mean, Dr. Turner. Look, we learned something interesting at the Hershbergers', and we're heading back into the office. Can I call you later?"

"It's not important. I'll see you tonight," Ezra offered, hoping she'd call anyway.

"Okay. Talk to you soon." Elizabeth sounded distracted. She hung up.

Ezra covered his eyes with his hands for a moment, telling himself it didn't mean anything. Everything was fine. His life was fine. He'd made his choices and they were good. He started his truck again and pulled away. He kept glancing at the young boy on the back of the horse in the rearview mirror until he was out of sight.

"It's sabotage," I said vehemently as I paced back and forth in Grady's office. "Someone deliberately fed a plant containing tremetol to those cows."

"We don't know that for certain," Glen hedged, sounding unsure of his own argument. "It could have just been a random tourist at the Hershbergers' place, like the kid said. As for the plant we found in the Fishers' barn, we need to wait for the lab reports to confirm that it actually contains tremetol."

I supposed I *was* getting ahead of myself. But I couldn't help the passion that made me feel I was finally on the right course. Furthermore, I didn't *want* to help it. Investigations are usually dull or intractable. When you find a spark, you grab it with both hands and you ride it for as long as you can, because it's that type of energy that gets things done.

I took a breath and forced myself to sound objective. "You're right. We won't know for certain that this is real until we get that lab report. *But* let's suppose for one minute that it comes back positive, that the traces of the plant found in the cows' trough at the Fishers' is a plant that contains tremetol. Right? Now let's further suppose that the DCNR doesn't find that plant anywhere in the Fishers' pasture. After all, they haven't found it yet, and they were out there all day."

I looked back and forth between Grady and Glen and summoned up the most confident professional demeanor I could. "Assuming those two things are true, that means someone *put* that poisonous plant in the cows' trough. That person either had to be a member of the Fisher family—who had no reason for doing so and every reason not to—or some unidentified person. A saboteur. And that makes sense with what Mark Hershberger saw. He saw a stranger feeding their cow something green over the fence the day before the cow got sick."

"It's interesting," Grady said dubiously. "But . . . I dunno, Harris. Seems pretty far-fetched."

"I agree. But you know the old line about how, when you eliminate the impossible, what's left must be true, no matter how improbable?" I ticked off points on my fingers. "The CDC hasn't found any tremetol in any of the feed or medicine that was given to the cows." Another finger. "The DCNR hasn't found any plant containing tremetol naturally growing at any of the affected farms—or anywhere else in Pennsylvania." Another finger. "This nonindigenous plant is supposed to have suddenly cropped up at these few farms, which aren't even close to each other, and which all happen to be Amish. I know you said birds could have carried it in their droppings, Glen, but that's some selective pooping."

Glen smiled at my wording.

"The plant could be on non-Amish farms though, right?" Grady put in. "Hell, it could be all over the place. But because most milk is pasteurized, we'd never know it, because there wouldn't have been any problems."

"That's not actually true," Glen said. "Pasteurization doesn't neutralize tremetol toxin, so if other dairy farms had been affected, we'd know."

I was unable to believe what I'd just heard. I must have been gawking stupidly at Glen. "Pasteurization doesn't neutralize the toxin?"

"No. That's why it's imperative we locate the source."

"But—in the press conference, the implication was that it was all about raw milk! And they've only banned raw milk sales. Now you're saying it could be in *any* milk?"

Glen looked uncomfortable. "That wasn't my call, Harris. It was the state's decision. I recommended they stop all milk sales from Lancaster County farms, and this was their compromise. Raw milk is the only place the toxin has actually shown up so far. And it's a small fraction of the dairy business, so it's less devastating to the economy and to the farmers."

"Oh my God," I said quietly. Ezra was right. The Amish made an easy target, didn't they? Blame it on them, blame it on their lack of regulation, and give the public a scapegoat.

"All right, all right," Grady said impatiently. "Forget about pasteurization for a minute. What else were you going to say about this possible sabotage business, Harris?"

I pulled myself together. There were only so many battles I

could fight at one time, but Glen's revelation left me with a very uneasy feeling. "Okay. We should have the test results on that plant matter tomorrow right?"

Glen nodded in confirmation. "I've rushed it. Shouldn't take more than twenty-four hours."

"Right. So if it does come back positive for tremetol, Grady, we need to open this as a homicide investigation. If this is a deliberate act, there are leads we should be following. Why *these* farms? How did the saboteur choose them? Is there a connection between the farms? And this plant doesn't exactly grow on the side of the road. Where did the killer get it? Also, we should interview the families involved again. Maybe someone else saw someone around their cow who shouldn't have been there, but didn't realize it was important at the time."

Grady tugged on his ear the way he did when he was making a decision. He sat up straight. "Right. Let's meet back up once you have those lab results, Dr. Turner. In the meantime, Harris, clean up anything that's urgent on your plate. You don't need to spend any more time on this until we know for certain there's something to it. But clean up what you can in case we do need to open up an official investigation. Got it?"

"Yes. Thank you," I said, relieved that Grady seemed to be taking the possibility seriously.

"Your gut's been right before." Grady gave me a knowing look. "I ignore it at my peril."

"If this does become a homicide investigation, I'd like to continue to work with Detective Harris on it," Glen put in.

"Don't you have . . . doctory, CDC stuff to be doing?" I asked. It wasn't that I minded Glen as a partner, but I was starting to wonder if his obvious interest in me was clouding his professional judgment.

"I have team members working on analysis, but right now my chief objective is to find the source of this toxin. This is the best lead we have on it right now." He muttered, lower, "Hell, it's the *only* lead."

"Anything we can do to help, Dr. Turner," Grady said. "Now get out of here. And Harris? I'm not convinced about this, but if someone *is* doing this deliberately? We need to rip that son of a bitch a new one."

"Yes, sir," I agreed. I'd promised someone else the same thing weeks ago, and it was long past time to make good on that promise.

I didn't get away from work until almost nine P.M. As I got into my car, I thought about calling Ezra to let him know I was on my way. That's when I remembered—Ezra had called me that morning when I was in the car with Glen. I'd told him I'd call him back, but I'd forgotten. *Damn it.* Ezra wasn't prone to calling me for no good reason, even though he'd insisted we could talk later.

I dialed Ezra before starting the car. "Hey! I'm just leaving work. Be home in twenty. I'm sorry I didn't get a chance to call you back today. Is everything all right?"

Ezra was silent for a moment. "All's well. I made some dinner I can warm up for you. Talk to you when you get here."

"Okay." But my heart beat a little faster at the weighted tone in Ezra's voice.

Ezra preferred to come out with things in his own time. So I ate my warmed-up roast and vegetables slowly and waited for him to talk. He was sitting in the chair across from me at our small kitchen table. His head was bowed, and the overhead light cast a shadow over his strong features. He played with a clean fork in his long fingers. Unhappiness radiated off him, making me more and more concerned.

"I saw my father today," he said at last.

I took a careful sip of water. *Oh.* "I take it that didn't go well?"

He huffed, twisting the fork in his fingers like an acrobat spinning around a pole. He started to speak, then just shook his head.

"I'm so sorry, babe," I offered.

"I wanted to warn them 'bout the milk. Don't know why I thought he might listen more if it was comin' from me. He didn't want to hear me. Didn't say a word." Ezra got up and put some water in the kettle for tea, his actions slow and angry.

I left my plate half-eaten and got up. I stopped his fussing by wrapping both arms around his waist from behind. My cheek rested on his warm, broad back. "I will never understand how a parent can disown their child. Or how anyone could not want *you* in their lives."

He remained tense in my arms, but he didn't pull away. He'd

been hurting like this all day, I realized, since he'd called me this morning, and I hadn't been there for him. I felt utterly inadequate. He covered one of my hands with one of his—large and warm. But he said nothing. I could feel the dampness of his body heat and the overly fast beat of his heart through his shirt. He was really upset. I squeezed him tighter.

"I'm sorry I didn't call you back earlier today. I was completely distracted by this milk case, but that's no excuse."

"You have your own life." Ezra's voice was distant. He probably didn't mean it as an accusation, but my guilt made me hear it as one.

I drew away, no longer sure of my welcome. He turned to face me and leaned back against the sink. I couldn't read a thing in his expression. I shivered and wrapped my arms around myself. "I . . . have my work. And yes, it can be very demanding at times. But that's not my whole life."

"I know what it demands of you. Can't say as I understand it."

I felt a sense of wrongness, like the floor was tilting under my feet. There had always been a hint of this between us. How could there not be? Ezra had grown up in a world where women stayed at home, did the cooking and the cleaning and a hundred other tasks around the homestead. They didn't go off to work ten to twelve hours a day. They didn't run after criminals, walk through bloody crime scenes, or carry a gun. They didn't say, "I'll call you back" when a member of their family was in pain and then totally forget to do so.

My hands found each other, and I clasped them together to resist reaching out to him again. Ezra's handsome face was closed off, and I didn't know how to make it right.

"The problem is not with you, Elizabeth," he said, his voice rough. "It's in me. I admire who you are. You know that. But I don't . . . I don't know who I am when I'm with you. Who am I? I'm not an Amish man anymore. I'm not a father. I'm not even a husband. And I don't take care of you. Even if I made enough money to do it, you make your own money and want to pay your own way. So what am I good for? Those mules out there are 'bout the only creatures on this earth that need me."

His face was bitter; his eyes glistened. He was as close to tears as Ezra Beiler probably ever got. I was exhausted after the near sleeplessness of the night before and the long day. So when my heart broke for him, it did so with surprisingly little effort or fuss, spilling a quiet, toxic grief.

"You, Ezra, are the man that I love. And I hope I'm the woman that you love. And the rest of it we'll build, Ezra. We will."

His shoulders relaxed a little, and his chin dropped to his chest. He looked up at me from under his blond eyelashes and quirked one eyebrow. "You sound pretty sure 'bout that."

"I am so damn sure," I answered adamantly.

He huffed and stared at me a moment longer. Then he sighed. It was enough to allow me to go to him. I wrapped my arms around his neck, and he opened up to receive me, putting his hands on my back.

"I'm so, so sorry I didn't call you back this morning. I hate how much they can hurt you, and I hate myself for not being able to prevent it."

"Not your mess," he said into my hair. "Not your fault."

It wasn't. Ezra had been preparing to leave the Amish before he'd even met me. But even so.

My body was tired, and my spirit too, but he needed me. He needed to feel loved, and I needed to make up for my thoughtlessness. I kissed him, pressing into him as he leaned against the counter. But it wasn't going to be that easy this time. After a moment, he reached up to unlace my arms from around his neck and push me gently away. With an unreadable look, he went to the back door, put on his hat, and went outside.

CHAPTER 9

The following day was a Friday. The CDC lab results on the plant matter found in Levi Fisher's barn came in at eleven A.M. At four P.M. Grady, Glen Turner, and I walked up the wide steps of the state capitol building in Harrisburg to meet with several state departments and an aide of the governor's.

It was the first time I'd ever been to the state capitol, and I was impressed. The stately building was made of ivory granite with a green dome. It was on a natural high point with views of the city, expansive grounds, spring flowers, and blooming trees. I was also anxious as hell. Glen would be doing the introductions, but I'd have to outline an initial plan and answer any questions about the case—a case which was less than five hours old.

"Oh, great," Grady muttered sourly. He paused on the steps.

"What's the matter?" I paused next to him.

He nodded with his chin. There were a dozen or so protesters near the front door of the capitol building. That probably wasn't a rare occurrence and I wondered why it had put Grady off. That's when I noticed the word "milk" on the protest signs. My gaze flickered from sign to sign. "My Body My Choice." "Food Freedom Now." "Keep Your Laws Off My Milk." "I Want It Raw." One woman who couldn't have been over twenty had a huge white sign that said, "I Drink Raw Milk. Arrest Me." The protesters were ordinary-looking people, young to middle-aged, and casually dressed. Amber Kruger would fit right in at a protest like this—if she weren't in the hospital fighting for her life.

"You've got to be kidding!" I said. "The press conference was only yesterday morning."

Glen spoke up. "The farmers will be out here soon too, if we can't get this ban lifted." He sounded calm about it.

"You must be used to this, working in the CDC," I said as we continued up the steps.

Glen gave a bitter laugh. "I've personally seen to the recall of thousands of pounds of meat and forced manufacturers to pull product from grocery stores worldwide. So, yes. Companies hate the CDC even more than they hate tax auditors, and protests tend to crop up when we're around."

"Good. Then I can place the blame on you," Grady said. He pulled open the heavy door and held it as we passed through.

"Well, personally, I'm glad you're here," I said. I meant it too. I didn't want to see anyone else die from this, and I was prepared to defend the raw-milk ban to anyone who would listen.

"Thanks." Glen looked at me warmly.

I ignored a wave of uneasiness and tried to get my mind back on what I planned to say.

The conference room had wood paneling and a mural of George Washington giving a speech. A fine-weave blue carpet covered the floor and an enormous round conference table was made of polished dark wood and surrounded by plush blue chairs. I recognized several of the state officials from the CDC debriefing at the station, but others I'd never met. Mitch Franklin was there from the Department of Agriculture and there were also people from the DCNR and the Department of Health. Margaret Foderman, the governor's middle-aged and smartly dressed aide, was the only other woman in the room.

She began the meeting. "Dr. Turner, can you give us a brief update on the situation? And then, I believe it was the Lancaster Police who requested this meeting."

"Yes, thank you, Ms. Foderman." Glen plugged his laptop into the projector and ran quickly through pictures of the farms that had been infected and a blown-up map of the county showing where the farms were located. He brought up the current total of victims. "As of thirty minutes ago, there are twenty-nine deceased and an additional forty-six that have gotten ill. We have one unconfirmed but suspected source of tremetol-poisoned milk—Aaron Knepp's farm in Paradise—and three confirmed cases. The confirmed cases are Samuel Hershberger in Paradise, the Kinderman family on Willow Street, and Levi Fisher in Bird-in-Hand.

"Right now, we have a handle on where it's been. Or we think we do. It's possible there are cases out there that have gone unreported. Unfortunately, we still haven't stopped the source of the tremetol. Which means it could crop up again anywhere, anytime. And probably will."

"Excuse me, but how is it possible you haven't found the source yet?" Mitch Franklin interrupted. "Those farms are hardly in a state of flux. That's as stable an environment as you could hope for. And I thought your people had been all over them."

"I didn't say we hadn't found the source. Only that we haven't *stopped* it. I'm going to let Detective Harris explain."

I got out of my chair and walked around the conference table to Glen's laptop, swallowing down my nerves. There was a lot more at stake here than my dislike of public speaking. Glen had shown me the pictures in his slideshow on the drive up here, so I knew the order. I clicked to a picture of the Fishers' cow trough.

"Yesterday, CDC investigators found a small amount of green plant matter in the cow trough on Levi Fisher's farm. It was tested by the CDC labs and came back this morning as positive for tremetol. The plant matter has been identified as white snakeroot, also called *Eupatorium rugosum*. In other words, we have evidence that the toxin was eaten by the cows, from their trough, in plant form. It was not in their feed or in their hay. And the plant was *not* found by the DCNR anywhere in the Fishers' pasture, just as it hasn't been found at the other farms where this sickness has cropped up."

"Isn't that a contradiction?" Margaret asked, looking confused.

"It's not a contradiction if someone brought that plant onto the farm and put it directly in the cow's trough. Levi Fisher claims to have no idea how the plant got there, so we're talking about someone, not a member of the family, coming onto the farm and feeding this to the cows. That's why this morning the Lancaster chief of police approved opening a criminal investigation." I looked at Grady.

He nodded. "That's correct. We believe there's enough suspicion of malicious intent to open it as a homicide case. Because the first big outbreak, the Kindermans, was in the jurisdiction of the Lancaster City Police, we'll be running the investigation from our violent crimes division. We have one of the most experienced and well-trained homicide detectives in the area—Detective Harris." He nodded at me. "She was a detective for the New York City Police Department, and she solved the Yoder/Travis case last year. She'll be heading up this investigation."

"Homicide?" This was clearly unexpected news to the state officials in the room. The reactions ranged from shock to surprise to disbelief.

After discussing it in whispers with his aide, Mitch Franklin stood up. His heavy, hanging-judge face wore a scowl. "Now, before we all get excited, I'd like to voice some skepticism. Just because no one's found the plant on the farms yet, doesn't mean it's not there. A cow can eat a plant down to the ground, can't it? You'd be left with stubs in that case, or even just roots. And . . . heck, are we confident that the team even knows what it's looking for? This seems pretty straightforward to me. The cow eats a plant, the plant makes the cow sick. I don't see a conspiracy here."

I pushed down my impatience and replied in a reasonable tone. "The DCNR team does know what it's looking for. Do you agree, Mr. Ellis?"

Dirk Ellis from the DCNR looked like a retired park ranger, still fit and handsome in his fifties. "Yes, we do, Mr. Franklin. My staff knows what to look for, and we haven't found it growing on any of these farms. Honestly, I'm not surprised. From what I understand, white snakeroot wouldn't be any cow's meal of choice. It normally grows in damp, shady areas and would be something cattle might eat during hard times, like in a drought, when other food sources weren't available. But these farms are flush with good spring grass."

"How can you know that when we haven't seen this plant here before?" Franklin asked.

"Because we do have access to history books and to conservationists in other states. I've been in touch with the chief conservationist in New Mexico, where they sometimes have issues with white-snakeroot poisoning. They've only seen it when cattle are allowed to forage in woodland areas."

Franklin shook his head as if not convinced, but he didn't argue.

"Also," Ellis continued, "if I may . . . with a plant like this, the stems are fairly woody, so it's unlikely it would be eaten down to the roots. Our people have been very thorough searching those pastures. I'm confident that it's not there."

Franklin gave a wary grunt. "Even if that's the case, it's still a leap to talk about homicide. What you really mean is a serial killer. Right, Detective?"

"Yes," I agreed. "He—or she, or they—is a murderer and, given the fact that they've hit multiple targets, a serial killer by definition. We believe we might have an eyewitness." I described what Mark Hershberger had seen—the man feeding their family cow from the road just before the family fell ill.

Ms. Foderman raised her hand and spoke up. "Detective Harris—if the plant was deliberately given to these animals, and the farmers don't know who's responsible, how do you propose finding the person?"

"Good question," I said. "We've outlined a number of lines of inquiry. We'll be interviewing the farmers' families again with this new information in mind. The killer may have a link to one or more of these farms, a reason why he—or she—targeted them specifically. Then there's method. White snakeroot isn't exactly easy to find in Pennsylvania. So we need to find out if any nurseries in the area grow it and check out their customer lists. The killer has to have access to the plant, and a considerable amount of it."

Franklin stood up from his seat, his bulk ponderous. "I have to say I'm concerned about the direction this is going. I think this is a monumental waste of time, and a deflection of expensive resources. The state of Pennsylvania is paying for this investigation, and, I'm sorry, Detective Harris, Detective Grady, but you haven't convinced me someone is deliberately poisoning random Amish cows." He said the last with considerable disdain, like we were blaming little green men.

But I'd faced plenty of bullies in my life, and I wasn't intimidated. I crossed my arms and stared right back. "That's what the investigation is for, Mr. Franklin, to convince you and everyone else, including, eventually, a jury."

Grady spoke up firmly. "We must follow this line of inquiry. I trust Detective Harris will be able to get everyone some kind of answer quickly."

"What I want to know is, what do we tell the press?" Ms. Foderman interjected. "The governor is already concerned about the media coverage. The deaths of the Kinderman family and the Philadelphia outbreak have made this national news. Foodborne illness can cause a public panic. We have protesters outside already. If people think this could be some sort of terrorist act, it's going to be a madhouse."

The words "terrorist act" hadn't been applied to the situation before, not even in my own mind. But Margaret Foderman was right. The press could spin it that way.

"Agreed!" Franklin barked. "If this *were* a case of deliberate poisoning, why, it could affect any farm at any time! We don't want to cause a boycott of all Pennsylvania food. Right now the scope is very limited. We need to maintain that perception."

Limited to Amish farms is what he means, I thought. And apparently that scope was fine with Mitch Franklin.

"Besides, what if the police are wrong?" he insisted. "We don't want to look like we have no idea what we're doing."

"Actually, I agree," I said. "I'd recommend that we keep this information quiet for the time being. First, because, no, we don't have unequivocal proof yet. I'd want more evidence before going public. But second, there's a better chance of catching this person—or persons—if they don't know we're looking for them."

I exchanged a look with Grady. He nodded.

"Well. I think that's resolved for now," Ms. Foderman said with the air of someone who fields crises on a daily basis. "Can we expect a daily update on your progress, Dr. Turner? Detective Harris?"

"Of course," Glen said.

That's not how I should be spending my time, I thought. But I nodded and said, "Absolutely."

On Saturday morning, the first full official day of the police investigation, Glen and I drove out to see the Knepps. They were one of the first families to have gotten ill, according to Hannah. They'd gotten sick even before the Hershbergers. It was past time to follow up with them in person. If they *had* been an early case of tremetol poisoning, they might hold an important missing clue.

Aaron Knepp was in his sixties and lived on a small farm of about twenty acres. As we drove up, we saw a Jersey cow, her udder ripe with milk, and a single goat. They were eating side by side in the pasture. Aaron Knepp said little as he motioned for us to sit on a hanging glider on the porch and took a chair opposite. His children, he explained, were grown but lived in the area. Since his wife's death, he lived on the farm alone.

"That sickness took my wife. She had a weak heart anyhow, and being so ill . . . She passed in her sleep." His voice was strangely devoid of emotion.

"I'm very sorry to hear that, Mr. Knepp," I said. "Did a doctor or coroner confirm the cause of death?"

Knepp nodded. "After I found her, I walked to the neighbors, and they called the doctor. He come right out that mornin' to make out the death certificate."

"Did he examine her?"

"Course. He made sure she was gone. Death certificate says it was her heart."

"Was there an autopsy?" Glen asked.

"No."

"Was she embalmed?"

"No." Knepp shook his head impatiently. "That's not our way."

I knew embalming was not mandatory in the state of Pennsylvania. All that was required was a death certificate by a licensed physician. Unless that doctor suspected foul play and insisted on an autopsy, that wasn't the Amish way either. They prepared the body at home, built a coffin, held the funeral within three days, and interred the body in one of their own cemeteries. They pretty much sidestepped the death industry altogether. And that was their right, as far as I was concerned. But it wasn't particularly helpful in this case.

"Where did they take your wife?" Glen asked.

"We buried her that Saturday in the Amish cemetery down there on Ronks Road."

I shared a look with Glen. His lips were set in a disappointed line. I shook my head minutely. *Nothing we can do about it now.*

"Did you notice anything wrong with your cow around that time?" I asked.

Knepp stroked his long gray beard, his gaze turned inward, as if remembering. "Ja. She was a little off for a few days round about then. I jus' heard today there was a sickness passing from cows through the milk, and it made sense to me that's where we got it. At the time, though, just thought we all had the flu."

"In what way was the cow 'off'?" Glen leaned forward, elbows on his knees. A light breeze ruffled his hair making him look boyishly young. Then I thought that was a weird thing to notice.

"Well . . . she just stood by the barn all day, sort of head down, instead of goin' off in the pasture like usual. So I knew she wasn't quite herself. I kept an eye on her, and she was all right after a few days. Course, we was all sick by then. My son's family too, my grandkids. I'd given 'em a gallon of that milk, and the whole family was sick as dogs. It only lasted a few days with them, though my daughter-in-law swears she still ain't right."

"Hmm. Did you notice the cow trembling at all?" Glen suggested. "Or maybe walking stiffly?"

"She weren't walkin' much at all. Maybe she was shakin', as I recollect. I thought she'd eatin' somethin' that upset her. The spring grass can upset their stomachs 'cause they eat so much of it, and they're not used to how rich it is."

Glen turned to me. "We should test the cow, and Mr. Knepp and his family too. I can get a team out here to examine the pasture and barn."

"Absolutely." I doubted they'd find much evidence in the barn, not this late, but we had to look. "Mr. Knepp, was there anyone around your cow in the day or two leading up to her sickness? Anyone you didn't know? Or even someone you did? A vet? A farrier? A tourist? Anyone?"

Knepp shook his shaggy head. "No. But I don't lock the barn, nor the house neither. Suppose someone could have gotten in at night while . . ." For the first time, I heard emotion in his voice. ". . . while the wife and I slept."

"What about the dog?" Glen asked, looking at the old black Lab at Knepp's feet.

"Oh, she's an old girl and deaf as a post. Sleeps in the mud room too." Knepp snapped his fingers, but the dog never looked at him. She continued to stare sleepily at me, head on her paws.

"One more thing, Mr. Knepp." I took a breath, feeling awkward. "I heard from Hannah Yoder that some people believe this sickness is a curse, a *hexerei*."

Knepp stared at me for a long moment as if surprised to hear an outsider speak of it. "'Tis so. I thought it was a curse. Not so sure now. People like you—youse don't understand."

"I'm hoping to," I said with a sympathetic smile. I ignored the questioning look Glen was giving me. "Hannah mentioned a *brauche* man, Henry Stoltzfus. Has Henry been by your farm at all?"

"Not for years. But he don't need to come by to lay a hex."

"I see. Well, is there bad blood between you and Henry Stoltzfus? Does he have reason to wish you, and maybe the Hershbergers and the Kindermans, any harm?"

"Guess you should ask him that. I can tell youse this—the bad blood's on his end." Knepp's face darkened with anger.

"Can you tell me what it's about?"

Knepp's lips worked into a bitter pout as he considered it. He looked at me and at Glen. I knew he must be thinking that we were with the police and he didn't want to talk to us. But maybe he was also considering the impact on his community this was all having. I tried to tip the scale in our favor.

"Maybe it was an argument Henry had with the church?" Hannah had told me that much.

That loosened Knepp's tongue. "He has a daughter, Henry does. Feebleminded. 'N' she got herself in the family way. She was unmarried. 'N' our church elders went to see Henry, wanted him to do somethin' about it. He refused. So he left the church.

Hard words were spoken. Now I understand the girl has another child too, and she's still not married." He shook his head in disgust. "Ungodly, they are. And Henry Stoltzfus practices *hexerei*. If he's not right with God, you can guess where that power is coming from."

I nodded thoughtfully. "Does Henry have any reason to dislike you specifically, Mr. Knepp?"

Knepp grunted. "You could say so. I'm one of the church elders, and so is Samuel Hershberger."

CHAPTER 10

We took a back road toward Manheim, where Henry Stoltzfus lived. I'd checked him out before but hadn't actually gone to see him. At this point, a talk with the *brauche* man was well past due. I could sense Glen's consternation as he drove. He opened his mouth to speak several times, then changed his mind. I held my tongue and waited for him to spit it out.

"So, uh . . . what's all this about hexes?" he finally asked. He seemed to be making an effort not to sound dubious.

"Stoltzfus has a grudge against the men whose cows were poisoned—at least Knepp and Hershberger. I'd say he's a suspect."

"But the Hershberger boy saw a man with a car. Isn't Stoltzfus Amish?"

"He's ex-Amish. I don't know if he has a car or not, but we'll find out."

Glen gave a "huh," and the atmosphere in the car lightened. Now he was just plain curious. "So what is a *hexerei*? Is this an Amish thing?"

I told him what Ezra had explained about the practice of powwow.

"So it's basically like folk remedies and prayers, for good or ill?"

"Sounds like it to me. Honestly, I don't know much other than what I just told you, which is what Ezra told me. He made it sound like not many Amish practice it anymore."

"That's more than I ever would have known," Glen said appreciatively.

I turned my head to look out the passenger window in case my skin was stupid enough to blush. Glen wasn't exactly moving on from his interest in me. If anything, it was getting worse. There were a dozen tells. It was there in the way I'd find him looking at me when he should be looking at the person we were interviewing, the way his hand lingered on the center console of the car while he drove, and in the smiles, winks, and warm looks he graced me with that were one step to the left of camaraderie. It wouldn't be the first time I'd dealt with a male partner being attracted to me. In the case of Glen, though, it left me feeling off, wrong-footed. He was good-looking, a doctor, employed by a prestigious agency—and he wasn't just staring at my breasts. He seemed to appreciate my intelligence, my work. It was flattering.

But he's not Ezra.

Things were definitely not what they should have been at

home. Last night, Ezra hadn't come to bed until late and he'd lain with his back toward me. He'd been polite this morning but distant. I missed him, odd as that sounded. I wanted to get us back to where we'd been before, but I wasn't sure how to accomplish that. I couldn't afford to be distracted from this case. There were lives at stake. Didn't he understand that?

"If this man is into herbal remedies, he might know about white snakeroot." Glen's voice was thoughtful.

"That's true." A spark of interest brought my mind back to the case.

"What about the Kindermans? Or Levi Fisher and his family? Would this Henry Stoltzfus have a grudge against them too?"

"I doubt they go to the same church. The Knepps and Hershbergers live relatively close together in Paradise, but the Kindermans were in Willow Creek and the Fishers are in Bird-in-Hand. They both live too far away to travel easily by buggy. I'll find out for sure, though. And he could have known them from somewhere else. If he practices folk medicine in the community, he could have customers from all over."

"See, I wouldn't have thought of that. I'm really glad to have you on this one," Glen commented. He added, as if feeling self-conscious, "Professionally, that is. I mean—" He cut himself off, biting his lower lip. It was a boyish tic, and it softened him.

Yes, he was attractive. In another time, another place . . .

"I'm glad to have your expertise as well," I said in a careful tone.

Please leave it at that, I thought. He did.

Henry Stoltzfus rented a house on a road outside of Manheim. It was a small bungalow in a neighborhood of similar homes that had probably been built in the forties or fifties. The house couldn't be more than twelve hundred square feet. There were children's toys scattered around the unkempt yard. The property was narrow but long, and it ran straight back behind the house. I could see a garden back there and a shed. In the gravel driveway was an old blue Ford sedan with a few rust spots on the sides.

I took pictures of the car with my iPhone and then nodded at Glen. We approached the front door and knocked.

A girl of about eight answered. Her light brown hair was pulled back in a sloppy ponytail, and her My Little Pony shirt was too small and stained with what looked like spaghetti sauce.

"Hi. What do you want?" she prompted smartly.

I smiled. "Hello. We're here to see Henry Stoltzfus."

"Pa-pa! Customer!" The girl disappeared, leaving the front door open, and Glen and I standing on the cracked cement slab of the front stoop.

Henry Stoltzfus came into the living room wiping his hands on a dishcloth. He was not what I'd expected. He wasn't terribly old, sixties at most. His thick hair was silver, and it was combed straight back with some kind of gel. His salt-and-pepper beard was closely trimmed, and his blue eyes were sharp. His face was still handsome and broad with Germanic strength. He was dressed in a worn brown work shirt and thick black pants that might have been Amish once upon a time. Otherwise, he didn't look particularly Amish now.

"Mr. Stoltzfus?" I held up my badge. "I'm Detective Harris with the Lancaster Police, and this is Dr. Turner from the Centers for Disease Control. We'd like to ask you some questions."

Henry hesitated, then tossed the dishcloth over one shoulder. "Youse are not here for remedying, I take it. In that case, we can talk in the house. Come on in."

He encouraged us to step inside the living room and shut the door, but he didn't invite us to sit down. He put his hands on his hips and raised an eyebrow, his face wary. "What can I do for the police?"

"Do you mind if I record this?" I asked, pulling my iPhone from my jacket pocket.

Henry frowned, as if not sure why I would want to record our conversation, but he gave a terse nod. I started the recorder. I preferred to be sitting, but I wasn't going to ask.

"This is Detective Elizabeth Harris. I'm with Dr. Glen Turner of the CDC. We're interviewing Henry Stoltzfus at his home on Power Road in Manheim, April eighteenth, 2015. Mr. Stoltzfus, do you know Samuel Hershberger of Paradise?"

Henry's mouth tightened into an unhappy line. "Know him to speak of."

"How would you describe your relationship with Mr. Hershberger?"

"Relationship? There ain't a relationship."

"Mr. Hershberger and his family went to the Amish church you used to attend in Paradise. Is that correct?"

"'Tis so."

"Do you still attend that church?"

"I do not." Henry straightened his back and folded his arms over his chest.

"Can you tell me why you left the church?"

Henry huffed and looked at the wall, his face darkening. "Do I have to answer your questions? Ain't done a thing wrong."

"You don't have to speak to us today, Mr. Stoltzfus. But if you refuse, it may raise questions later. And we can get a subpoena for an interview if need be."

Henry let out an angry breath. "God's sake, I got nothin' to hide." He met my gaze, his face stern. "I left the church because they're a lot of hypocrites. They wanted me to abandon my daughter. I would never do that."

"Why did they want you to abandon her?"

He grimaced. "My daughter, Rachel . . . she was born damaged in the head. She gets along well now, but she don't see things the way most people do. She don't understand why it's wrong to . . . to be with men. Got pregnant at sixteen. The church elders wanted me to shun her or lock her away. I've never penned up a dog in my life, and I sure as hell ain't gonna chain my daughter in her room—or send her to some damn asylum."

I felt Henry's passion and sympathized with him. But I'd been a police officer long enough not to take anyone's story at face value.

"The girl who answered the door? Was that your granddaughter?"

"Yes, and there's nothin' wrong with her," he said defensively. "What happened to my Rachel had to do with the way she was born, cord stuck around her neck for too long. It's not somethin' to be passed along from mother to child."

"I see."

"I have a grandson too. He's five years old. Won't be havin' no more now."

His words were both brusque and apologetic, as if justifying himself and not liking feeling that he had to do so. I wondered how he could be so sure there'd be no more grandchildren. Had Rachel had her tubes tied? Was she on the pill? The Amish didn't use birth control, but clearly Henry had divorced himself from those beliefs in plenty of other ways.

"How is Rachel doing now?" I asked.

His eyes softened. "She's doin' all right. Lives here with me, her and the children."

"Since your falling out with the church, have you been in contact with Samuel Hershberger or Aaron Knepp?" I asked, keeping my voice neutral.

Henry looked confused. "No. Why? Why are you here? If they said something, they're lying. I haven't had naught to do with them."

"Have you ever heard of milk sickness, Mr. Stoltzfus?" Glen asked. "It's sometimes called the trembles or the slows."

Henry nodded warily. "Heard of it."

I found that interesting. Not many people had a clue. "You mentioned 'remedying.' Is that what you do for a living? Remedy people? How do you do that exactly?"

Henry looked between Glen and me as if he wasn't sure what he could or should say. His face paled, and I could see the pieces clicking together in his mind, that this had something to do with sickness, and maybe something to do with his powwow practice, and the two of those things combined couldn't be good. He spoke hesitantly. "We make folk remedies. I work full-time at construction now. Mostly it's Rachel what does the remedying these days."

"Rachel does?" I repeated, surprised.

"Ja, she's a natural at it. She's not book smart, but she knows plants the way dogs know bones. It's a gift from God. She's got to earn her bread somehow."

Glen and I exchanged a look.

"I'd like to see your garden, Mr. Stoltzfus," Glen said in a polite but firm voice. "And also where you make your folk medicine. Please."

Henry wiped his brow nervously. "We ain't regulated. It's our own garden. And we make herbal treatments for friends is all."

I refrained from commenting on how quickly Stoltzfus had changed his tune. From Rachel "earning her bread" by remedying people to only treating "friends." But I wasn't with the FDA, and all I cared about was murder. "We're not here to fine you, Mr. Stoltzfus. We're looking into a different matter. I really would appreciate it if you showed Dr. Turner and me your garden and workroom, please."

With some grousing, Henry led us out the front door again and around the side of the house. The April garden was just getting going, much like Ezra's garden at home. I wasn't a gardener, but I recognized the young heads of lettuce and the tall, straight stalks of green onions. I left Glen to pore over the small plot of land with intense focus while Henry took me to the shed.

The shed was set back on the far end of the property, a worn old building of brown planks that was about the size of a one-car garage. The hair on the back of my neck prickled as we drew near. There were wooden flaps that served as windows, and they were propped open. Over the door and lintel were carved words and symbols. The words looked like German, and the symbols were odd, mystical-looking marks—a eye in a cloud, lightning bolts, symbols that looked almost like hieroglyphs, a sun with jagged lines, various types of crosses. It gave the little shed an ominous air, even in the bright light of day.

Henry pushed open the door, and I stepped inside. The air was redolent with sweet-smelling smoke as something dry and leafy burned in a stone chafing dish set over a flame. The ceiling was hung with bundles of dried plants and flowers, ropes of garlic, feathers, chicken feet, and other things I couldn't identify and didn't really want to. There was a huge wooden worktable that occupied the middle of the shed. A boy of about five was sitting perched up on a bare part of the table and focused on an electronic game in his hands, his tongue out as he worked. He barely glanced at me before going back to his game. A woman in her late twenties was working at the table, putting teaspoons of green stuff in little plastic bags.

"Rachel, this is Detective . . ."

"Harris."

"Sorry. My memory's not what it used to be."

"No problem."

Rachel finished filling and closing one of the little bags very deliberately and carefully before turning her attention to me. It was obvious at first look that Rachel was mentally handicapped. Her mouth hung open slightly, showing a gap between her front teeth. A bit of saliva lingered at one corner of her lips, and her eyes were dull. She wore a loose green print dress that went to mid-calf and rubber shoes. She wrung her hands and stepped from foot to foot, as if my presence made her excited. Despite all this, her black hair and pale skin gave the impression that she might have been a very beautiful girl, if not for the accident of birth Henry had described.

I smiled. "Hello, Rachel."

"'Lo." Rachel gave me a sunny smile. "Pretty." She reached out to touch a wisp of my hair that had come loose from my bun.

Henry intercepted Rachel's hand as if he were quite used to doing so. He held it gently in his. "Detective Harris wanted to see the shed, to see your work, Rachel."

"My work," Rachel repeated in a thick voice. She looked around and, pulling away from her father, snatched one of the filled baggies off the table. "Good tea. Good for sleep and—" Rachel waved at her nose and mouth with the hand that wasn't holding the baggie. "For a cold! If you have a cold."

"What's in it?" Glen asked politely as he appeared in the doorway behind me.

Rachel looked at her father for guidance.

"Chamomile, lavender, rose hips for the immune system, feverfew," he said. "She knows the plants on sight but not the names so good." He took the bag from Rachel and opened it, smelled the contents. "Mint too. You put mint in the tea?" he asked Rachel.

"Mint." Rachel nodded, smiling happily. "Good for your tummy." She circled her palm over her soft-looking belly.

"Where do you sell your herbal remedies?" I asked. I had my iPhone in my hand and was still recording.

"We set up at Root's Market on Tuesdays," Henry said. "I take that day off work and go along with Rachel. But most customers come here. Rachel knows what she's doin'. She's never hurt anyone. What is it exactly you're lookin' for? And what's this got to do with Knepp and Hershberger? They ain't never been customers of ours."

I glanced at Glen. He was peering closely at a shelf that had dozens of labeled glass bottles.

I decided I might as well be blunt. "The Knepps and Hershbergers were both quite ill with this sickness that's being transmitted in raw milk. Have you read about it or seen it on the news?"

Henry's eyes darted between me and Glen, who was still reading labels. "So? That's got nothing to do with Rachel and me. We don't even have a cow."

I debated internally what to say next. I spoke carefully. "You would know how to give a cow milk sickness though, wouldn't you, Mr. Stoltzfus?"

He blinked at me, his face shocked. "I—why would anyone want to do that?"

"Harris." Glen's voice was excited. He waved me over and pointed to a bottle on the shelf. The bottle was half full of a clear substance, and the label read: "Tall Boneset Extract."

"It's another name for white snakeroot," he muttered low in my ear.

I rubbed my lips, surprised and uneasy. It was certainly a breakthrough, but not one that was very gratifying. I only felt sad. Of course, this wasn't proof that Henry Stoltzfus had poisoned those cows. But he had the motive and the knowhow, and now we'd found the means—or at least *a* means. That many checkmarks rarely added up to coincidence.

Glen was watching me, his eyes asking how we should proceed. I straightened my shoulders and turned to Henry and Rachel.

"Mr. Stoltzfus, I'm going to have to ask you and Rachel to accompany us to the police station for questioning. You can refuse to go with me, but if you do, I *will* formally arrest you." I could arrest him now, but I preferred to wait until we had more to go on, something that directly linked Henry and the poisonings. Once I made an arrest, it would be on his record for life.

Henry went pale. As if his legs were weak, he grabbed the edge of the worktable for support. "My grandchildren . . ."

"We'll take them along. There's a playroom where they can wait at the station. I'll call a police car to come get you."

"Da? Wass wrong?" Rachel asked, studying her father's face. She looked confused and upset.

"It's fine, darlin'. We're just gonna take a little ride. Okay?" Henry rubbed her shoulder soothingly, his voice soft. "Come on, Billy." He held out his other hand to the boy, who now had his game machine tucked close to his chest and was watching the proceedings with a solemn face. The boy hopped off the table without a word.

I was touched by how gentle Henry was with his daughter and grandson. But I knew better than to let it cloud my duty. I opened the shed door and motioned for them to step out ahead of me.

"Need to grab Rachel's coat and purse from the house," Henry said quietly.

"I'm sorry, but I can't allow you to touch anything. While we're waiting, I'll go into the house and get your granddaughter and Rachel's things."

Henry closed his eyes and shook his head, as if he couldn't believe this was happening. But he didn't protest. Head down, holding Rachel's hand on one side and the boy's on the other, Henry Stoltzfus walked resolutely forward.

CHAPTER 11

I had a black-and-white pick up the Stoltzfus family, and I rode back to the station with Glen. We drove into the city from the south, and as we approached the center of downtown, the traffic grew congested.

The heart of the city of Lancaster is Penn Square, where the Soldiers and Sailors Monument—impressive, gothic, and ornate—stands in a small circle in the middle of the square. A roundabout directs the flow of traffic around the statue to the four intersecting streets. Penn Square is ringed by quaint shops in old colonial buildings of brick, stone, and wood, and I always enjoyed passing through it.

But today, the traffic was jammed up blocks before Penn Square. I texted with Grady to fill him in and get the interview room lined up, so I wasn't paying a lot of attention until Glen spoke up.

"Great. The governor will love this."

I looked up and took in the crowds on either side of the street. A few signs clued me in on what I was looking at. Among the Saturday tourists and shoppers were protesters. There had to be a hundred pro-raw-milk protesters with their signs and slogans. On one corner of Penn Square, a smaller group in opposition shouted at passing cars. They carried signs that read: "Pasteurization—Good for Farmers, Good for You" and "Raw Milk HURTS Dairy Farmers!"

"Oh no," I muttered. I was surprised by the number of people and surprised too by the passion I saw on the faces of those on both sides of the issue. "This is not good."

"No," Glen said tersely as the car crawled forward.

I already felt enormous pressure about this case. There was the meeting we'd had at the state capitol and the knowledge that the media and the state government were watching the case closely. But there was a greater stress that came from inside me, as if the walk-through I'd done at the Kinderman house was always lurking behind a thin veil in my mind. I'd do anything to prevent more children from dying, more Amish families from being poisoned on their own farms. I felt protective and fierce about the case, and I wanted to find whoever was responsible and make him pay.

However, the pressure the growing protests put on the police department was not at all helpful.

We rolled by a lovely brick building that I'd always admired. It was a real-estate office right on Penn Square, and it was across from a deli the police frequented. A man in white coveralls was in front of the brick wall with a bucket and scrub brush. Someone had defaced the building with graffiti in neon yellow. "Besnard," it said. Had the graffiti artist been trying to spell "bastard"? I hated to see the defacement of such a prominent property.

If you have to be an asshole, at least learn how to spell.

Then Glen braked hard as a group of young teens passed in front of his sedan. They wore T-shirts that showed the back end of a cartoon cow with a huge udder and, under that, the words "Do It Raw."

"Classy!" I muttered under my breath, and Glen burst out in a laugh.

The formal interview with Henry Stoltzfus and then Rachel was performed in one of the station's interrogation rooms and filmed through one-way glass. I ran the interviews, and Glen sat in. Though I couldn't see him, I knew Grady was watching from behind the mirror. I could feel his strong, calming presence as if he were in the room.

"Can you describe how you know the family of Aaron Knepp?" I asked Henry.

"Told you that already, at my house."

"I'd like you to tell me again."

No one ever enjoys being questioned by the police. Reactions run the gamut from fear to tears to anger and defiance. Habitual criminals often show no emotion at all, unless it's boredom or disdain. Henry was not an emotional man, and he wavered between bewilderment that this was happening at all, and irritation.

"We used to go to the same church. That was seven years ago. Ain't seen the man but a couple of times since."

He repeated the whole story, with prompting for more details from me this time. His wife had died giving birth to Rachel, and she was Henry's only child. When Rachel got pregnant at sixteen, and the church issued their ultimatum, he'd stuck by his daughter. He'd left the Amish church and the only life he'd ever known.

I couldn't help but admire Henry. I'd seen the way Katie Yoder's parents had written her off when they thought she'd left home and the Amish way. And then there was Ezra. Being shunned by his family hurt him in a soul-deep way that I was still trying to fully comprehend. With a low throb of anxiety, I remembered how upset he'd been two nights ago after he'd gone to see his father. It would have meant the world to Ezra to have his parents stand by him. Of course, they couldn't have done so without leaving the church, as Henry had.

But brave though Henry's actions might have been, it was clear that it hadn't been easy and that he still wasn't over it.

"Hypocrites is what they are," he said bitterly. "You're supposed to have compassion for the sick and disabled, but that's only if they're smart enough, or weak enough, to follow your rules. If they ain't, then to hell with 'em."

"You hold quite a grudge, Mr. Stoltzfus," I said.

"I'll hold a damn grudge as long as I want. I think I'm entitled. But I didn't do anything to Knepp or Hershberger nor to anyone else. I've got my own life to live. I don't have time to worry about theirs."

I changed tack. "Do you know Levi Fisher of Willow Run Farm in Bird-in-Hand?"

Henry shook his head. "Don't know him."

"Are you positive? We'll also ask Mr. Fisher. It won't look good if you withhold information now."

"I don't know him! Just because I was Amish don't mean I know every Amish there is. I know hardly any these days. We don't associate."

Henry wouldn't budge on the Kindermans either. He swore he didn't know them and had no reason to wish them harm. I'd follow up on that, of course. But for now, it was time to gain the upper hand.

I leaned forward, elbows on the desk, and gazed at Henry intently. "What is *hexerei*?"

"That's what this is? Those idiots told you I hexed them?"

"Just answer the question please. What is *hexerei*?"

He pinched his mouth closed, his eyes thunderous. He started to speak, stopped, and started again. "Powwow can be used for ill. But I have never used it as such. Yes, there are curses in the old books, *hexerei*. But never in my life have I laid one." He looked at me challengingly. "I have only ever done good with the word of God."

"How does a curse like that work? How is it done?" I asked, trying to sound curious.

Henry swallowed. He thought about it and shook his head. "I only read about it years ago. I have not studied it."

"But you have a general idea. Better than I would have anyway. Can you describe how it would work?"

Henry crossed his arms, his eyes fixed on the table in front of him, his face closed off. "To make a blessin', you draw certain figures and give special prayers to God, maybe use oil or plants, ashes, milk, and suchlike. To curse would be the same, only the words and intent change, the prayers call on God for justice and retribution maybe. I told you, I haven't ever done suchlike. My mother taught me powwow, and she warned against the curses. Evil comes back tenfold. It's God's place to punish the wicked, not ours."

"Would a curse ever involve putting something in someone's food? Or an animal's feed?"

"No." His blue eyes flashed angrily.

My gut believed him, but my mind remained suspicious. "So if someone came to you, a customer, and offered to pay you to curse someone, you wouldn't be interested? Even if he had a story you sympathized with? Or he offered you a great deal of money?"

"No one ever asked me to lay a hex, and I never would do," Henry said firmly.

"What if someone was hurting your family? Hurting Rachel?"

Henry merely shook his head. "I told you, it's playin' with fire to do such things. I'm not a foolish man."

I glanced at Glen, silently asking him what he thought.

"What about the tall boneset oil we found in your cabinet?" Glen asked. "Why do you have that?"

Henry's jaw clenched. "It's for faintin'. You burn the oil in a little pot. Put it under the person's nose. The smoke wakes 'em. Sometimes just a dab of oil under the nose will do it."

"So it's like smelling salts?" I asked.

Henry's eyes flickered to me. "Boneset has a very ugly scent. It'd wake the dead."

"It's also poisonous," Glen said, "to animals and humans."

"Don't use it like that," Henry said firmly. "Never have. And the children know not to touch anythin' in the shed."

What about Rachel? I thought. As my internal radar liked Henry for the crime less and less, my thoughts turned to his daughter. Rachel felt no moral conflict about sex. Would she feel guilt about hurting others? Was she capable of lashing out in anger? Henry said she knew plants instinctively. And he must have trained her, just as his mother had trained him. She would know what the boneset oil could do.

"Where did you get the oil? Do you grow the boneset plant, also called white snakeroot?" Glen asked.

"Never have grown it. Had that bottle for years. Not much call for it."

Glen narrowed his eyes. "You granted us permission to search your garden and shed, Mr. Stoltzfus. If you have the plant, we'll find it. So you may as well tell us now."

"If you find it, it'll be the first I knew of it," Henry insisted. He didn't appear worried.

The muscles in Glen's jaw twitched with annoyance. "You admitted you know how to give a cow milk sickness, and we found boneset oil in your possession. What do you expect us to make of that, Mr. Stoltzfus?"

Henry stared Glen down. "To do such a thing—this would never occur to me! You are a doctor. I'm just like you. Like you, I know how to kill a man if I wanted to. I could do it ten times over, in painful ways or in easy ways, quick or slow. But I never have and I never would. And to go the long way around? To kill a man through his cow? What madness is that? What purpose does it serve?"

It was an interesting question, I thought. And at least one answer was obvious. "It would serve very well if you wanted to kill not only the man, but his whole family," I pointed out.

"Ocht!" Henry made a dismissive gesture. "A man who would kill babies . . . he is the devil. I am not a perfect man, but I pray to God and I live the best I can. I am not such a man."

I wished I found Henry Stoltzfus less believable.

Rachel's interview was even less productive. She was upset when she came in and asked for her father in a panicky voice, refusing to calm down. We finally gave her hot chocolate and cookies, which got her to sit and eat, but she retained a stubborn silence. When questioned, she claimed, with shakes of her head, that she didn't recognize any of the victims' names. She wouldn't talk about the church she and her father used to attend, only shrugging and looking confused or talking about the "baby sheep at church," which I assumed had been something she'd seen at an Amish farm where they'd held a service. Talking to Rachel about powwow led to a recipe for making tea that she repeated like a broken record.

Giving up, we released Rachel to return to her children and father in a waiting room until we decided what to do with them. Glen and I stepped into Grady's office to hash it out.

"We could bring in a psychiatrist to talk to Rachel. Someone used to dealing with the mentally handicapped," Glen suggested.

"We could," I agreed. "But I'm not sure we'd learn much. If Henry did this, I doubt he'd tell Rachel. He's very protective of her. As for Rachel doing it, I . . . God, I just don't see it. Even if she was capable of the malice needed to poison a family, and knew how to do it using plants or boneset oil, I can't imagine her pulling off the kind of planning and cunning this would require. There's also quite a bit of traveling involved. Henry said she couldn't drive. And he's gone during the day, leaving the children with her at the house."

"What about Henry? What do you make of him?" Grady asked me. He was half-seated on the edge of his desk, his big arms folded across his chest.

I sighed. "He knows how to do it and had reason to hate at least two of the victims. That's means and motive. He drives, and he's away from home during the day, so he had the opportunity. He used to be Amish, so he'd know his way around those farms."

"But?" Grady prompted at the doubtful tone in my voice.

"It doesn't feel right to me. It's possible he has a grudge against the Amish because of what happened to him. Maybe he wants to hurt the community as a whole, but I don't really sense that in him." I shrugged minutely. "I'm far from crossing him off as a suspect though. We should see if Mark Hershberger can identify his car or Stoltzfus himself. And we need to check his alibis for the likely times the cows were poisoned."

"Right. So what's your call? Arrest him now, hold him as long as we can, or let him go?" Grady pressed.

"Hold him. He said we could search his property, so I'd like to go back out there today. Maybe we can find something that links Stoltzfus to the victims, and we need to check for white snakeroot plant. We know he has the boneset oil, but the cows were actually fed a plant. His property is pretty wild. It will take time to search."

"I can call DCNR and see if they'll meet you over there," Glen said.

"Great." I gave him a tired smile. "We can ask Henry if Rachel and her kids could go visit a friend until we're done. They'll be bored to death in the waiting room, and I don't see any reason to hold them."

"I'll get someone on it," Grady said briskly. He opened the door of his office and strode out. Meeting adjourned.

"I'd like to go along for the search of Stoltzfus's place," Glen said.

"If you have something more urgent to do, Doctor, I'm sure I can handle it."

Glen flushed and glanced at his watch. "Hmm. I really should check in with DC and my team. Will you call me if you find anything interesting? I can drive over."

"Will do."

"Thanks . . . Elizabeth." Glen gave me a lingering look before leaving the office.

I rolled my eyes. This was ridiculous. I had one man I was spending way too much time with and another I barely got to see. If only I could swap the two.

I checked the time. It was four already. It would be another late night. I'd hoped to get home a bit early tonight, see if I could get Ezra out of his funk, have some quiet time together. But that would have to be put off for another day.

I could only hope he was still there when I finally had time for him. For now, I had a property to search.

Ezra liked the little market down the road from their farm. He liked its gingham-lined shelves of health foods, bulk candy, and local produce. It was homey and far less overwhelming than the Giant market where Elizabeth preferred to shop. When she did shop. Not that he could remember the last time that had happened.

He didn't mind picking up the load when she was busy. He

liked to do things for her. She worked too hard. And there was only the two of them, so it wasn't like the household work was a bother, especially not with the dishwasher and the washer and dryer and all of those other time-saving devices he'd been getting used to. He was getting spoiled real fast.

No, it wasn't the work he minded. But he did mind doing it all by himself. He did mind that, right now, it felt like there was a space between he and Elizabeth like a crack in the earth, one that kept growing bigger.

Ezra had grown up in an Amish household with ten children. He'd never spent a single day of his life alone until his young wife, Mary, had died. But even then he'd had visitors three or four times a day during the grieving period. They had stopped by to check up on him or bring him food or just chat and "ease his sorrow." Then his sister Martha had moved in with him two months after Mary's funeral. It just wasn't the way in the Amish community to live alone.

Now he worked on his own farm raising mules and keeping up with his carpentry business, so some days he didn't see a living soul. Elizabeth was gone such long hours. He was alone far more than he was not, and it wasn't good, wasn't healthy. He knew it, but he didn't know what to do about it.

In front of him in the checkout line was an older Mennonite woman. She took her time, placing each of the items on the counter with care, making sure nothing had gotten damaged nor any of the price tags miraculously changed since she'd put them in her cart. Ezra wasn't in a hurry, and the woman reminded him a little of his grandmother. He smiled and met the eyes of the clerk at the register.

Huh.

Ezra knew him. The clerk was Amish, and he was Ezra's age. Ezra had seen him at sing-alongs and weddings here and there. They'd spoken but hadn't been particularly close.

For an instant, Ezra felt an ache of dread. His inner guard went up, and he steeled himself to be treated coldly or ignored. Then he realized that was unlikely. The man's beard was short, and his hair tapered in a modern style at his nape and was slicked back. He wore a store apron, but under that was a plain white shirt—with buttons. The man was no longer Amish.

When the older lady shuffled away, Ezra stepped up to the register.

The clerk smiled. "Ezra Beiler. Right?"

It felt good to be acknowledged. "Hello, Jacob."

Jacob looked him over, taking in his light tan pants and denim jacket. "You left too?"

"Yup."

Jacob started to scan Ezra's purchases, but he must have been doing this job for a while, because he was able to do it while chatting away. "I didn't know! How long has it been, then?"

"Since last April. You?"

"Comin' up on two years." Jacob said it proudly, as if he was talking about kicking alcohol or staying out of prison.

A spark of Ezra's humor returned. "Huh. Do they give you an award for that?" he teased in his dry fashion.

Jacob looked confused for a moment, then smiled. "Ocht! Yeah, the ceremony is at the county courthouse and everythin'."

"So you've met the president, then."

Jacob laughed. "I remember that about you, Ezra. You had a way of makin' people smile. If you wanna know the truth, the ex-Amish group I belong to will celebrate my anniversary with a potluck. But you know how we are. Any excuse to eat, don't say?"

Ezra felt a hopeful stirring of interest. "There's an ex-Amish group?"

"Oh, ja. Good-sized too. Maybe fifty people all told, though not all come at the same time. You know the Strausses from Soudersburg? Big family, all as redheaded as they come? Well, two of the Strauss brothers left the Amish. They're doin' carpentry for an RV company in Lititz. And you remember Leah Helmuth? She came up with you and me, and she's in the group. I'm datin' her now."

Jacob looked smug about that. Ezra did remember Leah. And the Strauss family sounded familiar too.

"You should come," Jacob said. "At least to say hello. Everyone'd be sure glad to see ya. There's a meetin' tonight."

"I'd like that." Ezra felt a wave of happiness, and he realized he really *would* like it. In fact, he looked forward to it more than he'd looked forward to anything in a long time.

And perhaps he revealed something in his tone or expression, because Jacob put Ezra's last purchase in the bag and looked him in the eye. He reached out a hand, steady and firm, and when

Ezra shook it, Jacob held it tight, his eyes warm. "It's real good seein' you, Ezra Beiler."

"It's good seein' you, Jacob Zook."

They held each other's gaze until Ezra, feeling self-conscious, released Jacob's hand.

"Lemme give you my number. Call or text me and I can give you the time and place." Jacob tore off Ezra's receipt and wrote it on the back.

Over the next week, the urgent desperation of a new case turned into the methodical clockwork of long hours, endless interviews, daily reports, and sifting through crumbs of evidence. The search of Henry Stoltzfus's property came up with nothing to tie him to any of the victims nor any trace of white snakeroot plant. The only thing we found that contained tremetol on the property was the tall boneset oil, which, according to tests of the bottle by forensics, did appear to be relatively old. Without further evidence with which to charge him, Stoltzfus, the *brauche* man, was released.

We spoke to all the affected families again, and their neighbors, but got no new insight into the saboteur. We rounded up and interviewed anyone we could think of to question. Amber Kruger came in as soon as she was discharged from the hospital. She'd have minor kidney damage and persistent weakness in her leg muscles for the rest of her life, but she was alive. She was a lucky woman.

I took Amber into a room at the station where we could do an official taped interview. The room was decorated in soothing blues and it was not particularly foreboding, but Amber seemed to find the process upsetting.

"Will I be charged with manslaughter? Will I go to jail?" she asked me as soon as she was seated. Her youthful, freckled face was pale, and she looked ready to faint from anxiety.

"Amber, you didn't know there was anything wrong with the milk, and neither did Levi Fisher. We're not looking to charge you at this time. However, the state is still reviewing the case, so I can't make any guarantees. And . . . you should probably get a lawyer. It wouldn't be unusual for relatives of the victims to file a civil suit even if there are no criminal charges." I explained this as gently as I could.

"Oh God." Amber put her hands over her face. Her chest rose and fell as she breathed hard.

"Are you all right?" I asked. "Can I get you something to drink?"

Amber shook her head and lowered her hands. Her eyes were dry, but somehow that was worse than tears, as if she'd already cried them all out days ago. "I was trying to do something good. I still believe in natural, local food. I do. My friends keep telling me this could happen to any food, that there's been lots of cases of processed food causing illness, like that spinach problem a few years ago. And I know that's true but . . . this is *me* and this is something *I* did. Children are dead because of the milk I sold in Philadelphia. How do I live with that?"

Amber looked so lost. I couldn't resist giving a squeeze to her cold, trembling hand. I knew something about living with guilt. "You do what you can to make it right and then you forgive yourself and let it go. It's not your fault, Amber."

She nodded, but she didn't seem to really take it to heart. She was rattled to her core, like a child who adored Santa Claus only to find the jolly old elf wielding a chainsaw in the living room.

"Can we begin? Maybe you know something that could help us."

"Yes," Amber said. "Anything."

She gave me a list of every Amish farm she'd ever been to in her quest to find products for her business. I was hoping to find some connection between Amber and all the farms where the poison had appeared. But Levi Fisher's farm was the only one Amber had ever had any interaction with. She knew nothing about the other victims or Henry Stoltzfus.

"Have you come across anyone who's passionately against raw milk? Maybe at the farmers' market?" I asked.

Amber appeared to mull it over. She took a shaky breath. "No. I've gotten some dirty looks, but it's hard to know why. No one's ever stopped and lectured me about it, if that's what you mean. My ex-husband is not a fan."

"Oh? In what sense?"

She gave an exasperated eye roll. "He didn't like me working in local foods. It didn't pay well enough to make him happy, and he just didn't get it. He's a Pizza Hut and Wonder Bread kind of guy. Not a fan of the Amish either. The more I got into the local food scene, the more we fought. We got divorced last year."

It sounded to me like the perfect recipe for anger and resentment. "What's his name?"

"Nate Kruger. He wanted me to take his name when we got married, so I did. I haven't messed with changing it back."

I wrote it down along with his address. "You say he's not a fan of the Amish. Can you explain in more detail?"

Amber looked uncomfortable. "Um. I don't know, really. He doesn't approve of their religious beliefs I guess."

"Would you say your ex-husband has an interest in seeing your business fail?"

Amber frowned. "I don't understand why you're asking. I thought this was about an invasive plant species. What does that have to do with my ex-husband?"

I had to tread carefully. So far no one outside of our internal team knew about the possible saboteur, and I wanted to keep it that way. "It's just routine. We have to look into every possible avenue." I changed the subject. "Tell me about your interactions at the Fisher farm. Did you ever see anyone else there? Did you talk about that farm with your friends? Did anyone ever go out there with you, your ex or anyone else?

"The only person I ever took out there was my intern, Rob. As for who I saw there, um, there was a vet there once. And sometimes there would be other Amish visiting at the house. And customers for the farm store . . ."

Amber's interview lasted three hours and added four people to my contact list.

Amber's ex-husband, Nate Kruger, was a good-looking thirty-year-old. He worked as an accountant for a local tile manufacturing plant, and he was nothing at all like his ex-wife.

"Amber is totally obsessed with food. She won't even go out to a restaurant. No GMOs, no 'factory farm' meat, nothing pasteurized, no corn syrup . . . She's completely paranoid!" Nate complained, exasperated. "I grew up on a farm in Lancaster, and my mother made cookies and TV dinners sometimes. Macaroni casseroles. Hell, she'd fry up Spam once in a while. There's nothing wrong with regular food!"

I made no comment. "Did you ever go with Amber to visit any Amish farms?"

Nate looked uneasy, as if wondering how much he should admit. "She kept going on about how great it was, so, yeah, I let her drag me a few times."

"Do you recall visiting the Levi Fisher farm in Bird-in-Hand?"

Nate rubbed at the tabletop with his thumb. "I dunno. I don't remember the names. They're all alike, aren't they?"

I didn't care for the way he wouldn't meet my eyes. I was pretty sure he was lying.

"And what did you think of the Amish farms Amber took you to?"

Nate scratched his forehead, then, obviously nervous, he rubbed the table some more.

"Mr. Kruger?"

"Look, Amber probably told you how much she loves the Amish. And that I don't. I'm going to an evangelical church in Mount Joy. The minister there says the Amish are a cult. God never asked us not to use modern conveniences. I mean, he gave us the brains to invent them, didn't he? He doesn't ask us to toil needlessly. And the Bible says 'be in the world but not of it.' They just hide from the world. We're supposed to be *in* the world, bear testimony, not shut everyone else out."

I studied Nate. I didn't like him. His everyone-else-is-wrong attitude rubbed me the wrong way. But did he have a deep enough hatred to kill? Could he resent his ex-wife's business with the Amish that much?

I gave him a tight smile. "Do you know much about plants, Mr. Kruger?"

"What? Plants? Not really. Why?"

"Never done any gardening?"

"No." Nate snorted as if the mere idea was ridiculous.

"Have you ever heard of a plant called white snakeroot?" I kept my expression neutral.

Nate licked his lips, uneasy. "It's been in the news the past few days. That's what got into the milk, right? The cows eat it and it poisons the milk? I told Amber she was setting herself up for a liability selling that stuff right off the farm. She never listened to me."

"Are you sure you never heard of white snakeroot before it was on the news recently?"

"No. Why would I? Look, if you're implying that I had something to do with the poisoned milk Amber sold, that's . . . that's ridiculous! That's total—*excuse me*—bullshit!" He laughed, but it was a bitter sound.

I stared at him for a long moment, watching him squirm. "It would help us eliminate you as a person of interest, Mr. Kruger, if you gave us permission to search your home and car. Just to verify that there's nothing that links you to this case. I also have a list of dates for which you'll need to provide a full account of your time." I took a form with dates from my notebook and pushed it to Nate across the table.

He glanced at the form. "You're kidding. Right?"

"If you have nothing to hide, you have nothing to worry about." I leaned my elbows on the table, my gaze steady.

Nate swallowed hard and pushed the form back to me. "I want to talk to a lawyer."

Rob Myers, Amber's intern, was the opposite of Nate Kruger. He was open and friendly, almost too friendly. He was short, about five foot five, dark-haired, and skinny. He was twenty but still had the acne of a teenager. His only attractive features were striking light blue eyes that glimmered with intelligence and a ready smile.

"This whole thing is so awful," he said sincerely when we interviewed him at the station. "Poor Amber. She must be beside herself, what with all those people dead. Are you going to arrest her?"

Rob's face was a study in sympathy. I thought, *You were selling that milk at the farmers' market too, kid*, but I didn't say it. Was Rob nervous that he could be in trouble? I decided I didn't need to threaten him with that. Not yet, anyway.

"That Tuesday morning when you picked up the milk and produce at Levi Fisher's farm, did you notice anything unusual?"

"Like what?"

"Anything different about how Mr. Fisher was acting? Anybody on the property you didn't recognize. Footprints. Trash. Animals acting strangely. Anything at all?"

Rob *hummed* and appeared to think about it. "No. Honestly, I'm not all that with it early in the morning. We were there at, like, seven o'clock. I remember it being just like any other day." He gave an apologetic smile. "Sorry. I wish I knew how to help."

"Amber didn't seem any different that day?"

Rob blew out a heavy breath. "Not until we were driving home. She got sick on the drive back. I offered to take her straight to the ER, but she wanted to go home. Guess maybe I should have insisted." He looked regretful.

"And you never got ill yourself?"

Rob shook his head. "No. I drink nonfat milk, so I don't drink the stuff we get at the farms. Gotta watch the diet, you know?" He patted his stomach with a conspiratorial smile. Said stomach was nonexistent as far as I could tell and in any case was hidden under an oversized Pittsburgh Steelers T-shirt.

"How did you come to work for Amber, Rob?"

"Um, I'm taking computer repair classes at a vo-tech college in Lancaster. But I thought I might want to be a farmer someday. You know, once I've saved up some money from a computer job. My dad was a farmer. It'd be nice to be your own boss, you know? Not have to punch a clock."

"And you met Amber how?"

"Oh. Well, anyway, if I ever do go into farming, I want to do organics. 'Cause that's where the money is, right? You can hardly make a living these days in regular farming, but people like that organic stuff, and if you sell it direct you cut out the middle man. Amber put up a job notice at the vo-tech 'cause there's a farm program there. I saw it and thought it might be good experience, just to see what it was like. And . . . yeah. It's been good. Very educational." Rob frowned. "Do you think Amber will keep her business? I know it means a lot to her. She's very dedicated, you know?"

"You'll have to talk to Amber about that."

"Right. Of course."

We ran through the other farmers—the Knepps, the Hershbergers, the Kindermans. But Rob didn't know any of them. He said that all the Amish farmers he'd met were "nice" and that he "could learn a lot from them probably." He didn't seem to harbor any emotion about them one way or the other. Or if he did, he was good at hiding it.

"Have you ever heard of a plant called white snakeroot?" I asked.

Rob tilted his head with a curious look. "No. What is it?"

"You haven't heard it mentioned on the news recently?"

Rob shrugged. "I don't watch TV much."

I wrote that down slowly. I found it odd, considering that Rob was closely involved with the deaths in Philadelphia. Most people would have followed the news stories about it obsessively. Then again, college students could be incredibly insular. "And where do you live, Rob?"

"I live with my mom right now. My dad isn't with us anymore, and she needs the help. Plus it saves money while I'm in school." He tapped the table restlessly, maybe embarrassed to still be living at home, despite his straightforward rationale.

"I'd like your address, please. And your cell phone number. I also have a list of dates. I'd like you to describe, to the best of your ability, everything you did on those days." I passed Rob the form.

"Absolutely. I'd be happy to," Rob enthused. "Anything for Amber."

CHAPTER 12

At noon on Friday, I was in the car with Glen as we drove back to Lancaster from Harrisburg. We'd given our update to Margaret Foderman, Mitch Franklin, Dirk Ellis of the DCNR, and the rest of the state officials who were interested in the raw-milk case. There'd been pressure placed on us but no more than was already there. It had only been a week since we'd opened the murder case officially, but frustration with the lack of progress was rising fast. Fortunately, the press still thought the deaths had to do with an "invasive plant" problem. It was only a matter of time, though, before the killer figured out we were looking for him.

"So . . . I hear you used to live in New York," Glen said, breaking the silence in the car.

"I did. I lived there a little over ten years."

"Living here must be quite a change for you. Why'd you move?"

I hesitated. I didn't feel like sharing the story of my husband's death with Glen. It was a private story and would make me more vulnerable than I cared to be with him. But not telling him, when he'd asked, felt like a denial of Terry. And that felt wrong.

"I was getting tired of the city anyway. Then my husband was killed. It was a random holdup at a convenience store. The perps shot him and two other people who were in the store at the time."

"I'm sorry," Glen said with quiet sincerity.

"Thank you."

I offered nothing more, and after a moment Glen spoke again. "I understand the desire to get away. Believe me. But . . . doesn't it get boring as all hell working in a small city and living out in the country?"

I shot him a disbelieving look. "You can ask that, with this case we're on?"

Glen made a face, acknowledging my point. "But this isn't the norm, right? And I'm not just talking about work. Culture. Nightlife. A real city. Don't tell me you don't miss it."

I looked out over the open countryside. It was scenic, especially in late spring, with the crazy neon green of new growth and the farmhouses tucked among the fields. Did I miss Manhattan? I missed things about it. I missed my favorite Indian food place, just a block from the apartment I'd shared with Terry. I missed the off-beat film festivals he'd dragged me to. I missed Central Park. I missed the lights of downtown at night. But if I was there, I'd miss here more. And I couldn't begin to picture Ezra in Manhattan.

An image came to mind of him, beautiful and strong and grounded to the earth, working out in the pasture with the mules. Things between us were a bit rocky at the moment, but that had no impact on how I held him in my heart. And I felt... important to this community in a way I hadn't felt in Manhattan, like I made a difference. Maybe it was an illusion, but it was a damned nice one.

"Nope. I'm good," I said.

"I have a few friends with the DC police. They're always looking for good officers. If you . . . I mean, if you'd have any interest in checking it out. It's a solid force. Good leadership. Excellent benefits. And DC is an exciting city."

I looked at him curiously. He kept his eyes on the road, his hands tight on the wheel. He was uncomfortable, probably because he was pushing in a rather obvious way.

"I appreciate the thought. But I'm not looking to make a move."

"Well... if you change your mind." Glen took his eyes off the road to give me a hopeful smile.

I thought he was going to say something more, something about how it would be nice to have me close by, maybe. His eyes said as much. I was relieved when he didn't put it into words. Words are tricky things, and you can't take them back.

We left the highway and crossed a small bridge just outside the city limits. Something caught my consciousness like a cast line. "Hang on," I said, sitting up straighter.

"What is it?"

"Pull over!"

Glen pulled onto the grassy shoulder, and I got out of the car. I jogged back to the bridge and stared down into the stream below. Lancaster County was riddled with streams, and I had no idea what this one was called. But it was at least ten feet across and still running high from the winter snow melt and spring rains.

"What's wrong?" Glen asked, joining me at the bridge.

I pointed. My eyes hadn't been playing tricks on me. I knew immediately what it was. And my brain leaped from that recognition to the implications in the space between one terrified heartbeat and the next.

Churning through the stream were swaths of white, like liquid ghosts. It was an unnerving sight, almost apocalyptic, only instead of the rivers running with blood they were running with milk.

"What the hell?" Glen sounded more confused than horrified. He hadn't gotten it yet.

I already had my phone out and was dialing Grady.

That morning, Ezra had made sure Elizabeth got some coffee, eggs, and toast before she headed out for a meeting in Harrisburg. Then he drove to Lancaster County Central Park to meet up with the ex-Amish group. He'd only been to one of the group's meetings, but he was looking forward to seeing them again. The park was crowded with cars, rows and rows of buggies, and large tour buses. It took a while to find a spot and to make his way to the rendezvous point on foot.

He hadn't told Elizabeth about this. He knew she'd be angry. The raw-milk protest had been growing like spring weeds with high emotions on both sides. Elizabeth had complained about it several times—the mess it was making of downtown and the pressure it was putting on the investigation. Now the Amish were organizing their own protest, which would only add fuel to the fire. Jacob Zook had heard about it from his older brother. Samuel Zook was still Amish but talked to Jacob a little anyhow.

Jacob had brought it up at the ex-Amish group meeting on Wednesday. "I guess we have every reason not to support them. But I think . . . yeah. I want to be better than that. I want to show I can support them even if they don't support me. And everyone is welcome at this thing, English too. That's what Samuel says."

I can support them even if they won't support me. Those words had stuck with Ezra. He'd made the decision to come today in full knowledge that Elizabeth wouldn't like it one bit. He was willing to give a lot for her, but there were times when a man had to do what he felt was right no matter who disagreed.

There were at least two hundred people gathered at the park pavilion where the protest was being held. It was on a grassy lawn bordered by steep woods on one side and a pretty bend in a stream on the other. People were milling about the area. The group was primarily Amish, but there were dozens of English there too, standing around waiting, some holding protest signs in favor of raw milk.

Ezra recognized some of the Amish in the crowd. Their gazes lingered on him a moment before moving away. But it felt all right. He was not their concern today. The men were busy moving around large kegs on dollies from a flat-bottom wagon. And a group of Amish women stood in a circle, holding hands and praying.

Jacob Zook saw him and came over with Leah.

"Hey, Ezra. Good to see you." He shook Ezra's hand with a smile.

"Jacob, Leah. Good to see you too."

"We have eleven here from our group. Wanna come stand with us?"

"I'd like that."

Jacob led the way. The Strauss brothers were there with their English wives. Ezra hadn't known any of the others in the group in his previous life, but they'd all felt like kin immediately. The younger ones had the look he thought he himself probably wore—like someone walking out onto the ice in a pair of skates for the very first time. There was a nice older woman, Mary, who was a nurse. She'd been out of the Amish community for twenty years. She'd left, she told Ezra, to get an education. She'd never taken the vows the way Ezra had, so her leaving wasn't considered as much of a sin. Her family still talked to her some. There was an older man, too, who'd left the Amish on religious grounds. Ben was now "born again." They all greeted Ezra and he shook hands all around.

It was . . . nice. It was hopeful to have a group to stand with, like he was less of a castoff. But they were all castoffs, he supposed. They were the in-betweens. They were no longer Amish, but they knew the life as second nature. It held no mystery or undue romance. They were not like the English in the crowd who either stared at the Amish or tried so hard not to that they stuck out like red poppies in a field.

The mood in the crowd was serious. Hardly anyone spoke as the Amish rolled large barrels over to the stream bank.

"Do you know what they're plannin'?" Ezra asked Jacob in a whisper.

"Not exactly," Jacob replied with a wary shrug. "But I'm guessin' there's milk in those barrels."

It was one of the Amish men who finally spoke. Ezra didn't know him, but he was likely an elder. He had a full, long white beard and a kind face. There was a sparkle in his eye and sympathy in his open nature that made him a good spokesman. He stood in front of the array of barrels, his booming voice carrying easily through the crowd. "Can I have your attention, if you please! Please, come gather round. Come on in. Don't be shy."

He motioned with his hands, and everyone moved in. The crowd had grown since Ezra arrived, and now there was a news van too. A man with a huge camera over his shoulder moved in close to get the speech on film.

"So this here is a peaceful demonstration. Those of you who are visitors may have heard that we Amish do not believe in violence. We won't serve in the military. We won't go to war. But sometimes, it's our duty to protest in a peaceful way. And this is one of those times."

Ezra was nudged forward as people in the back tried to get closer to hear.

"Here's how we see it: Men have been livin' on homesteads for thousands of years, raising stock and crops, and bartering with their neighbors with the fruits of their labor and the blessings the good Lord gives us. In the past fifty years, we've had to fight to keep our rights to raise food and sell food in the way we believe God means for us to live—simply and with as little intervention in the natural way of things as possible."

There were appreciative murmurs from the crowd.

"We would never knowingly sell anything to anyone that would do them harm. We want to get to the bottom of what happened as much as anybody. Our hearts go out to the victims, and it is heartbreakin' what happened to them, to the folks in Philadelphia, to Levi Fisher's customers, Will Hershberger, and the Kinderman family. But so far, the police haven't been able to tell us anythin' that makes sense about this tragedy. They say the sickness was due to a plant the cows ate, but they haven't found the plant, not in a single place." He paused while that sank in.

"Now, there were only three farms affected. Two of 'em didn't sell milk to anyone, but only drank their own cows' milk. Yet Amish dairymen all over Lancaster County are havin' their milk turned away by the same dairies they've supplied for years. The dairies don't want our milk, even though there's nothin' to say our milk's been affected. Two men farmin' land side by side—the English man gets his milk picked up as usual and the Amish man does not. That's thousands of gallons of good food the Lord gave us that's goin' to waste every single day. And families that earn their livin' from the milk have nowhere to turn. So today we're here to say this cannot go on without hurtin' the entire Amish community, and in turn all good people of conscience."

It was what Ezra had feared when he'd seen that press conference about the raw-milk ban. The dairies were now boycotting *all* Amish milk. It wasn't easy to make a living as a farmer anymore. Many Amish youths had to get jobs in construction or tourism or anywhere else they could find them. Dairy was an important chunk of what was left of traditional Amish farming. This would be devastating.

"We want to show people just what is bein' wasted. We want people to feel the waste—the heartbreak and the sin of it, and to know that the milk is perfectly safe. So we brought our milk here." He waved to the barrels. "All of this milk was tested. The farmers, their families, and those in our community, all drank some of every single batch of this milk two days ago and never got sick. So if you want to add your voice to the protest, you're welcome to have some milk from the open barrels we'll put out. There's no obligation to do so. Please, only take some if God moves your heart. Now I'd like to offer up a prayer that He will give us wisdom in this matter, that He will open people's eyes and hearts, and bless this demonstration."

The elder's prayer was long. Ezra figured most of the English people present were not religious, but no one made a peep. What happened afterward had the intimate air of communion.

The Amish women started to sing. They chose hymns that

would be familiar to everyone, not the German hymns they sang at church. "Amazing Grace" began soft and low and swelled as people joined in. Amish men opened up two large barrels at the front of the crowd. Amish women stood by them with dippers and a stack of plastic Dixie cups. First the Amish went up to the barrels and received cups of milk, which they drank. But soon everyone was lining up. And as the slow lines moved forward, a dozen or so Amish men began to open the rest of the barrels, one by one, and dump rich milk into the running stream.

"Amazing Grace" turned into "We Shall Overcome." And Ezra was enveloped with a thick, sacred sense of community. It had been a long time since he'd felt that, felt the invisible webbing that bound him to other people with its sticky threads. That binding could chafe. He knew that better than anyone. But it could also be a wonderful feeling, to be part of something so much bigger than yourself—a way, a people, a place, and a time.

For a moment, he glimpsed it again and was grateful.

With a faint smile, Jacob squeezed Ezra's shoulder and moved away to get into the milk line, his hand clasping Leah's. Before anyone else in their group could move, Ezra stepped forward and followed.

Deep in my heart I do believe that we shall overcome someday.

PART III

Poison

CHAPTER 13

Despite it being a Sunday morning, I drove in to work. Downtown Lancaster was quiet. Most businesses were closed on Sundays, a consequence of living in an area with strong religious roots. I detoured to pass through Penn Square. It was devoid of protesters for once, but the ghost of the protest lingered on every corner. There was a "Stop Big Brother Bullies" sign poking out of a too-small trashcan. Litter attested to the throngs that had stood around the Soldiers and Sailors Monument. And on that classic brick-front real estate building a new message was scrawled in graffiti—*Pritchard.*

I shook my head and drove the few blocks to the parking garage for the police station.

I wondered if even the liberal ACLU types took the Lord's

day seriously, or if protesting in Penn Square could no longer hold a candle to the Amish-led protest that had been going on at Lancaster County Central Park the past few days—the one that drove me bat-shit bonkers. Thousands of gallons of raw milk were being dumped into the local waterways, and there was nothing the police could do about it. Or, at least, there was nothing they *would* do about it.

"The elders say they're testing all the milk before they dump it, drinking samples two days before. So there's little chance there's any tremetol in it. And even if there were, it would get diluted in the water. Besides, the press is all over it, Harris. There are a dozen news vans out there now. Do you really want us to be on national news handcuffing a bunch of Amish? The governor doesn't want to touch this with a ten-foot pole!"

At home, Ezra had been quiet on the subject of the Amish protest, but I sensed he was in favor of it. Not that I'd seen much of him lately. Glen felt almost as strongly against the protest as I did, and he was trying to get an injunction to stop the dumping of milk on purely environmental grounds, but that was going to take time. Which meant there was just more pressure on us—on *me*—to find the goddamned source of the tremetol and stop it so all of this could end.

When I got to the station, the usual hodgepodge of drunks and desperate people were in the lobby. Back in the Violent Crimes room, I was the first one in. I sat down at my desk, but I wasn't quite ready to face it all yet so I hesitated to start up my computer. I got myself a cup of coffee and sat quietly for a minute, willing my brain to stop churning like a washer on "agitate."

By the time I finished my first cup, I'd achieved some level of mental quietude—except for one thing. There was something niggling at me, lurking just out of reach. It was something I'd seen or heard recently. What was it?

I stared at the desk with a frown, thinking over the morning. I'd thought about the case in the shower, of course. There'd been rumors that some anti–raw milk group, or maybe even the state, had deliberately poisoned the milk in order to ban raw-milk sales. Was that conspiratorial nonsense? Or was there something to it? Could someone like Mitch Franklin feel so passionately about government regulation that he would engineer a crisis like this? But it didn't feel right, didn't quite fit.

My thoughts moved on to a quick good-bye to Ezra out at the barn. There'd been a brief kiss on the cheek, something distant in Ezra's eyes. He was always extra quiet on Sunday mornings, as if he felt guilty about not being in church. Then my drive in . . .

The graffiti: *Pritchard.*

It's human nature to dismiss the expected, the mundane. There's so much data in the world, and we can only process so much of it. But this . . . it was ringing a distant bell.

I started my computer and googled it.

Pritchard Industries, Pritchard Lab, a law firm, scientists, people on Facebook . . . I drummed my fingers on the keyboard, dug into my memory. What else had been written on that same brick wall? I remembered something that should have been "bastard" but wasn't. *Besnard.* Right.

I typed it into Google: "Pritchard Besnard." Still, nothing relevant came up, at least not in the first three pages of the search results, and there were thousands of those.

I got myself another cup of coffee. My brain didn't want to let it go. It wouldn't be the first dead end I'd chased, but I didn't want to give up too soon. When was the first time I'd noticed that particular color and style of graffiti? Single words that seemed random, painted in big block letters with neon yellow paint. *Cotton.* It'd been written outside Amber Kruger's apartment on the street, a strange place for graffiti of any kind. I typed it in.

Pritchard Besnard Cotton.

This time, when the search returned, the first result made goose bumps break out all over my body. It was an article on famous poisoners. Dr. Pritchard was an Englishman who had poisoned his wife and mother-in-law with antimony. It had been a famous Victorian case.

Marie and Léon Besnard had killed multiple family members with arsenic in France in the early 1900s. Finally Marie had done away with Léon the same way, with rat poison in his food.

Mary Ann Cotton had poisoned four husbands and twice as many children with arsenic in the mid–1800s.

The website that told me all this, World's Most Lethal, had a black background and colorful graphics. With grisly glee it celebrated the notoriety of serial killers. The very tone of the website mocked me: *I am death and you can't catch me. Your kind never catches me until I've had my way again and again.*

I stood abruptly, causing my roller chair to spring away with a clang.

This is why the Amish. This is why so many bodies, so many *children.* He was taking trophies, the more horrifying the better. He wanted to be famous, a famous poisoner. And he'd written it on the streets of Lancaster cryptically, and he was probably smug about the fact that no one would make the connection until it was too late.

The little dark-haired Amish boy marched with exaggerated motions toward his family's barn. The watcher smiled, though there was no one to see it, hidden as he was behind the trees across the road. He wondered what the little boy was thinking, marching like that. Maybe in his head he was a soldier. True, he was Amish, who were dumb-shit pacifists. But maybe soldiering came naturally to males, even little boys like this one, who'd never heard of war, or even *Doom* or *Halo.*

Yeah. That sounded about right. The watcher loved violence, yearned to tear everything down, kick the carefully constructed sand castle in the fucking teeth. *Oh, yes.* Maybe this little boy did too. He wasn't yet old enough to have it all tamed and white-washed and beaten out of him.

The Amish boy went to the barn and pulled the heavy door

open with all of his slight weight. This family was a large one, popping out babies like there was a shortage of spit-up and dirty diapers and bad bowl haircuts in the world. His dad used to bitch about that: *I'd make a profit too, if I had all that free labor. But* my *wife ain't no brood mare.*

They all looked so much alike, these kids. The watcher pictured them standing stiffly, all those Amish boys and girls, standing in a field like stalks of corn, waiting for the scythe to cut them off. He, *he,* was a big fucking scythe. They were so ripe for adding to his body count. Would anyone miss another ten, twenty, fifty identical Amish kids? There were more where they came from. And children—children made it so much worse. And thus, *so. Much. Better.*

The watcher didn't know this family but he knew their name from the mailbox—*Troyer.* Wayne Troyer and his free labor had a farm on a rural road south of Lancaster toward Holtwood. These people were like ducks in a barrel, really. All you had to do was drive around and pick a farm. Wayne Troyer lived just far south enough that maybe the cops hadn't been around here yet with their raw-milk message. And even if they had, this didn't look like a family that would throw out good food. They had just the one cow and a calf. The calf was kept separate in a white pen, probably destined to be veal piccata. And when the boy left the barn with the evening's milk, it was in just one, heavy-looking covered bucket. A gallon, probably, maybe a gallon and a half. A family this size would have that all drunk up by morning. The family dog, a mottled and hairy mutt, followed the boy into the house.

The watcher hummed with pleasure. Oh, this one would work. It would be just like the Kindermans. And hadn't *that* been fucking perfect? Another four or five like that, plus the Philadelphia horror, and he'd be famous all over the world. He would tear down the biggest fucking sand castle he could before he was caught. Once *he* decided it was time to be caught.

It would be a while. He had a legacy to build. Besides, it was fun.

The little boy disappeared into the house. The sun was almost down. They'd be having supper next. The watcher considered. He could wait until it was full dark and they were all asleep in their little beds. But maybe the dog would be out then. And he had no fucking patience.

He watched for another five minutes, and when he saw no one else, he decided they must really all be at the dinner table. He took advantage of a tree with a branch that hung over the fence to get himself into the pasture without being visible from the house, then he slipped into the barn.

The brown cow stood in a stall chewing hay from her trough. She chewed and she stared at him. She didn't seem alarmed.

"I have something for you much tastier than that," the watcher said, slipping his black backpack off his black hoodie sweatshirt. Under the raised hood he had his hair stuffed under a crappy paper cap he'd had to wear when he'd worked at McDonald's. On his hands he wore the thinnest rubber gloves he could find at Kmart. He wasn't an idiot. He watched *CSI*. He opened his backpack and pulled out a plastic grocery bag stuffed full of green leaves and stems.

It had taken him a few tries to figure out the lethal dosage and also how to get the damn cows to eat the stuff. It wasn't their favorite food, but if he doctored it with a spray he'd concocted of powdered alfalfa and molasses, the cows ate it eagerly. And wasn't Google grand?

He was nervous as he held out the first handful and the cow smelled it, tasted it with her thick tongue, then began to eat, not remotely shyly. As she munched away he grew more and more worried that someone was going to come in. He didn't want to be caught. Not yet.

Where's your fucking backbone? Be a man.

He felt the urge to dump the bag in her trough and run for it. She'd probably eat it all, probably before anyone came back into the barn. But he wasn't going to reach his goals by being a fucking coward. He was pretty sure the police didn't yet know that he even existed. He'd like to get the body count to at least one hundred before they figured it out. And that meant he couldn't risk his "product" being found in the barn. He had to make sure she consumed it all or take away what she didn't.

"Eat up, shithead," he told the cow in a sweet voice. He eased his mind by going to the door and opening it a bit, peeking out where he could watch the house and see if anyone was coming. "Eat up," he said again under his breath.

He reminded himself: He was fucking *invincible.*

CHAPTER 14

The call came in early on Wednesday morning, April 29, twenty-three days after the Kinderman family had been found dead, fourteen days after the deaths in Philadelphia. At five thirty A.M., Ezra and I were asleep, and the buzzing of my cellphone on the nightstand woke us up. Blinking awake, Ezra handed me the phone. It was Grady.

"There's been another large Amish family hit. Multiple dead. I'm on my way there now."

"Text me the address." I was already out of bed and reaching for a dresser drawer.

"Yup. Can you call Dr. Turner and let him know?"

"I will."

By the time I'd run through the shower and dressed, Ezra was in the kitchen with a sandwich wrapped in a paper towel and coffee ready for me in a thermos mug.

"More deaths?" he asked, looking worried.

I nodded, upset. "Grady says it's a big Amish family, but I don't have the details."

"Do you know the name?" Ezra's words shook a little. The victims could be people he knew.

I checked the text on my cellphone. "Wayne Troyer, off Drytown Road near Holtwood."

Ezra shook his head. He didn't know them.

"You can't say anything to anyone, all right? Not until the news goes public."

"I won't," Ezra said solemnly. "Be careful, Elizabeth. And let me know when you're . . ."

Done with the bodies? Recovered? Out of the path of a serial killer?

". . . back in the office," Ezra finished awkwardly.

"I will."

I looked at him for a heartbeat and then took the two steps to where he stood on the kitchen's hardwood floor. I wrapped my arms around him and he held me tightly, his face buried in my hair. Silent apologies passed between us. Death has a way of making arguments feel trivial, and I wasn't even sure what we'd been arguing about. I found his mouth and kissed him deeply for one brief moment. Then I left him in the kitchen and hurried to my car.

I tried to steel myself on the drive, my stomach clenching around sips of coffee. Grady had said "multiple dead" and that it was a family. There'd be children, like at the Kindermans'. That was not a scene I'd ever wanted to see again in my lifetime. But seeing it—seeing *them*, the victims—was my job.

The farm was well off the beaten path, not even on Drytown Road, which was edged by farms for miles, but down a dirt road off that. I passed fields of unused land thick with weeds. Approaching the Troyer farm, there was an overgrown pasture surrounded by an old post-and-barbed-wire fence. The two-story brown barn looked halfway to falling down, but the farmhouse was neat, with rows of tulips around the porch.

God, there were still clothes hanging on the line. Their flat and empty aspect felt sinister as they billowed in a light breeze like fabric ghosts.

The driveway was crowded with an ambulance, three black-and-whites, the coroner's van, and Grady's car. All this, and the sun was barely over the horizon. It didn't look like Glen was here yet, but I'd texted him. He was on his way.

The mood was solemn as I approached the house. I passed several uniformed officers, who looked at my badge and then away again without saying a word. They seemed shaken. At the front door I closed my eyes and blew out a long breath. I took a pair of latex gloves and paper booties from a box on the porch, put them on, and went inside.

The Wayne Troyer family had been dead for over twenty-four hours. They'd died early Tuesday morning, before dawn, and within a few hours of each other. One of them, a teenage girl, had been found in the back field, apparently attempting to reach a neighbor's farm. She must have been going for help. She didn't make it.

The others—mother, father, an older female relative, and seven other children ranging from two to fourteen—were all found in the house. The place was ripe with the smell of decomposing bodies, and I was forced to dab some Vicks under my nose as I went about my work.

I looked over each body, recording my observations into my cell phone. This time there was a hard line inside my chest that kept my feelings distant. It felt almost surreal. I had the idea that if I were truly to feel it, I'd be incapable of doing my job. So I accepted the numbness and did what I had to do.

Glen was beside me at some point, pulling up the eyelids on an Amish boy, maybe eight years old. Something about signs of acidosis. I was barely aware of it when he walked away. I kept recording.

I saw Grady in the house, and the coroner, even Glen again, but no one seemed inclined to talk. It was the quietest crime scene I'd ever attended. There was no doubt about what had killed the Troyers or how. There was only the task of witnessing and recording the lives passed, one by one. When I'd seen all of the dead in the house, I went down to the kitchen. Glen and Elaine from the CDC were there. The refrigerator door was open, and Elaine was taking samples from a Tupperware bowl that looked like leftover casserole. She acknowledged me with her gaze, but neither of us smiled or said a word.

Glen waved his hand at a large glass gallon jar on the counter. On the bottom was a scant half inch of creamy white.

"We'll sample everything in the kitchen, but my guess is this milk is the culprit. Looks like they had it with one of their last meals, but God knows how long it's been poisoning them."

"He's getting too good at this," I said. "The timing of it, and the amount. He's got it down to a science."

Glen nodded, his brow furrowed and his eyes upset. He wasn't having much luck keeping this strictly professional either. "I was just going to check the barn. Want to come?"

I nodded in answer. There was little room for words in the thick atmosphere of tragedy that hung over the house, and my throat felt too tight to form any sentences that weren't absolutely necessary. Glen seemed to be feeling the same, because we said nothing more as we left the kitchen through the back door and walked to the barn.

We found the cow, a pretty Jersey, in a stall in the barn. The large door to the pasture was closed, and the sour stench of manure and sickness hung in the confined space. The cow lay on her side in a straw-strewn stall. She was panting, and her udder was so huge and distended that it looked like she had a beach ball between her legs. There was dried foam and mucus over her nose and mouth. Her brown eyes, dull and glazed, rolled to look at us, but she didn't try to rise.

I felt sick. "Oh God! Poor thing. She must have gotten a heavy dose of it."

"Looks like she hasn't been fed or milked since the family died," Glen said. "We should call the ASPCA."

"I have the number of that vet who was at the Fisher farm. He's familiar with milk sickness."

"Even better. Can you call him now?"

I stepped out of the barn to call Dr. Richmond. Anything was better than looking at that suffering animal. Nevertheless, after getting the vet's assurance he was coming straightaway, I made myself go back into the barn. I found Glen kneeling by the cow. He stroked her head with one hand and checked her mouth with the other.

"We need to check everywhere, especially in the stall and around the food trough. There has to be some trace of white snakeroot," I said. "If not in here, then by the fence line. He could have fed her over the fence. If we're lucky, we can find some trace of our killer too. Footprints. Fibers. As soon as the crime scene team is done inside, I'll get them out here."

"I don't see any traces of plant matter in her mouth," Glen said quietly. He put his hand assessingly on the cow's trembling flank.

I began to examine the feeding trough in the stall. The lighting was dim, so I pulled a small flashlight from a pocket and studied the smooth metal surface carefully.

"It's just so hard to believe," Glen said, "that someone would deliberately do this. I mean, if they wanted to poison a family, why not just put arsenic in the milk? Or in the well for that matter. Aren't all these farms on wells?"

"Now you're thinking like a homicide detective," I said, my gaze intently focused on my search. "And for that, I am truly sorry."

I glanced at him, and he gave me a sad smile. "A week ago I would have said I had no naïveté left."

"There are always things, people, that can shock you. Seems like there are always people who find a way to be worse than you can possibly imagine." At this moment, that weighed more heavily on me than it had in a long time. It felt like I had a ship's anchor tied to my soul.

The last time I'd felt like this, I'd considered giving up being a detective, finding some profession where I could hide from the darkest side of life. Flower arranging maybe. Trail guide. Bubble-bath salesman. Instead, I'd moved here to a rural paradise. But there was evil here in Lancaster County. It just hid better.

Dr. Richmond showed up and began, with the grimly unpleasant demeanor he'd shown before, to treat the Troyers' cow. Between him and the crime-scene crew, the barn was overcrowded. There was nothing more I could do now but wait for the results. I walked to a slight rise in the pasture and looked out over the farm. From here I could see the farmhouse, the barn, the driveway, and the dirt road. Across the road was a parcel of native growth with tall pine trees mixed with deciduous ones. The bright green leaves of spring danced in a slight breeze as if the trees were vain about them.

Why here?

The Knepps, the Hershbergers, the Kindermans, the Fishers, now the Troyers. I'd been looking for something that connected them all to Henry Stoltzfus or some other suspect, or even to Amber Kruger. But if the killer truly was a serial killer, a poisoner, the connection might not be there. It was even harder to imagine the Troyer family, living well away from the heart of Lancaster County, was connected to any of the others.

So why here? How does he choose them?

The Troyers were the most remote family yet. And the white snakeroot was given to their cow only a few days ago, after the press conference, after the protest had started, after the deaths had become major headlines.

Was the killer going farther afield to look for a family who wouldn't have heard the news, who would still be drinking their cow's milk? Unfortunately, I had the feeling that, despite our best efforts , there were hundreds of Amish families like that in Lancaster County. But how had the killer found this one? The Hershbergers' cow had been fed the poison plant at the fence line near a road. That could have been opportunistic. The killer could have seen the cow while out driving around and just decided it was an easy target.

And here, at the Troyers'? Had he just been driving around looking for . . . what?

They were all Amish families. *Large* Amish families. Lots of children. Was that why he'd targeted them?

I let my instinct guide me. *He's not Amish himself, or ex-Amish. He sees them as "other," expendable.* That felt right, though maybe it didn't go far enough. *He hates the Amish.* Hmmm. I supposed he had to hate them to kill them so ruthlessly. But was the poisoner a sociopath who hated everyone, or the Amish specifically? If so, why? Had he had bad dealings with the Amish? Did he resent them on religious grounds?

And why the children? Did he have an issue with how many children the Amish had? Did he have sadistic pedophilic tendencies? Did the idea of innocent children suffering satisfy him in some way?

It didn't quite fit. If he was a sadist or pedophile, wouldn't he want to see the children suffer in person? My eyes shifted to the house, contemplating the possibility that he had watched from the windows as the family died or even entered the house to see up close.

But we had nothing that indicated that was the case. Other than Mark Hershberger seeing the man at the road, none of the survivors had seen any strangers lurking about. And I'd seen no evidence of an intruder at the Kindermans' or here, no indications that the bodies had been disturbed after they'd died. There was something else, something I wasn't seeing.

My eyes wandered to the woods across the road. If he'd watched the Troyers, studied them to determine if they were a good target, that would be the ideal place from which to do it. I could almost picture him there, looking back at me from the cover of the trees. I pictured him the way Mark Hershberger had described, wearing a black sweatshirt, hood up, face obscured.

We needed to search those woods.

"We're on to you, asshole," I muttered under my breath. "I *will* find you."

CHAPTER 15

I couldn't find the poisoner.

The police and the CDC had pored over the Troyer farm and had little to show for it. We discovered a few leaves under the trough that were positively identified as white snakeroot. And the crime-scene team found shoe prints from Converse tennis shoes in the woods across from the Troyers' land. But the shoes were a popular variety and also not found in the thick matted grass of the Troyers' pasture or the cement floor of their barn. He was careful. And smart.

The death of another large Amish family had the press in a frenzy. And now the protesters at the state capitol building in Harrisburg and Penn Square in Lancaster had been joined by a new faction—one that demanded action from the police and state government, one that pointed the finger of blame at the police and thus, essentially, at me, since I was in charge of the investigation.

No, I wasn't the only one second-guessing my leadership, but the voice of my own internal critic was the loudest.

I was poring over my files again on Friday afternoon.

Someone who knows the history of milk sickness and how to cause it.

Someone who hates the Amish.

Someone who wants public fame, who fancies himself a poisoner on a historic level.

Henry Stoltzfus would not have left the graffiti. The FBI profiler I'd talked to said our perp was male, likely under thirty. Single. Bright. He could have a political agenda about the raw milk or the Amish, but even if he did, it was a thin veil for an ultimately sociopathic and megalomaniacal wish for fame and notoriety, a notoriety he believed he deserved because he was smarter and more ruthless than most people.

I went through my list of all persons of interest but was only able to eliminate an unfortunately small number of them with certainty.

Someone hovered over my desk. I raised my head to see Hernandez. His expression was sympathetic. "Hey. I'm gonna run out and pick up some sandwiches. You wanna go? Get some fresh air?"

I glanced at the time stamp on my monitor. It was after one P.M. "No thanks. I'm in the middle of this. But I'll take a sandwich if you're buying."

"No way, Harris. You gotta go along. I need to fill you in on some stuff. You can stretch your legs and work at the same time. How's that? Anyway, I'm always happy for your company, ma'am."

I gave him a dubious look. "Are you ordering me around or sucking up? You seem confused, Hernandez."

"Yes to both, ma'am." Hernandez grinned.

I rolled my eyes, but I grabbed my wallet without further thought and we headed out. He was right. I did need some air. I'd been looking at the same damn data until I was cross-eyed.

It was a very warm April day, and the sunlight made me feel like a mole emerging from hibernation. At a crosswalk, we stopped behind a handsome young blond father holding an adorable baby in his arms. The baby stared at me curiously.

And suddenly, my mind shifted tracks.

Who am I? I'm not a father. I'm not a husband.

Ezra's words came back to me, low and frustrated. He wasn't happy. It was like he was anchorless, and I . . . I was not enough to anchor him. Would he feel less adrift if we were married? If we had a child? Or would he feel trapped in a life he didn't want? With my job, the bulk of the child-rearing would be on his shoulders. Would that make him feel more needed? Or just resentful?

Then I wondered: Why *hadn't* he asked me to marry him?

We'd been together for just over a year. It was a lifetime in one sense, a heartbeat in another. It wasn't like I had dreams of a white dress and a church wedding. I was a widow, after all. I thought I had a realistic view of marriage. I was in no hurry to make it official. But Ezra was a traditional man. In the world he came from, you didn't just shack up with your sweetheart. So why hadn't he asked? Was he unsure if he wanted to be shackled to a modern woman? One who was not only rarely home but couldn't even return his phone call when he needed her?

I still bore guilt over my marriage with Terry. I'd worked so many late nights and weekends, and Terry was—mostly—understanding. He'd been considerably older than me, and he'd had his own life. And then he'd been the victim of a random shooting. And any chance to make up all those lost hours with him was abruptly gone.

My work wasn't like this all the time. Months would go by with only routine cases and almost normal hours. But something like this . . . I couldn't bring myself to regret my ability to focus so intensely. It was that obsessive focus that enabled me to solve cases. And my work wasn't just about me. I *avenged the dead.* I put people away so they couldn't hurt anyone else. It was something I could do, something I contributed, that went beyond the narrow twists and turns of my own life. I didn't want to give it up.

But Ezra . . . He was a gorgeous man—tall, broad, blond, and strong. He was funny and good-hearted, utterly honest and loyal, gentle and passionate in bed. He deserved a woman who could give him everything. It hurt knowing it wasn't me.

"Harris!"

The blond father and his precocious offspring were long gone, and I was still standing on the curb, blocking access to the crosswalk. Hernandez was looking at me funny. I stepped aside and let a group of protesters past. They were stocky-looking men, probably farmers, and they had on black T-shirts with the slogan "Safe, Legal, PASTEURIZED Milk!" I gave Hernandez an unhappy glance, and he nodded his head, indicating we should abandon the crosswalk and continue on our current side of the street.

He led me on an out-of-the-way path down an alley to avoid the crowds. I was relieved. I knew the protesters were there and what they wanted—for me to solve the case, even if they didn't know it. I didn't need the reminder.

Fortunately, our usual deli wasn't too busy. Hernandez ordered a dozen sandwiches to go for the team, and I placed my own order. As we waited, we watched the passersby through the window.

"So, I was thinkin'. . . ." Hernandez began.

"Yeah? You mentioned you had something to tell me." I perked up. When Hernandez had something to say, it was worth listening to.

"I've been doing a lot of research. You know, this milk sickness was a thing, back in the pioneer days. Lots of people died of it before they figured out it was caused by a plant their cows were eating."

"Yeah, Glen—Dr. Turner told us that."

"Glen, huh?" Hernandez raised one eyebrow knowingly.

I rolled my eyes. "That's what he asked me to call him. Anyway, what were you going to say?"

"Did you know that Lincoln's mother died of milk sickness?"

"Oh yeah?"

"Yeah. So, I was thinking. . . ." He paused.

"You're doing a lot of thinking," I pointed out dryly.

"Aw, Harris. Don't bust my chops, man. No, listen. Most people alive now have never heard of milk sickness. So how'd our perp find out about it? What if it has to do with Lincoln's mother?"

"I don't think she's doing much talking these days," I said, unable to help myself. It felt good to joke around with Hernandez for a few minutes and take a break from the gravity of the police station.

Hernandez made a *pfft* sound, the barest possible laugh. "No, seriously. Like, what if the perp read it in a biography on Lincoln, or maybe heard about it in school?"

"Yeah. I get it. Or even a TV documentary or something. Sounds like a pretty big haystack though."

"What else is new? I called around to a bunch of libraries in the area. Got their research librarians to do a check for books that might have that tidbit about Lincoln's mother in it and send me a list of people who have checked them out."

"That's really good." I was impressed. It might not turn up anything, but it was worth a shot.

Hernandez smiled at the compliment. "Yeah, and I also contacted all the high schools around here and talked to history teachers. Asked if they ever talked about milk sickness or Lincoln's mother in class. 'Cause you discovered all that poisoner graffiti, and the profile says someone like that, he's probably young. So I figured, schools, you know?"

I'd been leaning one hip on the counter. I straightened up. That idea made the eddies in my mind stir in a new way.

"And? Have you heard back from the high school teachers yet?" I asked.

"Yup. Most of them said they don't cover that. The general complaint seems to be too much material, too few school days. In fact, most of 'em had never even heard about it, which kind of surprised me. Hey, Harris, do you think the public school system is doing its job?"

I could tell by the sparkle in his eye that Hernandez was yanking my chain. He must have something good to make me wait for it like this. I crossed my arms and gave him a glare. "But you did find a teacher *who* . . ." I prompted.

He grinned. "Yeah, I did find a history teacher who covers it. At Donegal High School in Mount Joy. Said she does a section on the dangers faced by the pioneers moving into lands they didn't know. She talks about milk sickness *and* Lincoln's mother dying of it. She's been teaching the section for a while too. Eleven years at that school."

My heart beat a little faster. Holy shit, this felt like a good lead. "Can we get a list of all the students who have been in her class during that time?"

"Yeah. But I thought you might want to talk to her too."

"Can we go over there right after lunch?"

Hernandez's eyes twinkled at my eagerness. "Yes, ma'am. I thought you'd never ask."

We made it to Donegal High School just as the last bell of the day rang. I was with Hernandez. When we'd gotten back from the deli, Glen was on his cell phone in one of the police station's conference rooms, and I decided not to disturb him. He'd been eager to be involved in every step of our investigation, but for now, this was a long shot.

Except I hoped it really wasn't.

Besides, Hernandez was chomping at the bit to get away from the desk research and out on the street. I couldn't blame him. Glen had been hogging shotgun on this case since it started.

The lady at the school office told us where to find Mrs. Roberts, the history teacher. She was upstairs in room 203. Hernandez and I navigated the hallways, which were noisy with chatter and the clang of lockers and crowded with very animated teenagers. It felt bizarre to be in a high school again. At that age, I'd been quiet, focused on classes and my after-school job, and focused on getting the hell out of Pennsylvania. I hadn't been unpopular or picked on. I was pretty enough to escape bullying. But I hadn't been part of a big social circle either.

"Dang, this place is gonna give me nightmares," Hernandez muttered.

"Worse than curry," I agreed. I hoped I didn't have one of those dreams where I went to class in a see-through Disney princess nightie.

Hernandez looked around in awe. "Man, I thought my high school was nice."

It was a brand-new school building. Everything was fresh and new and of excellent quality. The classroom doors were heavy wood and had honest-to-God signs on them. It was certainly nicer than Solanco High School in Quarryville, where I'd graduated.

"Where did you go to high school, Hernandez?"

"McCaskey in Lancaster."

"Seriously? Didn't realize you were such a homeboy."

"Been here all my life, 'cept when I was in the Marines," Hernandez said proudly.

We reached room 203. The door was closed. I knocked lightly and got a quick "Come in!"

Mrs. Roberts looked every inch the schoolteacher. She appeared to be in her forties and had a thick pageboy haircut that was dyed a deep brown. She wore glasses and had on a knitted Fair Isle vest over a striped button-down shirt and gray wool-blend trousers.

"You must be the detectives!" she said with a big smile, like she was thrilled.

"Hello, Mrs. Roberts. I'm Detective Harris and this is Detective Hernandez, Lancaster Police." I reached out a hand and the teacher shook it, and then Hernandez's, with vigor.

"Wonderful! Well, as I told Detective Hernandez on the phone, I'm happy to help in any way I can. I've always been interested in criminal justice. Even sat on a murder trial jury once. That was really something!"

"Good. Well, thank you for serving."

Mrs. Robert's enthusiasm was a nice change. Most people I talked to were not happy to meet me. But the teacher's high energy was a bit like a steamroller.

"Now, you mentioned milk sickness on the phone," Mrs. Roberts said briskly to Hernandez. "It's so odd, you know. When I first heard about this recent outbreak on the news, that it was caused by tremetol, I could hardly believe it! I've been teaching about that in my history of the American West section for years! And here it is happening right in Lancaster County. My students have been very curious about it, I must say. And of course the whole school's gone off milk!"

"Mrs. Roberts," I said, trying to get ahold of the conversation, "do you mind if I record this?"

"Of course not! Be my guest."

I brought out my phone and started the recorder. "This is Detective Harris. I'm interviewing Mrs. Roberts, a history teacher at Donegal High School. With me is Detective Hernandez."

Mrs. Roberts was still smiling eagerly.

"Mrs. Roberts, can you describe in more detail what you teach your students about milk sickness?"

"Certainly. I have a section on the pioneer movement into the American West, the logistics of it, the Oregon Trail, the Mormon migration, all of that. Then the next section is about the difficulties the pioneers faced in their new homes. Now, that section ends with the dust bowl, which of course you know was caused by the fact that the farmers who moved into those plains states didn't understand the land. They plowed up all that buffalo grass, which nature had put there for a good reason, and disturbed the natural ecosystem. That's why the winds were able to just pick up all that freshly turned top soil and—"

"I'm sorry," I interrupted. "Can you get to the part about the milk sickness, please?"

"Oh, I do apologize." Mrs. Roberts blushed. "Occupational hazard. *Anyway.* The point of that section is how the Native Americans knew the land because they'd been living there for centuries, but the pioneers and homesteaders tried to treat it like the land they were used to on the east coast, or even back in the old country. And that could be quite dangerous. They often let their cattle just roam, for example, and they'd end up eating toxic plants that the homesteaders didn't even know existed. You know, thousands died of milk sickness before they figured out what was causing it. Lincoln's mother was the most famous victim but, gosh, it wasn't at all uncommon back then."

"I see. And how many students a year do you teach this section to?"

Mrs. Roberts had to think about it. "Let's see. I have about thirty students in a class and three history classes a day, plus two semesters . . . I guess about a hundred and eighty students a year."

"And you've taught about milk sickness for how many years?"

Mrs. Roberts looked a little abashed. "Well, of course, I do upgrade my class materials every single summer, but the core of it stays the same. I would say I've been discussing milk sickness in my American West unit since I came to this school, eleven years ago now."

That was quite a lot of students to follow up on, especially considering that it was only tangentially related to the case. Hernandez and I exchanged a hard look.

"You said on the phone you had some class materials you could share with us?" Hernandez spoke, his voice soft.

"Yes! I made copies for you." Mrs. Roberts went over to her desk and picked up two manila folders. She passed them to Hernandez and me like she was passing out an assignment. It gave me an uneasy sense of déjà vu. "There you go! I won't even make a crack about a pop quiz." She tittered nervously.

"Do you recall any particular student who had an interest in milk sickness?" I asked.

"Hmm." Mrs. Roberts looked thoughtful. "It is a popular lecture. You know, I find that anything death-related perks teenagers right up. But that's natural for kids. In fact, there's a paper due at the end of that section, and several of my students wrote theirs on milk sickness. It does grab the imagination."

I sat up straighter. "Do you keep those papers, Mrs. Roberts?" I tried not to sound too eager.

"Well, no. Once they're graded, and the grades entered into my computer, I hand them back to the students."

Damn it.

"Any chance you remember the students who did a paper on milk sickness?"

"Yes, let's see. . . . I'm pretty good with students' names. And of course, some of them you *never* forget!" she said warmly. Then she muttered in a drier tone, "Even if you'd want to." She laughed at her own joke, and I smiled. "But let's see . . . milk sickness. As I recall, a boy named James Westley did a very good paper on milk sickness. A bit morbid, but well researched. He was a straight-A student, James was."

"Do you know what year that was?"

"Yes, he was a senior two years ago. I suspect he's off to college somewhere now."

"And what did he write about milk sickness, do you remember?"

Mrs. Roberts sighed. "I read so many. Let me think. . . ." She went quiet, her eyes turning inward. A minute later, she smiled. "Yes, I remember now. James Westley wrote that the Native Americans could have used white snakeroot to poison whole pioneer communities, by deliberately feeding it to their cows, and the settlers would have been none the wiser. In fact, there were some deaths he'd researched that had unknown causes that he attributed to just that—deliberate poisoning by the local Indian tribes. Very imaginative boy, James! He did take care to separate fact from speculation. It was an excellent paper, especially considering the grading curve here. We have a lot of students who—"

I clicked off my phone and stood abruptly. "Mrs. Roberts, thank you so much for your time. If you remember anything else, any other student who expressed a strong interest in milk sickness, or wrote a paper on it, will you please give Detective Hernandez a call?"

Mrs. Roberts looked a little taken aback. "Ah . . . of course."

"Thank you. I imagine the office has records of past students and their contact information?"

"I'm sure they do."

"You've been very helpful." I took her hand again and pressed it warmly. "Thank you again."

Mrs. Roberts nodded, but her brow furrowed in a worried frown.

CHAPTER 16

On Saturday morning, I dragged myself from bed at eight A.M., which was late enough but still far too early. My body wanted more sleep. I'd gotten home at eleven the night before, which wasn't too bad. But it had taken hours to wind down, and for a long time I'd lain next to Ezra in the darkness of the bedroom unable to shut off my internal dialogue. I'd considered waking him and making love—that would have hopefully been diversion enough for my case-soaked brain. But he was sleeping deeply, and it felt like a selfish thing to do. I was also not entirely sure I'd be welcome.

There was coffee on in the kitchen, but Ezra wasn't there. The sun was shining in through the windows, and the sky was a clear blue. I decided to wander out to the barn in my robe. I found

Ezra mucking out stalls. I didn't dare leave the central aisle in my bare feet.

"Mornin'," Ezra said, taking in my robe with a slight smile. "Glad you slept in. You worked such a long day yesterday."

"Too long." I stepped up to the half wall of the stall and leaned against it, pursing my lips.

Ezra came over and gave me a kiss, but he leaned into it warily. "I'm a mess from muckin'."

"Your mouth looks very presentable, if you ask me."

"Glad to hear it."

He kissed me again, still leaning forward so the only part of us touching were our lips. But at least he lingered this time, kissed me with tongue and with heart. My toes curled on the rough wooden floor.

He broke the kiss, a twinkle in his eye. "Give me forty minutes, and I'll come in and take a shower. Make you some breakfast if you like. Or provide some other useful service."

I smiled at his sexy tone, feeling a trickle of delight in my tired body. "God, I'd love that. But I have to work to—"

"Damn it, Elizabeth!"

I drew back from his anger. "I'm sorry, babe! But we have a big lead. We found this kid yesterday who wrote a paper on milk sickness and how it could be used to poison people. We tracked him down last night. He goes to college at PSU. This morning we're going to drive up to State College to talk to him face-to-face."

Ezra leaned against the pitchfork he was holding and let out a long sigh. "You shoulda told me. I could at least have had breakfast with you this morning, made sure you got something to eat. Now I'm . . ." He looked down at his filthy clothes.

"It's all right. I don't have much time anyway. I'll just grab some toast. And I'll try not to be late tonight. Okay?"

Before Ezra could answer, I leaned forward over the stall to give him another quick kiss. I turned back for the house.

Twenty minutes later, I banged out the front door with a thermos coffee mug in one hand. I wore a gray suit and my hair, still wet from the shower, was up in its policewoman bun. Glen was waiting for me in the driveway, leaning against the passenger's-side door of his car. We'd decided last night that we didn't need to drive two cars up to State College, which made total sense. But as we pulled out of the farm, I noticed Ezra in the barn's doorway watching us, hands folded over his chest. He did not look happy. At all. Maybe having Glen pick me up wasn't the best idea I'd ever had.

I'll make it up to him tonight, I thought, but I felt a stab of guilt knowing I'd probably get wrapped up at work again. *I'll make it up to him as soon as this case is done*, I told myself more firmly. And I damn well meant it.

"Guy's name is James Westley. He has no criminal record. His dad works in management for Westinghouse, mom is a homemaker, two younger siblings, good student. He came in third place in a state-level competition for science projects when he was a senior. Guess what his science project was on?"

Glen glanced at me curiously as he drove. "Um . . . milk sickness?"

I huffed. "Wouldn't that be nice? No, sorry to get you excited. It was about digging for Native American artifacts in Pennsylvania, which apparently is something James did regularly. Sounds like he's really into Native American history, given how he suggested that they could have poisoned the settlers using white snakeroot."

"Sounds pretty on-target to me. Our guy has to be smart. So do you plan to arrest this James Westley today?"

"No. All we have right now is proof that he would have known *how* to do it. I just want to feel the guy out, in person. And I want to see what he's got in the way of alibis for the times those cows were poisoned."

The CDC had continued to refine the windows when they thought the cows had been fed the white snakeroot. Unfortunately, the windows were pretty wide open with the Hershbergers and Kindermans, over twenty-four hours. But with the Levi Fisher case we were in luck. They'd been able to get dated milk containers for every milking from the day of the Philadelphia outbreak moving backward. The first appearance of the tremetol, and also its heaviest concentration, was in the milk from Tuesday morning the fourteenth. Based on the research the CDC did on how long it took substances to go from a cow's stomach to her milk supply, they'd narrowed down the ingestion to Monday the thirteenth, sometime between eight P.M. and midnight.

That time frame made sense with the traffic at the farm too. It would be easiest for the perp to avoid getting caught if he did it after sunset. It was over a two-and-a-half hour drive each way from the town of State College to the Fisher farm in Bird-in-Hand. If James Westley had driven it that evening in order to poison the Fisher cows, he would have been gone for hours. Someone might have seen him leave or come back.

"Maybe we'll get lucky and he'll do a runner," Glen said. "Or you could offer him a glass of milk and get him to confess."

I tsked. "Black humor from you, Doctor? I'm shocked."

"Oh, yeah?" Glen smiled at me slyly. "I'll have to strive to achieve that more often. I like shocking you."

It was only a mildly flirtatious comment, easy enough to ignore. But maybe I'd been ignoring Glen's little forays too much. I remembered Ezra's face as he watched us pull out of the driveway this morning. It was time to remind my temporary partner that I was in a committed relationship. "Glen—"

As if he knew what I was going to say, he cut me off. "So has Hernandez had any luck tracking down plant sources?"

I cleared my throat. "There's an herbal nursery that grows white snakeroot near Lancaster, but they have a small supply and say they haven't sold any in bulk or had any go missing. Unfortunately, there are a number of heirloom seed places online where you can buy the seeds. Apparently, some people use it in perennial borders. Hernandez has been tracking them all down and asking them for lists of sales in Pennsylvania in the past few years, but that will take a while to check, especially the PO boxes."

"He seems like a good guy, Hernandez," Glen said. "I've

actually been impressed by your department overall. I like Grady too."

"So do I. He's a great boss."

Weirdly, Glen didn't look too happy about it. He frowned at the road. "There are good people in DC too."

"I'm sure there are."

He started to speak, hesitated, then took a deep breath. "Are you *really* happy here, Elizabeth? In such a rural area? With . . . with a man who . . . who is basically a farmer? I know it's none of my business, but I guess it's pretty obvious that . . . I'd like a shot with you. You're intelligent, beautiful, and dedicated. I think you deserve better."

Well there it was, all laid out. And I found that I didn't feel conflicted at all. I liked Glen, and it had been flattering to be the focus of his attention. But the only thing I felt in my heart was a longing for the man who had kissed me in the barn this morning, the man who worked hard at his craft, could put together a mind-blowing potato salad, and still made my toes curl.

"I have everything that I want right here."

He sighed and shook his head. "If you ever change your mind . . ."

"I won't," I said, and smiled.

James Westley was a wiry kid with lumpy brown hair that was cut short but still managed to be in disarray. We found him in his dorm room, where he was playing a video game with another guy, the door wide open. James clearly wasn't thrilled about being interrupted during his Saturday morning playtime.

"Detective Harris from the Lancaster Police and Dr. Turner from the CDC. We're here to ask you a few questions." I showed James my badge.

"Wow. I'm out of here," his friend said. "Whatever he did, I wasn't there." He seemed to be joking.

"Asshole!" James shouted at the guy's back as he took off down the hall. James was apparently also joking. Or perhaps not. He flushed when he looked back at Glen and me. "Um . . ."

"We can step inside, James, or would you prefer to talk here in the hall? Or perhaps you'd like to go down to the lobby?" I suggested briskly. Not talking to us at all was not an option I mentioned.

James stepped aside and let us into his room. He gave a nervous glance down the hall before shutting the door.

The dorm room wasn't exactly neat, but it wasn't a pigsty either. The bed was made. Pillows slumped on the floor from where James and his friend had been gaming. A bag of Doritos and several energy drink cans were arranged on the desk, which seemed otherwise dedicated to a TV monitor and a PlayStation 4.

"So . . . you came up from Lancaster? I'm from there," James offered with a reluctant attempt at friendliness.

"Yes, we know you are," I said.

"So why are you here? Shit. Is this about my family?" James suddenly looked scared.

"No, James. As far as we know, your family is fine. We're here about another matter. Have you heard about the recent deaths in Philadelphia and Lancaster County? The ones caused by milk?"

James's face lit up. "Yeah, I saw that online! You know, the weird thing is, I wrote a paper once on milk sickness. It was for a history class."

I studied his face, trying to discern if he was playing me. "We know that. That's why we're here."

James looked confused. "Huh. Well . . . I'm not an expert or anything. You should talk to my teacher, Mrs.—"

"Roberts. Yes, we did. We're not here to ask for your expert advice." I managed to keep the verbal eye roll from my tone.

James's mouth shut, and he looked from me to Glen, a frown between his brow. "So what's this about then?"

"Do you have a car, James?"

"Yeah. Well, it's optimistic to call it a car, but it runs. I don't use it much."

"When was the last time you were in Lancaster County?"

James looked uneasy. He shuffled from one foot to the other. "I, um, went down for Valentine's Day. That's my mom's birthday too, so it's sort of a family thing. Went down for the weekend."

"You haven't been back there since mid-February?"

"No."

"Are you sure?" I pressed, my tone cool. "Because we will be able to track your car via the highway camera system." It was a bluff mostly. Yes, we could look for his car on the video feed if he'd taken Interstate 76. But there were faster routes he could have taken that didn't have video coverage.

James folded his arms over his chest. "Of course I'm sure! I don't leave campus very often because gas costs money and I'm too busy anyway. You can ask any of the guys who live here, and they'll tell you. What's this about?"

I exchanged a look with Glen. I wasn't getting any guilty vibes from James. If he knew anything about the crimes in Lancaster, he was doing a remarkable job of faking innocence. I was disappointed, but I wasn't done yet. What at first glance seemed like a dead end could still have a hidden egress or two.

I chose my words carefully. "We have to investigate all possible causes of the milk sickness in Lancaster County, no matter how remote. That includes the possibility that someone is introducing the poison deliberately."

I stopped there, watching his face. His brow furrowed deeper as he tried to figure out what I meant, then cleared. His eyes widened. "You think—" He stopped, biting his lip.

"Go on. What were you going to say?"

"You think someone's feeding the cows . . ."

"Go on."

". . . white snakeroot. Right? Is that what you mean?"

I just looked at him.

"Man, that is fucked up!" James looked worried but also scared. And his expression grew more scared by the moment as he studied our faces. "Look, if you think it could have been *me* . . . I mean, that's nuts! Just because I wrote that stupid paper, like, years ago! I haven't even left campus. You can check."

"Oh, we will," I said smoothly.

"And I wouldn't . . . I mean, *Christ.*"

"The paper you wrote, James," Glen said. "Did you read that out loud in class by any chance?"

"No." He shook his head hard. "That's, like, grade-school shit. We just turned the papers in. We didn't have to get up and do a speech or anything."

"Where did you get the idea?" I asked. "Especially the one about Native Americans feeding white snakeroot to the settlers' cows in order to poison them?"

James shifted from foot to foot. He stuffed his hands into his pockets. "I dunno. It just occurred to me. The Indians knew about the plant. And eventually they told some doctor, and the settlers figured it out. So that made me think, like, did the Indians know before that, know that's why people were dying, and just didn't say anything? Like, 'Ha ha, you took our land and now it's biting you in the ass, dickwad.'"

"So that was entirely your own idea? You didn't read it anywhere? Or maybe someone suggested it?"

"No. I told you how I thought of it."

"Did you discuss it with any of your friends? Talk about how cool that would have been? Or maybe you shared your paper with someone?"

James blinked. A spark appeared in his eyes, as if something had occurred to him. But he shifted his gaze to the floor. "Nah. I dunno. I don't remember. It wasn't a major deal at the time. Just one more paper. Like, who would give a shit? We had other stuff to talk about."

I studied James's downturned face and the way he was examining the toe of one grubby tennis shoe. He was wearing beat-up Nike running shoes, not Converses like the ones that left the print at the Troyer farm. He turned the tip of the shoe this way and that as if suddenly finding it fascinating. I'd bet anything he was lying. But about what, and whether or not it was relevant—that was another question.

"James?" I waited until he looked up at me, his eyes wary. I took a steadying breath and tried to appeal to his humanity. "People are dying. Children are dying. They're drinking poisoned milk and dying a very painful death. Do you understand that?"

James shrugged, uncomfortable. "That sucks. But there's nothing I can do about it." He raised a hand to his mouth and began biting at a nail.

I studied him a moment longer, then sighed. I nodded at Glen, who brought out the form the CDC had put together. It listed the days and hours in which the known and suspected poisonings had taken place. "Please fill out this paperwork and write down what you were doing for the times noted, in detail. And if you remember anything at all, will you call me?" I took out a card and held it out.

"Sure," James said, but he didn't meet my eyes as he took the card.

CHAPTER 17

When Glen and I arrived back at the Lancaster police station, it was midafternoon. I wasn't surprised to see most of the Violent Crimes team at their desks. Everyone, even the detectives who normally worked drug and gang crime, was putting in extra hours on the raw-milk case. They were on the phones and the Internet following up leads for Hernandez—tracing anyone who had bought white snakeroot seeds from the suppliers he'd found and running down library patrons. I was grateful. Everyone cared about this case. A lot. Surely it was just a matter of time before we got a break.

I'd barely put down my things when Grady pulled me into his office along with Hernandez and Glen Turner. He paced behind his desk.

"The chief called me this morning after *he'd* talked to the mayor, who'd been called by the governor. They're looking at introducing a bill on Monday in the state house, an emergency measure that will make it illegal for anyone to give children under eighteen raw milk. We banned selling it, but this would mean no one who owns a cow could give the milk even to their own kids. I don't care if we get lawyered up the ass. If we can't stop the Amish adults from drinking the damn stuff, we can at least make them think twice before giving it to their children. I don't want to find any more dead kids!"

I sympathized with Grady's anger. We'd all been devastated at the Troyer house, knowing we should have been able to prevent the tragedy and had failed. But I also felt pretty clear that being more heavy-handed wasn't the way to go.

"Hang on a minute," I said, putting a hand on Grady's arm as he passed. He paused instead of shaking me off, which was a good sign that he would at least listen. "What we have is a lone poisoner targeting vulnerable-looking Amish farms. There's only so much damage he can do."

Grady looked incredulous. "We just found a dead family of eleven! That's plenty enough damage as far as I'm concerned."

"Sorry. That's not what I mean." I took a deep breath, trying to organize my thoughts. "I mean, we have an intimate situation—one killer."

"And literally thousands of Amish farms," Grady pointed out roughly.

"Yes. But." I sighed again. "What we need to do is not go after *all* milk or *all* Amish farms. What we need to do is catch *one killer*."

Grady huffed. "I thought that's what we were trying to do."

"We don't need to blow up this conflict with the Amish any more. The more we try to tell them what they can't do on their own farms, the more they're going to feel like outside authority is coming down on them, trying to force them to go against their beliefs. That's not going to help."

Glen nodded. "She's right, Grady. We need to be working *with* the Amish on this. We have another press conference Monday morning. What if we release the news about the poisoner? Ask the Amish to be on the lookout for him?"

Grady grunted. "That would mean the killer would also know we've figured it out. But at this point—"

"No," I said firmly. "He's targeting Amish farms, and the Amish won't watch the press conference anyway. All that will accomplish is to tell everyone *else* what we're looking for—including the killer. He'll just get harder to find. Yes, we should warn the Amish about him, but not through the press." I started pacing myself. I met Hernandez's gaze.

"We need to catch him in the act," Hernandez said.

"Right. We need to lure him out somehow," I agreed.

"But how would we know where he's going to strike?" Grady asked, his tone more thoughtful now. "There're way too many vulnerable farms out there. We can't watch them all."

No, we *can't.* I tapped my chin as my mind worked it over. "Look, can you give me a few hours?" I glanced at my watch. "We can reconvene at five. I'd like to talk to Ezra and a few of the other Amish I know. I have an idea, but I need to make sure it's solid."

Grady rubbed his jaw doubtfully. "Five is too late. I'm sure the chief and the mayor are going to want to hear a plan today."

"Four then." I was already reaching for the office door.

Glen stepped forward. "Do you want company?" He clearly wanted to go along.

"No. Sorry. I need to do this alone. See you at four."

The beautiful farm on Lynwood Road in Bird-in-Hand glowed in the Sunday morning light, its house and large barn a gleaming white. Ezra and I pulled into the driveway. The center area between the house and barn was crammed tight with sleek black buggies and horses. An Amish boy motioned for Ezra to park on the lawn, and he did, rolling slowly to avoid damaging the grass.

I took a nervous breath, wondering if I was really ready for the plan we'd agreed to yesterday afternoon in Grady's office.

I'd dressed as conservatively as my closet allowed this morning—a full black skirt that reached the middle of my calves, boots, and a white silk high-necked blouse under a black suit jacket. My hair was back in the bun I normally wore for work, and I had even less makeup on than usual.

Beside me, Ezra was tense.

"You don't have to go inside," I said, offering him an out for the third time that morning.

He shook his head, as if there were no point in discussing it, and opened the driver's door.

Ezra had helped me devise the plan I'd presented to Grady.

And he felt strongly about it and wanted to be there, even though, in his words, "It may do you more harm than good to be seen with me." I didn't agree. Even if the Amish shunned Ezra because he'd turned his back on the Amish way of life, they still knew he was one of their own. I most certainly was not. Besides, I wanted Ezra's read on how this went this morning. He could understand the German dialect the Amish spoke, and knew how to interpret their body language and expressions better than I ever would.

The Amish don't believe in spending a lot of money on church buildings. They hold services in a different congregant's home each Sunday. This farmhouse had been built recently, no more than twenty years ago. And it appeared to have been built with this kind of gathering in mind. Just inside the front door was a small foyer that opened to a large room that was probably a living room and dining room most of the time. The furniture had been moved out to provide room for rows of portable wooden benches. There was no podium in the front, but different Amish men got up to speak to the crowd.

I couldn't understand a word of the thick German, but I glanced at Ezra occasionally and he didn't seem particularly bothered by the sermons. I was glad the elders hadn't taken the opportunity to preach at Ezra in a veiled fashion, to try to make him feel guilty. But really, other than some curious glances, no one paid much attention to Ezra and me as we stood in the back of the room.

After the interminable sermons came more singing. There was no musical accompaniment, and the hymns were sonorous and slow, more solemn than joyous. But the raised voices and harmonies were beautiful, and I found my chest growing tight.

How strange it was to be here, witnessing a life so foreign to my own, to what I'd seen in my years in Manhattan. It was hard to believe that such pockets existed, relatively unchanged from the way they'd been several hundred years ago. There was a peace in it that I would never be able to access. But I knew now that there was no such thing as an idyllic way of life or a place where cruelty didn't exist. And I knew too that I was too independent, too questioning to ever have a place in a regimented world like this one.

Finally, when I was beginning to wonder if the service would ever end, an elder got up and spoke in English.

"We have someone here today to speak with us. It is Detective Elizabeth Harris with the Lancaster Police. She helped last year in that sad business with the murder of Katie Yoder and her English friend Jessica Travis. So please listen up to what she has to say now."

It was a warmer introduction than I'd expected, and I was grateful. I made my way up to the front of the room feeling all eyes upon me. I hadn't brought along muti-media materials because I knew they'd only distance me from this audience. But without them I felt a bit at sea.

"I'm sure you have all heard about the poisoned milk that's killed a number of Amish in the area, sickened others, and has created a lot of fear in the public and bad press for farmers."

Dozens of blank Amish faces stared at me. The men, with their long beards, were intimidating. And the women were hard to understand. At least I'd gotten to know Hannah well enough to know there was no malice behind those women's eyes, only reserve. I represented a world they didn't want their children to know.

"I'm speaking to you today in confidence. What I'm going to tell you is something we don't want the newspapers, or the general public, to know. The truth is, we need your help to put an end to this problem before more people die. You see, there's a person—we believe he is not Amish but an outsider—who is deliberately giving your cows this poisonous plant and causing the milk to become deadly."

I had their attention now. There were murmurs in the crowd, and then men began talking to each other in harsh German words.

"Please!" I raised my voice to get their attention. "Please let me explain."

When they were quiet again, I explained about what Mark Hershberger had seen: the man feeding the family cow at the fence the day before the family fell ill. I explained about finding traces of the plant in the trough at Levi Fisher's farm and the Troyers', and the shoe prints found in the woods across the road from the Troyer farm.

"We need your help. If anyone has seen any strangers lurking around their farms, parked cars in places where they shouldn't be, or especially anyone trying to feed or pet your animals, please come talk to me after the service. Any description of the person we're looking for will help. If you see someone suspicious in the future, it's probably best not to try to detain them or let them know they've been seen. If someone in your family or neighborhood has a cell phone for work purposes, call me. We'll get there as soon as we can."

I met the eyes of as many men as I could in the audience. They were definitely interested now, a few leaning forward and regarding me intently.

"Also, until we've caught this person, I'd like to ask you to be extra vigilant with your cows. Don't allow them to wander out in a pasture without supervision. And when they're in the barn, lock the barn doors. Make sure no one can get inside while the family is sleeping, or even post guards if you have the manpower. Watch closely for any signs that your animals have been infected—panting, trembling in the legs or flanks, mucus or foam around the nose or mouth. If you see this, call us immediately and we can have the animal tested." I studied their faces, hoping they could sense my sincerity. "I'm not going to ask you not to drink your cows' milk. That's a decision each of you must make for yourselves and for your children. But please know that until we can catch this poisoner, this danger is out there. If anyone in your family becomes ill, this sickness *is* treatable, but only if you get to the hospital right away. At the first sign of muscle aches, weakness, vomiting, or diarrhea, please go to your closest emergency room. Are there any questions?"

A younger Amish man with a long dark beard stood up. "Can't youse tell the public about this outsider? So they know it's not a fault of our milk, or the way we're farmin'?"

There were murmurs of assent. I nodded. "I know this has been very hard on your livelihood. The public is afraid, and that probably has hurt your sales in any number of ways."

"I've been selling my milk to Heinz Dairy for fifteen years. Now they won' take it," another farmer said, shaking his head.

"We could tell the newspapers about the poisoner," I agreed, "but I'm not sure that would make the public feel safer. In fact, it might make them more afraid, knowing there's someone out there putting poison in Amish foods. After all, if he can poison the milk, he could poison something else."

A lot of unhappy faces seemed to agree with me.

"What we want to do is put an end to this once and for all and catch this person. And that will be easier for us to do if he doesn't realize we know what he's up to. If he hears that we're looking for him, he may stop targeting your farms. And while that's good for your families, it won't put the public's mind at rest, because he could start up again at any time. That's why we need to catch him and put him in jail and then let people know exactly what happened.

"And please, you can help by passing this word along to all your Amish friends and relatives. We need to get the word out there to the entire Amish community."

Glen Turner was speaking at another worship service today, and Isaac Yoder at his congregant's service in Paradise. Hopefully that would be enough to disseminate the message.

"I believe what she said makes gut sense." The elder who'd introduced me stepped forward. He stroked his white beard with a weathered hand. "We should pray that God grants us the wisdom and strength to face this person who is intent on doing so much evil. We are lucky to have gut friends to help us. Let us pray."

On the way home, Ezra was quiet, but it was an easy stillness. His face was relaxed, and he looked at peace.

"Thank you for helping to arrange that and for going with me. Are you all right?" I asked.

"I am."

Ezra had one hand on the steering wheel; the other relaxed on the center console. I took that hand and he didn't pull away. I threaded our fingers together.

"Half a dozen people nodded at me," Ezra said. "Men I came up with. Two ladies who'd known my wife, Mary."

"I'm glad." I really was relieved this morning hadn't been a disaster for Ezra. He'd been so low lately. I didn't want him to be unhappy, and I didn't want to lose him either.

"You know . . ." he began slowly. "Bein' there made me realize all over again that I could never go back. I'm not . . . Maybe I never was that person. But I couldn't even fake it now."

I listened, rubbing my thumb over his strong hand.

"I don't want that," he said firmly, shaking his head. "And . . . and I truly am in love with you, Elizabeth Harris. I was proud of you today."

His words were warm, and they brought a lump to my throat. I looked out at the countryside as we drove, determined not to reveal myself as a total sap. I could be a hard-ass when I needed to be. But Ezra Beiler? He could push every single one of my schmaltzy, puppies-and-kittens buttons.

"Maybe you'd be better off with some fancy doctor like that Glen guy, but, the truth is, I'm too selfish to let you go," Ezra added roughly. "That is, if you still wanna stay."

"Oh, babe, I don't want him or anyone else. You're all I want."

He smiled sweetly. "Then I'm a lucky man. And it's time I acted like it."

"I know I've been at work all hours with this case, and I haven't been there for you—"

"Stop." Ezra shot me a stern look as he drove. "I'd be a selfish fool to expect you to be home with me at six o'clock when you're helping so many other people with your work."

"It's not always like this," I reminded him.

"I know that. And when you're needed, you're needed. The least I can do is take care of things at home and provide whatever support to you I can."

I sniffled and wiped at my wet lashes. Damn hormones. Damn mascara. "I know that's not the type of woman you grew up with. And it has to be hard for you to accept me being away from home all hours. But I love you so much."

He abruptly pulled the car off onto a wide dirt shoulder that bordered a cornfield, turned to me, and took both my hands in his.

"If I'd wanted that kind of wife, I could have stayed with the Amish."

I nodded as if I knew that, but, honestly, I needed to hear those words from him today. I gave him a smile.

He looked down as if self-conscious. "Listen, what's been wrong with me lately is about me, not you. I was cut off from everythin' I knew, and you were all I had. That's too much burden to put on any one person."

"But I want to be there for you."

"You are there for me." He squeezed my hands gently. "But nobody can find a man's happiness but the man himself. I learned that from Mary."

I swallowed and nodded.

"Just be patient with me. I'm taking steps. . . . I found a group of ex-Amish, and it's been real good to have someone to talk to about things."

"You have?" I asked, surprised.

"Yes. As soon as you find this killer, I'd like to take you to one of the meetings with me. I'd be glad for you to meet them."

"I'd like that."

"And . . . one of the ex-Amish, Jacob, he and his girlfriend go to this small church. Lutheran. I might try it out. I'm not so sure about God and me, but I feel like I need to make peace with that too, one way or the other."

I nodded. "Okay."

Ezra raised an eyebrow, a sparkle coming into his eyes. "You can't agree with me on everythin', Elizabeth. Makes me suspicious. I know your ornery nature."

I laughed. "I'm sure I can find something I disagree with. Just keep talking."

He grunted and released my hands, slipped his arms around my waist—rather awkwardly given the seatbelt. I leaned into him and he placed a kiss on my hair. "I meant what I said. I'm real proud of you. You sacrifice yourself to help other people. You're like . . . like a guardian angel, I guess."

I snorted. "Okay, *that* I disagree with. I'm no angel."

He rubbed my back. "Good works through you though. That's all I need to know."

Good works through you. God, there went those damn hormones. I couldn't love this man any more than I did at that moment. And I had a few hours before I had to report in at the office. Lucky me.

"Let's go home," I said, kissing his neck. "I've missed you so much. I want to hold you for a while, Mr. Beiler."

He gave me a last squeeze before pulling away. "Time to break a few speed limits, then."

I had no objections.

CHAPTER 18

The watcher wanted to flip off the Amish man who drove toward him in a buggy and stared at him. Instead he dredged up a wide-eyed smile and a wave, hoping to pass as a clueless tourist. The buggy went by, and the watcher observed it through his rearview mirror until it was well past him. He slowed down on the country road, scanning the farms to his right.

He was getting pissed off. It was Tuesday afternoon and the second day he'd wasted *hours* driving around the back roads of Lancaster County. Yesterday he'd tried south, around Quarryville. Today he'd gone in the opposite direction and was now up north near Denver. He still wasn't having any luck.

It was easy enough to tell which farms were Amish. Most of them had clothes hanging out on a line. Some had windmills or buggies parked outside. And unless the weather was shitty, there were usually people hanging around, especially kids. But something had changed. Some paranoia had poured through the community like red paint, making his life much more difficult.

They were watching.

Before, it had always seemed to him that they ignored the cars that passed by, belonging, as they did, to outsiders. They ignored the cars and they ignored the drivers, dismissing his relevance from their reality. That had always annoyed him, as if he wasn't good enough to be acknowledged. But he knew it was stupid to be annoyed. Why should the fox complain if the chickens chose to pretend it wasn't there?

The problem was, they weren't doing that anymore. As his '04 Corolla cruised past farms, people stopped what they were doing and watched him go by, as if they were making sure he drove on and was gone. And that wasn't all.

Yesterday he'd seen three Amish kids in the yard of a farmhouse and a lone cow in the pasture. He'd noted the address and had driven back there at sunset. He'd parked down the road a ways to watch. For the first time, he felt nervous and exposed parking on the side of the road, even though he had a cover story about being lost (map on the passenger seat) if anyone approached him. He trained binoculars on the house. His mother had gotten the cheap pair for him for his twelfth birthday. At the time, he'd made up a story about wanting to learn bird calls, but the truth was, he'd been hoping to see the woman who lived next door naked.

Through the somewhat fuzzy lenses he watched a man and

boy come out of the house and walk to the barn. The boy was carrying a lidded bucket, obviously for the milking. The watcher leaned forward with interest. He was astonished to see them reach the barn door and the man fiddle around with . . . *a lock.*

There was a large padlock on the barn door. The man opened it with a key and went into the barn with the boy.

Fucking hell. He'd never seen the Amish lock up anything. Was this a one-off? Maybe the farmer kept something valuable in the barn. But the watcher didn't like it. In the gathering gloom of dusk, he shoved his car into gear and drove by a few other farms with dairy cows he'd noticed previously that day, slowing down to train the binoculars on the barns. Locks. He saw more locks.

Feeling a surge of rage, he slammed on the accelerator and peeled away, heading back toward Route 23 and Lancaster. He was *done.*

As he drove he slowly calmed down. He didn't get angry often. Bullshit emotions. He was above all that. *Don't get mad, get even.* That's what the strong did, right? Like Ragnar on *Vikings.* Calmly take it all in without saying jack shit. Then, when it's time to act, have no mercy. But today had been surprising, and it fucked with his head.

The more he thought about it though, the more he figured maybe it wasn't such a bad thing.

The Amish were afraid. That made him smile. He was having an impact. That's what he'd wanted, wasn't it?

But if they were watching out for strangers, locking up

their barns, that meant they were on the lookout for a person, not a plant. And if they'd figured that out, the police probably had too.

Or maybe not. The Amish didn't necessarily listen to the police, much less tell them their business.

And maybe it was time he upped his game anyway. He was clever, wasn't he? If they thought he couldn't get past a padlock or two, they were dumber than a pig running after a bacon truck. He just had to figure out how to adapt his strategy. And when he did, the scythe would fall.

Two days after I'd met with the Amish congregation, Grady and I agreed on the final details of a plan. He insisted we run it by Lumbaker, the chief of police, just to get "an objective opinion." But really, I figured, it was to cover our asses. I was not averse to getting Lumbaker's input. I needed all the professional objectivity I could find. And when Lumbaker agreed to what I outlined, I was almost sorry.

Good works through you.

I hoped to God Ezra was right and that my existence on this planet wasn't about to become a liability for a family I cared about very much. I tried not to second-guess myself. I knew the plan made sense. But it was one thing in theory—another thing entirely face-to-face.

Grady went with me to the Yoders' home, and we were soon seated at the kitchen table. There we sat: tough guy Grady, me, and a middle-aged Amish couple: Hannah and Isaac Yoder. It was like a gathering of mismatched odds and ends, certainly no one's idea of a dream crime-fighting team. I turned down Hannah's offer of coffee. My stomach was a mess already.

Grady nodded at me, and I laid out my plan, trying to keep my voice steady and reasonable.

"So . . . you want us to lure the killer here?" Isaac summed up. He spoke slowly, as if he doubted he'd heard me right.

My hands gripped each other in my lap. "I hate to ask it of you. I realize it sounds desperate, but I guess we are. We need a way to *find* him. The area's too big; there are too many farms. We need to be able to guess where he's going to strike next. I thought of you because I know you're strong and reliable, both of you. And I hope there's some trust between us."

I was going to go on, to repeat our reassurances for their safety, but Hannah spoke up, her voice firm. "Of course. Please let us help. None of us will feel safe as long as he's out there."

Isaac nodded. "We must help. I wanna see you catch this man once and for all. He should face the consequences of his actions. We'll do whatever you say."

I breathed a shaky exhalation of relief and gratitude. There was a lump in my throat. "Thank you."

"If the good Lord can use us to stop this, who are we to say no?" Isaac asked.

Amen to that. Only, for God's sake, let nothing go wrong.

"Yo, James! Where are you, Mars? I said, what're ya doing this weekend?" James Westley's roommate, Billy, waved a hand in front of James's face. He'd been sitting at his desk in their dorm room, so lost in thought that he hadn't even heard Billy come in.

"Sorry," James muttered. "Studying, I guess. Laundry."

"Dude! Way to live on the edge. You gotta slow down. That fast lane'll kill ya."

"LOL," James said flatly. He smoothed the pages of the textbook under his hand. He had to read three chapters by tomorrow, but he couldn't focus.

Billy snorted. "What's up? Something's been bugging you for the past few days."

If even Billy noticed, it was pretty damn obvious. Billy's attention was usually reserved for things that wore pink panties or had a head of foam. James had tried to put his fears in the back of his mind, but they kept floating up like a piece of shit in a toilet. James had lied to that hot female detective, Harris. The thing is, James wasn't a rat. He *really* wasn't a rat.

In his sophomore year of high school, he'd hung around with a group of guys who liked to party. They'd smoked in the third floor boy's bathroom at school. The teachers could never catch them at it because they would stand in a circle and pass around one cigarette. The minute a teacher walked into the bathroom, whoever had the butt would toss it in a toilet. And then they'd all lie their asses off. It was the sort of thing where you had to be caught with the ciggy in your hand to get written up.

Well, one day, James had the cigarette, and he was telling a story and he got distracted. So did his friends. The next thing he knew, he had the butt between two fingers and was staring right into the face of a teacher. Busted.

The asshole principal had offered James a choice: provide a list of all of the boys he'd seen smoking in the bathroom or take ten days detention with no ability to make up his work. James had taken the detention, and he'd been a hero for it with his friends.

James Westley didn't rat.

People are dead. Children.

It wasn't his business anyway. He was in college now. And probably what he knew had no relevance to anything. He *didn't* know the killer. He couldn't. The person he knew would never do that. It was a coincidence. Just because he'd discussed that paper with someone back in high school didn't mean they had anything to do with the deaths in Lancaster. He'd just cause a lot of grief for an old friend. Well, not a friend exactly, but . . .

Someone *did it. Probably someone no one would suspect.*

"Earth to James!" Billy yelled.

"Huh?"

"I asked if you wanted to go to karaoke night at the Shandygaff on Wednesday. A bunch of us are going."

"I dunno. Maybe. Hey, can I ask you something?"

Billy sat down on his bed, giving James a curious look. "Sure. What is it?"

James heaved a sigh and scooted around in his chair. "Okay, so let's say hypothetically there's this guy. . . ."

On Friday, the eighth of May, almost seven weeks after the death of Will Hershberger, a Harrisburg news crew broadcast a special segment from Lancaster Central Park. The reporter, Juliet Lindsay, interviewed a serious-looking Amish man on camera.

"Hi, can you tell us your name?"

"I'm Isaac Yoder."

"Are you a dairy farmer, Mr. Yoder?"

"I farm lots of things, but I do have a half dozen cows we milk, 'tis so."

"And how has this milk crisis been affecting you?"

"I sell to a dairy, and the dairy stopped takin' my milk. They say their customers are afraid of Amish milk, even though they pasteurize it."

"I'm sure that's having a real impact." Juliet, her blonde hair neatly sprayed into a bob, nodded sympathetically.

"There's nothin' wrong with the milk." Yoder shook his head grimly. "I've got ten children at home, and we're all drinkin' it right from the cow. There's nothin' healthier for youse. And what we don't drink, I bring here to the protest now that I can't sell it."

"What kind of impact have these tragic deaths—particularly the Kinderman family and the Troyers—had on the Amish community?"

Yoder wiped his face wearily. "We have terrible sorrow over these deaths, especially the children. We pray for God's mercy that no more will have to go through such things."

Juliet awkwardly patted Yoder's arm. "Me too, sir, me too. Do you live close to any of the farms that were affected?"

Yoder shook his head. "Not at all. People don't realize how big an area this is. I live on Harvest Drive in Paradise. My neighbors are all Amish, and they haven't had any trouble either, thank the good Lord."

"Thank you for speaking to us, Mr. Yoder. I wish you the best."

"You're welcome. God bless."

There wasn't good cover across from the farm, only an open cornfield, its green stalks still too low to hide more than a small dog. The watcher cut the engine on his car and rolled it to a stop on the shoulder just far enough down the road that he could still study the farm without drawing their attention.

He got out and pretended to fiddle with his phone. It was a sunny day in May, and it grew warm in the late afternoon, which sucked since he was wearing his black hoodie. It was too warm already, and his scalp grew increasingly hot and itchy, but he kept the hood up just in case. Only a loser couldn't suck it up when he had to. The watcher sat on the front of his car pretend texting with his phone in case anyone passed. He watched the farm from under his hood.

The Amish guy who owned the farm, Yoder, had been on the news yesterday. It was almost too good to be true. Maybe it *was* too good to be true, but he had to at least check it out. You saw an opportunity, you grabbed it. That didn't mean you had to be stupid about it. He wasn't moving in until he was sure it was safe.

But Amish didn't lie, right? And they didn't pull ambushes. He was pretty sure Yoder was exactly what he appeared to be. It made sense that the guy was going to talk about how safe his milk was—he sold the shit. He had to look like he trusted his own product, right? That's probably why his family was still drinking it, and why he'd agreed to be interviewed on TV. Money talks, even to the Amish.

Ten kids. That meant a body count of at least twelve, maybe more if they had gran or gramps living with them.

The farmer, his wife, and his cookie-cutter offspring came and went from the house to the barn and fields. They were like ants on a hill from where he was sitting. A little girl of about seven skipped around with a basket in her hands, her feet bare. She was pretty with dark brown hair. He watched her until her mother opened the door and yelled something. The little Amish girl ran inside.

Oh, the watcher wanted this one. He wanted it bad. But he felt uneasy. He couldn't stop looking behind himself, down the road and across the fields, half expecting to be approached by the police or even just neighbors.

Hold it together. Don't be a candyass.

There was nothing illegal about stopping on the side of the road. He had a story ready about a call from a sick family member. He'd say he didn't want to drive while he was upset, so he was waiting for a call back. That was what a good citizen would do, right? That was fucking responsible.

He did have white snakeroot in the car, which they might

find if they searched it. But why would they? And anyway, it was hidden in the spare tire compartment. There was no danger at all in simply parking here. *Suck it up.*

So he watched for over an hour. There was no sign of cops or anyone else. The Yoders didn't have any locks on the barn. He didn't see a dog either.

The father took out some farm wagon, put a couple horses on it, and took off for one of the fields. Two boys went on the wagon with him. Later, two women in Amish dresses came out and put clothes on the line, and there was a different young girl too, maybe twelve.

Any of them could see him, parked as he was down the road, if they only looked. But they didn't seem to be paying any attention. Finally. They were acting like they *should* be acting. Maybe it was the watchfulness that had been a fluke. Maybe he was getting paranoid.

The sun sat low in the sky like a bloated, diseased orange by the time the father drove the wagon back and he and the boys started unhitching the horses. By then, the watcher's shoulders had relaxed and he felt perfect—calm and so fucking clear. He felt like he could do *anything.*

After dark, he decided. Sunset was around eight P.M. He'd looked it up. These farmers went to bed early, especially since they had no TV or computers. He'd wait until nine P.M. It would be dark around the barn. Very dark. Then, if it still looked clear, he'd make his move. For now, it was time to disappear.

CHAPTER 19

The hardest thing I've ever done was to watch the killer drive away. Grady and I discussed it over the headset. I was in the Yoder's barn, watching out of one of the windows in the hay loft. Grady was in the house.

"He might have something incriminating on him. What do you think, Harris?" Grady had sounded edgy, ready to move.

God, I wanted to grab him as well. What if we'd been made? What if he didn't come back? This might be the closest we ever got to him. And it *was* him. I knew it.

But the guy didn't seem to notice anything wrong. He hung out by his car for over two hours. If he'd known he was being watched, he would have left right away.

The old conundrum of cats and cops everywhere—pounce now? Or wait?

"He's doing recon. He might not have the snakeroot on him," I said in a low voice over the headset. "And even if he does, a smart lawyer might be able to explain it away. I think we should wait. He'll be back. And I want to nail this bastard with such an airtight case he won't be able to shift to scratch his ass." Ah, yes. These tense situations did bring out the colorful lingo I'd learned as a New York cop.

"You want a selfie with him, the plant, and the cow?" Grady half teased.

I smiled. "Yes, sir, that's what I want. We have someone down the road to grab his license plate number, right?" His car didn't have a front plate, so I hadn't been able to get more than the basic make and model through the binocs.

"Yeah, we'll get it. We've got someone walking a dog at the end of the road."

"Then we can trace him if we have to. But for God's sake, let's not scare him away now."

"Roger, Harris. We'll wait."

He was about to sign off. I spoke up. "Everyone okay in there?"

"Everyone's fine, don't worry. The family's inside for the day now, and no one's getting past the uniforms in the front room. Over and out."

Good. Grady and I had debated the merits of sending the children away for the entire operation. But we both knew the killer was drawn to kids. It was important that the family looked normal from the outside. And our killer wasn't a gunman. He shouldn't be a direct danger to anyone on the property except the cows. I was still glad Grady and two uniformed officers were in the house.

In my pocket, my cell phone vibrated. I put one hand on it but didn't get it out. My attention was focused on the road. The Corolla drove out of sight at a leisurely speed. *Please get the license plate number*, I thought, *and don't make him suspicious.*

The guy would be back. We'd left too tempting a target.

With a sigh, I took my cell phone out of my pocket and checked the screen. It was a number I didn't recognize. It was the second time today that number had dialed me and not left a message. We were in the middle of the most important sting of my career. If it wasn't urgent, I wasn't going to allow myself to be distracted by it. I put the phone back in my pocket.

One of the police techs came up to the loft by the ladder and regarded me.

"Are the lights set up?" I asked.

"Yup. All rigged to go off with a single click."

"And they're well hidden?"

"The best we could manage, which is pretty damn good. This barn has more nooks and crannies than a Triscuit." The tech laughed at his own joke. "Wanna come look?"

I did.

The watcher parked his car near a tree a few hundred yards from the Yoder farm at nine P.M. exactly. The sunset had faded to inky darkness. There was only a sliver of a moon in the sky, and the country road had no lighting. The only lights visible as far as the eye could see were the dim lantern lights in the windows of the farmhouse and those of the farmhouse of a distant neighbor. There was no light in or around the barn.

The watcher got out of his car and removed his backpack from the trunk as quietly as he could. He started toward the farm at a jog, sticking to the grassy shoulder.

There was no one around. No one at all.

He was nervous, scared. It seemed like, every time he did this, it felt more dangerous. Part of him wanted to turn around, go back to his car, and drive away. But the thought of another large family, of adding ten or more to his body count, drove him onward. Fuck it. No guts, no glory.

When he reached the farm's driveway, he paused, checking everything out one more time. He didn't see a living soul outside the house. No sign of life in the barn. No barking dog. He darted across the gravel drive in the shadows and headed for the closed barn door. He carefully squeezed the iron latch, opened the door, and slipped inside.

He heard the cows before he saw them. Yoder had a small herd, at least six. They were in a stall at the back of the barn. The watcher moved toward them over the cool concrete floor. The darkness inside the barn gave him confidence. He could barely make out the aisle in front of him, but that meant he couldn't be seen either.

He reached the stall and saw big dark cow eyes staring at him. He slung his backpack off his back, unzipped it.

"Hey, cows!" he whispered. "Guess what I have for—"

The lights went on like a thousand suns, blinding him. From beyond the glare he heard a man's voice shouting, "Freeze!"

We got him!

I had my gun out and trained on the figure in the black hooded sweatshirt. The lights our tech crew had strung up in the barn were even brighter than I'd anticipated, and my eyes were fighting to adjust. I blinked rapidly, not wanting to lose sight of our perp for a second. I didn't dare turn my head to look for Hernandez on my left, or Schmidt, a uniformed cop, on my right. The perp hadn't moved, hadn't raised his hands, just stood absolutely still, his back to us, a partially unzipped backpack in his hands.

What if he had a gun in there?

"Drop it!" I yelled. "Drop the backpack! Now!"

"Harris," Grady's voice crackled in my ear.

"We've got him," I muttered, not wanting to be distracted. The guy still hadn't moved. He was slightly built, but something in the tension of his body told me he was capable of lethal violence.

"Be careful," came Grady's voice, urgent. "One of the Yoder kids got out somehow. Get that guy cuffed and then *guns down.*"

Oh shit. Oh no. Hannah and her family were supposed to be well guarded and safe. I'd promised Hannah personally. The possible ways this could turn disastrous flashed through my mind in an instant, more instinctual knowing than words or even mental pictures.

"Drop the backpack!" I screamed again. "Drop it or we'll shoot!"

I saw Sadie at the same instant the perp did. Unfortunately, he was much closer to her, and he was fast.

There was another barn entrance near the cow stall, and they'd taken care of that door. One of the uniformed cops, Davis, was supposed to have locked it from the outside as soon as the perp entered the barn so he couldn't escape that way. Davis was also supposed to be watching the outside of the barn to make sure no one got in or out.

But Sadie was small, and she knew the barn the way only a child could know it. Somehow she'd gotten past Davis. There was a heavy rubber flap in the wooden barn wall on the feeding aisle, not far from where the perp stood. It pushed inward, and Sadie crawled through, back legs first.

Oh God, no!

Before I could shout a warning to Sadie or make up my mind to just shoot and wound the perp, he moved. He hurled the backpack toward us as a distraction and dove for Sadie.

"Don't shoot!" I shouted. My voice sounded amazingly calm. "There's a child! Don't shoot!"

Then he had her. He picked Sadie up and clutched her to his chest as a shield. His face was still hidden by the hood, and now by Sadie's head as well. One eye looked past Sadie toward me, but it was mostly in shadow. He held a large knife at Sadie's throat. She froze, her eyes round with shock.

Oh God, please, no.

It was my worst nightmare. He held not just any Amish child, but Sadie Yoder, a little girl I adored, and Katie's sister. And it was my fault. I'd used Hannah's friendship to orchestrate this. Sadie had probably come out to the barn looking for me.

I didn't pray often, but a prayer erupted in my mind. *Please, God, don't let him kill Sadie. Please let me stop him. Please.*

Three guns were trained on the man in the hoodie and the child, including, I realized, my own. I took a deep breath and slowly lowered my gun.

"You're gonna let me go. I walk away or the girl dies," the perp said. They were his first words, and he was talking low, clearly trying to disguise his voice. But there was a quaver of fear there. "Back off or I'll do it. I swear to God I will."

I knew he would. He'd kill Sadie with absolutely no remorse. But I also knew that if we let him walk, if we let him escape by using her as a human shield, if he got her into his car, he'd kill her anyway. As far as I was concerned, there was no way in hell he was taking Sadie Yoder out of this barn.

I risked a glance at Hernandez. He looked back, his face rigid with determination. I shook my head slightly. Then I took one step forward so the perp would focus on me. I let the gun go lax in my hand, hanging down at my side. Suddenly, the knot of terror in my stomach eased, and I felt a warm wave of calm.

"Rob Myers!" I called out. "We know who you are. Even if you escape this room, it's over."

That surprised him. I heard him gasp, and he drew back half a step. The hand that held the knife shook dangerously. "How?

How did you know?" Strangely, he sounded curious, even pleased.

I'd found out an hour ago, when I couldn't stop thinking about the calls from that unrecognized number and had decided to return them. The caller had been James Westley. He reluctantly told me a story about a guy in his high school who'd wanted to talk about James's paper on milk sickness after he'd presented it in class. The guy had been obsessed about it. That high school student was now Amber Kruger's intern.

"That doesn't matter, Rob. The point is, we know who you are, we know your car, and we know where you live. We know your mother."

"Then I've got nothing to lose, cunt!" He sounded angry now. He pushed the knife tighter against Sadie's throat. She whimpered, her big eyes pleading with me. But she didn't struggle, didn't move, didn't cry out. *Good girl.*

I spoke fast. "Rob, wait! If you hurt that little girl, if you even start to use that knife, we *will* shoot you. Dead. That's not what you want, is it? You want to be able to tell your story. The famous raw-milk poisoner. Maybe there'll even be books and movies. You'll want to be around for that. If you die now, you lose it all."

Rob hesitated. That one eye stared at me.

"Come on." I lifted my chin with more casual confidence than I felt. "Don't be foolish. You've done all this work, now you're not gonna benefit from it? Was that really your plan?"

He tightened his grip on Sadie, but the knife, I noticed,

moved farther away from her throat. "You'll shoot me anyway," he said doubtfully.

"No, Rob. We won't shoot an unarmed man. Toss the knife down and let me come over to you. I'll stand in front of you while you put Sadie down. Then I'll handcuff you. I swear, no one will shoot you. We'll put you in a squad car and take you to the station. All right?"

He glared at me, shifting from foot to foot. His eyes darted to Hernandez and then to Schmidt, both of whom still had their guns trained on him. *Keep calm, boys. But keep the pressure on.*

"This is it, Rob," I urged softly. "You either die right here, or you go to jail."

"I'm not done. I wanted a higher body count."

I felt a wave of absolute hatred. *Body count.* All of those dead individuals were nothing to him but notches on his belt. But I couldn't let it show. "You are done, Rob. There's no way we'll let you continue now. It's done tonight, one way or the other. Die in this barn or surrender now. Your choice."

He thought about it a few seconds more. "Okay. But you walk over here first. Without your gun. I'm not tossing my knife until you're in front of me, blocking their shots."

"I can do that."

I heard Hernandez hiss my name, but I ignored him. And, yes, with a psychopath like this, it wouldn't be beyond the realm of possibility that he'd think that adding a female cop to his *body count* would be a good way to check out. But I had to take that chance.

"I'm just going to put my gun down and get my cuffs." Slowly, I bent my knees and placed my gun on the floor, both of my hands visible. Then I raised one hand, and with the other slowly fished a pair of cuffs from my pocket and held them up. "All right?"

Jerkily, he nodded, still holding Sadie and the knife.

It felt like I crossed a football field one slow step at a time to get to them, worried that at any moment he'd change his mind and kill Sadie. The knife was so close to her throat. The other cops wouldn't be able to stop him, not with me in the way.

Finally, I was close enough to hold up the cuffs. "Okay? Let go of the knife and then Sadie. Turn around and let me cuff you, and you'll walk out of here, Rob. I promise."

I could make out his face now, under the hood. He looked back at me, his light blue eyes darting nervously between me and the cops behind me. Such an ordinary-looking young man.

If you're going to go for broke and kill anyone, come after me, I thought.

But Rob gave a jerky nod. He opened his hand and let the knife fall to the floor, where it landed with a clang. He let Sadie go, pushing her away and turning quickly. He held his hands behind his back, shoving them up, fingers splayed as if to show he was unarmed. He seemed anxious to get cuffed so he wouldn't be shot. His faith in the police department was almost touching. For a second, the images and smells from the Kinderman home roared through my mind and I wanted to kill him anyway. I could pick up the knife and do it. It would be easy. But the urge lasted only a second before reason caused it to dissipate. I wasn't the only person he'd hurt, and whatever justice he had coming, it wasn't mine alone to dispense. Besides, I would never leave Sadie with a memory like that.

I cuffed him. And if I tightened the steel bands a bit too much, who could blame me?

Hernandez was there to grab Rob. He looked at me to see if I wanted to do the honors, but I just motioned for him to take Rob out of the barn. I had more important things to do.

As Hernandez started reading Rob his rights, I picked up Sadie Yoder and held her tight.

EPILOGUE

Rob got his wish. He was famous. The story unraveled in the media hour by hour, each source adding some small spot of detail to the horrific picture.

Rob's father had been a dairy farmer who'd gone bankrupt. He'd hated the Amish because he said they hurt his business, that customers wanted Amish goods because they thought them "quaint" when really they were "dirty hillbillies." After he'd lost his farm, Rob's father had worked in a factory for a short time before abandoning his wife and son for parts unknown.

Their dairy farm had been in Paradise, not far from the Knepps and the Hershbergers, Rob's first and second attempts to use white snakeroot.

Rob was supposedly fascinated with Native American culture and stories of the Wild West and thought Indians had poisoned settlers with white snakeroot. He'd written a paper on it once, the media wrongly claimed. They got most other things right though.

Rob was a straight-A student at his vo-tech school, where he studied computer repair. He became Amber Kruger's intern looking for easy targets, and her work with the Amish promised the opportunity to find them. He was a regular poster on three websites that glorified serial killers. Two books and a film on Columbine were found in his room along with videotapes he'd made recounting his kills. He kept his body count list in a spiral notebook with a black cover he'd doodled on, graffiti-like, with metallic pens.

Rob still lived at home. He'd grown white snakeroot from seeds under grow lights in the basement of his mother's house and planted it in her backyard. She'd approved of his interest in gardening.

She continued to believe he was innocent.

After a while, I tuned it all out. I'd understood the media attention on the case when it was open, but it had always made me feel pressured and anxious. Now, knowing this was just what Rob had wanted, it made me deeply uneasy and slightly ill. How could we stop future copycats in this age of selfies and reality-show stars if we gave these bastards so much attention?

I had no control over it, so I focused on wrapping up the case paperwork. I received an almost-hug from a grateful Margaret Foderman, aide to the governor, and a meaty handshake and a "Good work!" from Mitch Franklin. I said my good-byes to Dr.

Glen Turner for what I assumed would be the last time ever, barring any future E. coli outbreaks in Lancaster County.

I wished Glen good luck in the parking garage at the police station, turned away, and went inside. I didn't look back.

I stood under the hot rush of water in the shower for countless minutes, letting it stream over my face. When the hot water ran out, I toweled off and wrapped myself up in my terrycloth robe with nothing underneath. I padded out to the kitchen in my bare feet to find Ezra waiting for me. He was leaning back with his feet crossed, hands braced on the counter. The smell of something tantalizing like beef gravy hung in the air. My stomach gurgled in delight.

I lingered in the kitchen doorway, looking at the pots on the stove and the plates on the table and, lastly, at my man. Ezra's expression was soft and warm and full of things that I wasn't sure I knew how to deserve—love and pride and forever. My eyes stung. It was exhaustion, I told myself. But, damn, I was grateful to be here. To have this.

"You always take care of me," I said, forcing a wobbly smile.

He held out his arms, and I went to him and let him wrap me up tight. He felt so strong and solid and as warm as a sunny day.

"Somebody has to. 'Cause you're too busy taking care of everyone else. Besides, it makes me feel useful."

I went up on my tiptoes and put my arms around his neck so I could get even closer. I was tall for a woman, but Ezra was taller.

"You are more than useful. But it's my turn to take care of you. Grady says I can have a week off."

"Yeah?" He sounded happy. He rubbed my back.

"Yup. I owe you some quality time." I turned my head so I could snuggle into his neck, smell the clean, earthy scent of him.

"What on earth will you do with a whole week off?" he teased. "You'll be arresting squirrels for putting acorns in the gutter pipes and ticketing groundhogs. Not that they don't deserve it."

I laughed, the sound vibrating against his throat. "I'm not interested in groundhogs or squirrels, but I might have to put you under house arrest for a day or two. Or bedroom arrest," I added in a sultry tone.

He squeezed me tight, but he didn't laugh. In fact, he grew a little tense in my arms. I felt him swallow. "I hear you can get married pretty quick. Think a week would be long enough for that?"

Shocked into silence, I drew back to look at his face.

He studied me warily. "Or . . . maybe you'd prefer to take your time with somethin' like that. If ya wanna do it at all."

I blinked, feeling joy and fear and—*damn*, life was amazing and sad and tragic and so beautiful too that my chest hurt.

"I love you, Ezra Beiler. And I will marry you—next week or the week after, it doesn't matter. Just . . . yes."

He smiled, his eyes a little damp. He said nothing more but took my face gently in both hands and kissed me.

Keep reading for an excerpt of Jane Jensen's first book in the Elizabeth Harris Novels . . .

KINGDOM COME

Available from Berkley Prime Crime!

The Dead Girl

"It's . . . sensitive," Grady had said on the phone, his voice tight.

Now I understood why. My car crawled down a rural road thick with new snow. It was still dark and way too damn early on a Wednesday morning. The address he'd given me was on Grimlace Lane. Turned out the place was an Amish farm in the middle of a whole lot of other Amish farms in the borough of Paradise, Pennsylvania.

Sensitive like a broken tooth. Murders didn't happen here, not here. The last dregs of sleep and yet another nightmare in which I'd been holding my husband's cold, dead hand in the rain evaporated under a surge of adrenaline. Oh yes, I was wide-awake now.

I spotted cars—Grady's and two black-and-whites—in the driveway of a farm and pulled in. The CSI team and the coroner had not yet arrived. I didn't live far from the murder site and I was glad for the head start and the quiet.

Even before I parked, my mind started generating theories and scenarios. *Dead girl*, Grady had said. If it'd been natural causes or an accident, like falling down the stairs, he wouldn't have called me in. It had to be murder or at least a suspicious death. A father disciplining his daughter a little too hard? Doddering Grandma dipping into the rat poison rather than the flour?

I got out and stood quietly in the frigid air to get a sense of place. The interior of the barn glowed in the dark of a winter morning. I took in the classic white shape of a two-story bank barn, the snowy fields behind, and the glow of lanterns coming from the huge, barely open barn door. . . . It looked like one of those quaint paintings you see hanging in the local tourist shops, something with a title like *Winter Dawn*. I'd only moved back to Pennsylvania eight months ago after spending ten years in Manhattan. I still felt a pang at the quiet beauty of it.

Until I opened the door and stepped inside.

It wasn't what I expected. It was like some bizarre and horrific game of mixed-up pictures. The warmth of the rough barn wood was lit by a half dozen oil lanterns. Add in the scattered straw, two Jersey cows, and twice as many horses, all watching the proceedings with bland interest from various stalls, and it felt like a cozy step back in time. That vibe did not compute with the dead girl on the floor. She was most definitely not Amish, which was the first surprise. She was young and beautiful, like something out of a '50s pulp magazine. She had long, honey-blonde hair and a face that still had the blush of life thanks to the heavy makeup she wore. She had on a candy-pink sweater that molded over taut breasts and a short gray wool skirt that was pushed up to her hips. She still wore pink underwear, though it looked roughly twisted. Her nails were the same shade as her sweater. Her bare feet, thighs, and hands were blue-white with death, and her neck too, at the line below her jaw where the makeup stopped.

The whole scene felt unreal, like some pretentious performance art, the kind in those Soho galleries Terry had dragged me to. But then, death always looked unreal.

"Coat? Shoes?" I asked, already taking inventory. Maybe knee-high boots, I thought, reconstructing it in my mind. And thick tights to go with that wool skirt. I'd *been* a teenage girl living in Lancaster County, Pennsylvania. I knew what it meant to care more about looks than the weather. But even at the height of my girlish vanity, I wouldn't have gone bare-legged in January.

"They're not here. We looked." Grady's voice was tense. I finally spared him a glance. His face was drawn in a way I'd never seen before, like he was digesting a meal of ground glass.

In that instant, I saw the media attention this could get, the politics of it. I remembered that Amish school shooting a few years back. I hadn't lived here then, but I'd seen the press. Who hadn't?

"You sure you want me on this?" I asked him quietly.

"You're the most experienced homicide detective I've got," Grady said. "I need you, Harris. And I need this wrapped up quickly."

"Yeah." I wasn't agreeing that it could be. My gut said this wasn't going to be an open-and-shut case, but I agreed it would be nice. "Who found her? Do we know who she is?"

"Jacob Miller, eleven years old. He's the son of the Amish farmer who lives here. Poor kid. Came out to milk the cows this morning and found her just like that. The family says they've got no idea who she is or how she got here."

"How many people live on the property?"

"Amos Miller, his wife, and their six children. The oldest, a boy, is fifteen. The youngest is three."

More vehicles pulled up outside. The forensics team, no doubt. I was gratified that Grady had called me in first. It was good to see the scene before it turned into a lab.

"Can you hold them outside for five minutes?" I asked Grady.

He nodded and went out.

I pulled on some latex gloves, then looked at the body, bending down to get as close to it as I could without touching it. The left side of her head, toward the back, was matted with blood and had the look of a compromised skull. The death blow? I tried to imagine what had happened. The killer—he or she—had probably come up behind the victim, struck her with something heavy. The autopsy would tell us more. I didn't think it had happened here. There were no signs of a disturbance or the blood you'd expect from a head wound. I carefully pulled up her leg a bit and looked at the underside of her thigh. Very minor lividity. She hadn't been in this position long. And I noticed something else—her clothes were wet. I rubbed a bit of her wool skirt and sweater between my fingers to be sure—and came away with dampness on the latex. She wasn't soaked now, and her skin was dry, so she'd been here long enough to dry out, but she'd been very wet at some point. I could see now that her hair wasn't just styled in a casual damp-dry curl, it had been recently wet, probably postmortem along with her clothes.

I straightened, frowning. It was odd. We'd had two inches of snow the previous afternoon, but it was too cold for rain. If the body had been left outside in the snow, would it have gotten this wet? Maybe the ME could tell me.

Since I was sure she hadn't been killed in the barn, I checked the floor for drag marks. The floor was of wooden planks kept so clean that there was no straw or dirt in which drag marks would show, but there were traces of wet prints. Then again, the boy who'd found the body had been in the barn and so had Grady and the uniforms, and me too. I carefully examined the girl's bare feet. There was no broken skin, no sign her feet had been dragged through the snow or across rough boards.

The killer was strong, then. He'd carried her in here and laid her down. Which meant he'd arranged her like this—pulled up her skirt, splayed her thighs. He'd wanted it to look sexual. Why?

The doors opened. Grady and the forensics team stood in the doorway.

"Blacklight this whole area," I requested. "And this floor—see if you can get any prints or traffic patterns off it. Don't let anyone in until that's done. I'm going to check outside." I looked at Grady. "The coroner?"

"Should be here any minute."

"Good. Make sure she's tested for any signs of penetration, consensual or otherwise."

"Right."

Grady barked orders. The crime-scene technicians pulled on blue coveralls and booties just outside the door. This was only the sixth homicide needing real investigation I'd been on since moving back to Lancaster. I was still impressed that the department had decent tools and protocol, even though I knew that was just big-city arrogance talking.

I left them to it and went out to find my killer's tracks in the snow.

This winter had been harsh. In fact, it was shaping up to be the worst in decades. We'd had a white Christmas and then it never really left. The fresh two inches we'd gotten the day before had covered up an older foot or two of dirty snow and ice. Thanks to a low in the twenties, the fresh snow had a dry, powdery surface that showed no signs of melting. It still wasn't fun to walk on, due to the underlying grunge. It said a lot about the killer if he'd carried her body over any distance.

There was a neatly shoveled path from the house to the barn. The snow in the central open area in the driveway had been stomped down. But it didn't take me long to spot a deep set of prints heading off across an open field that was otherwise pristine. The line of prints came and went. They showed a sole like that of a work boot and they were large. They came from, and returned to, a distant copse of trees. I bent over to examine one of the prints close to the barn. It had definitely been made since the last snowfall.

A few minutes later, I got my first look at Amos Miller, the Amish farmer who owned the property. Grady called him out and showed him the tracks. Miller looked to be in his mid-forties with dark brown hair and a long, unkempt beard. His face was round and solemn. I said nothing for now, just observed.

They say the first forty-eight hours are critical on a homicide case, and that's true, but, frankly, a lot of murders can be solved in the first eight. Sometimes it's obvious—the boyfriend standing there with a guilty look and blood under his nails rambling about a "masked robber." Sometimes the neighbors can tell you they heard a knock-down, drag-out fight. And sometimes . . . there are tracks in the snow.

"Nah. I didn't make them prints and ain't no reason for my boys to be out there," Amos told Grady. He said "there" as *dah*, his German accent as broad as his face. "But lemme ask 'em just to be sure."

He started to stomp away. I called after him. "Bring the boys out here, please."

Amos Miller shot me a confused look, like he hadn't expected me to be giving orders. I arched an eyebrow at him—*Well?*—and he nodded once. I was used to dealing with men who didn't take a female cop very seriously. And I wanted to see the boys—wanted to see their faces as they looked at those tracks.

My first impression of Amos Miller? He looked worried. Then again, he was an Amish farmer with two boys in their teens. A beautiful young English girl—the Amish called everyone who was not Amish "English"—was dead and spread-eagled in his barn. I'd be worried too.

He came back with three boys. The youngest was small and still a child. That was probably Jacob, the eleven-year-old who'd found the body. His face was blank, like he was in shock. The next oldest looked to be around thirteen, just starting puberty. He was thin with a rather awkward nose and oversized hands he still hadn't grown into. His father introduced him as Ham. The oldest, Wayne, had to be the fifteen-year-old that Grady mentioned, the oldest child. All three were decent-looking boys in that wholesome, bowl-cut way of Amish youth. The older two looked excited but not guilty. I suppose it was quite an event, having a dead body found on your farm. I wondered if the older boys had gone into the barn to get a good long look at the girl since their little brother's discovery. Knowing how large families worked, I couldn't imagine they hadn't.

Each of the boys glanced at the tracks in the snow and shook his head. "Nah," the oldest added for good measure. "Ain't from me."

"Any of you recognize that print?" I asked. "Does it look like boots you've seen before?"

They all craned forward to look. Amos stroked his beard. "Just look like boots, maybe. You can check all ours if you like. We've nothin' to hide."

I lifted my chin at Grady. We'd definitely want the crime team to inventory every pair of shoes and boots in the house.

"Would you all mind stepping over here for me, please?" I led them over to the other side of the ice-and-gravel drive, where there was some untouched snow. "Youngest to oldest, one at a time."

The youngest stepped forward into the snow with both feet, then back. The others mimicked his actions obediently, including Amos Miller.

"Thank you. That's all for now. We'll want to speak to you a bit later, so please stay home."

They went back inside and Grady and I compared the tracks. All three of the boys had smaller feet than the tracks in the snow. Amos's prints were large enough but didn't have the same sole pattern. Besides, I was sure Grady wasn't missing the fact that the prints came and went *from* the trees, since the prints heading in that direction overlaid the ones approaching the barn.

"I think Ronks Road is over there beyond those woods." Grady sounded hopeful as he pointed across the field. "Can it be that easy?"

"Don't!"

Grady cocked an eyebrow at me.

"You'll jinx it. Never say the word 'easy.' That's inviting Murphy, his six ex-wives, and their lawyers."

Grady smirked. "Well, if the killer dumped her here, he had to come from somewhere."

I hummed. I knew what Grady was thinking. I was thinking

it too. A car full of rowdy youths, or maybe just a guy and his hot date, out joyriding in the country. A girl ends up dead and someone gets the bright idea to dump her on an Amish farm. They drive out here, park, cross a snowy cornfield, and leave her in a random barn.

It sounded like a stupid teenage prank, only it was murder and possibly an attempt to frame someone else. That was a lot of prison years of serious. A story like that—it would make the press happy and Grady fucking ecstatic, especially if we could nab the guy who wore those boots by tonight.

"Get a photographer and a recorder and let's go," I said, feeling only a moment's silent regret over my good black leather boots. I should have worn my wellies.

It wasn't that easy.

The tracks crossed the field and went into the trees. They continued about ten feet before they ended—at a creek. It hadn't been visible from the barn, but there was running water here, a good twelve feet across. The land dipped down to it, as if carved out over time. The snow grew muddy and trampled at the creek bank. The boot prints entered the water. They didn't reemerge on the opposite side.

"Cattle use this creek?" I asked Grady, looking at the mess of mud and snow and hoofprints along the bank.

Grady sighed. "Hell. It's not legal, but a lot of the farmers do it, especially the Amish. It's hard to explain to a man whose family has farmed the same land for generations why politicians in Baltimore don't want his animals to have access to the free and plentiful water on his own land."

I really didn't give a toss about the pollution of Chesapeake Bay at the moment. But our possible killer's footprints, so clean in the snow, had vanished into a churned-up creek bed that had been literally ridden herd over. I walked up and down the bank as carefully as I could, trying not to step anywhere there might be evidence. There was chicken wire strung up across the creek to the north, and a matching wire wall glinted to the south. Presumably, this kept the farm's animals from escaping the property.

The freaky thing was, there were no signs of tracks on the other side of the creek anywhere between those two makeshift fences. I rubbed my forehead, a sense of frustration starting in my stomach.

"Damn it!" Grady cursed, apparently reaching the same conclusion.

"How far is the road?" I asked.

As if to answer my question, an SUV lumbered past, visible through the trees on the far side. There was a road maybe thirty feet beyond the other side of the creek.

In a righteous world, the boot prints would have climbed out on the opposite bank and led right to that road. In a righteous world, there'd be tire tracks off the side of the road over there, tire tracks we could attempt to trace.

No one had to tell me it wasn't a righteous world.

I looked at the creek again, then went back to look at the boot prints. The prints with the toes facing the creek definitely overlaid the prints with the toes facing away. Unless the killer had walked backward in both directions—one way carrying a dead body—he hadn't come from the farm.

Grady stood there shaking his head. I decided, *Screw it,* and shucked my boots and rolled up my pant legs. At least this suit was a trendy wash-and-wear and didn't require dry cleaning.

"You don't have to do that." Grady sounded uneasy.

I ignored him. If there was one thing I knew for sure about being a woman on the police force, it was that you didn't turn up your nose at getting physical or messy. You didn't wait for some guy to do it. If you wanted respect, you had to be willing to jump into the shit headfirst.

But, goddamn, this sucked. I waded into the ice water masquerading as a creek and followed the bank to the chicken-wire obstruction.

"Anything?" Grady called to me as I ran my hand along the chicken wire and stepped deeper into the creek.

When I reached the middle, the frigid water was streaming painfully around my upper thighs.

"Damn," I muttered as I felt along the fence.

A few inches below the surface of the water the wire ended. To be sure, I sent one leg forward on a foray. It swept through nothing but water. No wonder our Jane Doe had gotten wet. The killer had pushed her under these barriers and then likely followed by ducking under himself.

“Bastard walked through the creek,” I said, my voice shaking with cold and not a little disgust. “He came in and out under one of these fences, but he had to leave the water somewhere. We need to search the banks upstream and down from here. We’ll find his tracks.”

I sounded confident. And I did believe what I was saying. We were talking about a man, after all, not a superhuman, not a ghost.

I was wrong.